JUST IN TIME

AN OUT OF TIME STORY
BOOK TWO

PAULINE BAIRD JONES

ABOUT JUST IN TIME

Time Travel Romance by USA Today Bestselling Author Pauline Baird Jones

Delve into a romantic saga where love transcends time and space, and past, present, and future collide. Join a daring pilot from the present and an ingenious inventor from the past as they defy the odds to save their love and their lives.

Ty Granger, a dedicated scientist and military pilot, has joined the effort to fight those who would manipulate time for their own benefit. He travels back to 1954 to investigate a suspicious incident around the development of an innovative aircraft. But his mission takes an unexpected turn when he falls for the talented inventor of the device - a woman who will die by the end of the week.

Alice Merriweather is on a mission to validate her extraordinary creation's ability to soar the skies. But as suspicions of sabotage hover around her project, Alice takes a gamble and places her trust in the enigmatic man who sees her as his equal.

With history hanging by a thread, Ty grapples with the ticking clock, hoping to save his love from her impending doom.

Alice, deeply in love with the man from the future, is prepared to sacrifice her life, if it means her groundbreaking work and the man she loves will survive.

But with murky enemies threatening to erase Ty and Alice's existence, can their love story find its happily ever after?

Just in Time is the enthralling second installment in the *Out of Time Stories,* a clean & wholesome romantic science fiction series.

If you're drawn to paradox-filled plots, irresistible chemistry, and heart-wrenching moments, then you'll be captivated by Pauline Baird Jones' engrossing adventure.

Buy *Just in Time* today and embark on a romantic journey through time!

What others have said about *Just in Time:*

"Their romance is shown in brief swatches across the action of the three groups jumping time and space. I loved the historical accuracy and how it balanced with the imaginative futuristic technology. It was thrilling to read about the villainous Alastor and guess who sent the men in black to chase Rita. Fans of the television shows "The Time Traveler's Wife," "Fringe," or "Doctor Who" will love this book. I recommend this series as a whole for hopeless romantics who are fans of science fiction, time travel, and page turners." N.N. Light's Book Heaven

"**Just in Time**, Pauline Baird Jones' long awaited sequel to **Out of Time** contains the critical elements of a Jones book that I look for: an action-packed complex plot, engaging, smart characters and that signature sense of humor that I love." Whiskey With My Book

"Just in Time will appeal to a reader who wants to be on the edge of their seat for hours on end. The book simply draws the reader in and will keep you invested to the very end. Fans of great espionage films and books will love this book. Fans of historical plane development will love this book." NN Light Book Heaven

"Highly recommended for those who enjoy a good love story, time travel, and the suspense involved in trying to stay one jump ahead of their time tampering-foes (SOMEBODY is trying to stop them but it is unclear exactly who is friend or foe), etc." Amazon reviewer

"A delightful, twisty, turny time travel read!!! I'm hoping we get another in this exciting series!!!!!" Amazon reviewer

"What a heart pumping, exhilarating ride!!!" Amazon reviewer

"Many levels of deception and adventure....a good old fashioned spy-like read."

"...contains the critical elements of a Jones book that I look for: an action-packed complex plot, engaging, smart characters and that signature sense of humor that I love." Reader

CHAPTER 1

*E*dwards Air Force Base, August, 1952

Alice Merriweather climbed out of the car and shielded her eyes the better to study their new home. The horizon wavered in the intense heat, though it failed to hide how unforgiving the desert was that surrounded the base, broken only by the coolly distant San Gabriel Mountains.

No breeze lifted the damp strands of hair from off her face, and the scarf she'd tied over her hair did nothing to ease the rays from the sun. It felt as if she'd burst into flames at any moment. She lifted a hand holding a handkerchief and dabbed delicately at her neck. Then she resolved not to do that again. Movement of any kind felt as if it only made the heat worse.

She tried to define the scent of the place absent the smell of gasoline, and decided that while it might not be a smell, it still smelled hot.

All through the drive to Edwards Air Force Base, she'd stared out at the bleak sea of scrub and sand, backed by the far too distant mountains. She glanced up. There was so much cloudless sky dominated by the remorseless sun.

"Are you all right, Miss Merriweather?" the Captain asked,

standing by the gate to their new residence. He'd accompanied them to the base, but Alice couldn't remember his name. An airman had scrambled out from the driver's seat to open their doors for them. "It gets pretty hot this time of year."

Alice glanced at her father, noting the anxiety in his rather pale gray eyes. "I'm fine," she said. "I hardly feel the heat," she added the lie. It wouldn't be her first or last, she guessed.

With an inner stiffening of her courage, she turned to face the bungalow where they'd be living for—well, she was not certain how long they'd be there. So much depended on her father and this opportunity to build his dream.

The small house looked as defeated as she felt after the long, hot drive. The small gate stuck for a minute before it opened with a squeak, then the men gestured for her to go first. Drifted sand half hid the sidewalk. The knob was hot to the touch but opened without a key. She paused to look back. The street was silent, almost deserted, except for a dark car. A man leaned against it, his arms crossed over his chest. His clothes were dark, too, and sunglasses obscured his gaze, but Alice felt a prickle along her nerve endings.

Her shoulders straightened an inch more. She turned and stepped inside.

* * *

PRESENT DAY, *Time-resistant Bunker in an Undisclosed Location*

"What if it's a trap?" Melanie "Mel" Morton Hamilton asked.

She turned from the map dominating the entire wall. It was dotted with newspaper clippings, notes—both handwritten and printed—and a myriad of red lines running in a variety of directions. But most of them headed to one location.

Edwards Air Force Base.

The two men on the other side of the room glanced at each

other then returned their attention to her with carefully neutral expressions.

"It's what we're doing," she pointed out. "We're looking for them." If it was a trap, their unknown foe had baited it well. It had the most indications of time tampering of any other event they'd been tracking.

Her husband, Jack, gave a half shrug in acknowledgement of her point. Mel turned her attention to the other man in the room, because looking at Jack made her heart kick up and distracted her from the task at hand. Plus, it was unprofessional to look sappy at work. Out of the corner of her eye, she saw Jack's lips twitch, as if he knew.

Jack's companion, Dr. Tyson Granger, was also good looking —in a quietly powerful way that didn't move her heart dial at all. His build was broader than Jack's, a different kind of lethal rumbled under there, hiding behind eyes as deeply compelling and soulful as a St. Bernard's.

"That's why I'm going," Granger said. He had a deep, soothing voice to go with his "trust me" eyes. Between eyes and voice, even his most outrageous assertions sounded entirely logical and reasonable. Granger was a pilot, like Jack, but not really like Jack. Both were total geeks, though neither of them looked like geeks. No glasses or pocket protectors. Jack had the pilot swagger and a belief in his own immortality. Granger was so focused and delib-erate, Mel had to remind herself he was, in his own way, as reck-less as Jack. Or her, she conceded wryly.

Mel didn't disagree with his assertion he was making the trip, even though the trip hadn't been approved yet. She wasn't going, that was for sure. She and Jack had barely made it back alive from their last attempt to track the rogue time travelers. It was just a theory, of course, but Jack believed it was because they'd tried to track them into the future. Not that traveling into the past had been without its smackdowns.

"If they are after you—" Granger began.

"They could just be trying to tamper with the timeline," Jack cut in.

Just. Mel almost snorted.

The room in the center of their specially designed bunker shook as if there'd been some kind of explosion or seismic event. They all glanced at their seismic monitor, but it hadn't registered anything. Their time sensor was going nuts—if it worked properly. This would be the first serious test if Jack approved Granger to go.

If.

Had Jack hesitated this long before sending Mel back in time? Okay, probably, since he'd had almost eighty years to think about it, but still, this mission had more riding on it than just a time machine test. This was about the time tampering; it was an attempt to get an handle on who was doing it. And if the perps were from the future? One step at a time, Jack said, though it was more like a leap at a time.

Granger's legs were long enough for leaping. And it was a truth—possibly a universal one—that a man determined to travel back in time would find a way to make that happen. Granger had taken everything they'd thrown at him. The physical training, the high-altitude parachute drops, the psych evaluations—he'd immersed himself in the target time period, and never once looked flustered. If there was a perfect time traveler, Tyson Granger was the poster dude.

As the resident expert on time travel, Mel felt—not doubts exactly—but concern for sure. She'd been there and done it. She knew how freaking hard it was. And she'd changed her past history and Jack's to some extent. At least from what they knew. It was the parts they didn't know that worried both of them. She'd had a front-row seat to see time rippling through her life. She'd returned with two distinct and separate memories of her personal timeline. It made for some weird *faux pas* in her encounters with friends and family.

Jack had postulated that the reason she remembered both timelines was because of her photographic memory. It wasn't a bad theory except for the trip into the past she didn't remember. Jack claimed she didn't remember that first trip because he'd sent her back into the past the second time before the first time happened.

This is why her eyes twitched a lot. Even worse, time travel, if you thought about it too much, also made your head want to explode. Paradoxes and timeline changes and…

Another time tremor rattled the structure, causing the lights to flicker. She tasted something metallic in her mouth and her skin tingled. No question the tremors had worsened as they'd closed in on the suspected time tampering. Mel turned back to the map and touched the tip of her finger to the red circle, their suspected ground zero. The tremor almost shook her off her feet. She took her finger off the map, rubbing the zinged tip, and the tremor eased.

Whether it was time tampering or a time trap, something was building—had built—at Edwards Air Force base in the past. They could act and change heavens knew what, or do nothing and—they didn't know what would happen if they did nothing. Nothing might happen. Something might happen when it was too late to do something. Yeah, eye twitch time.

When Jack had sent Mel back in time, it had been personal. He hadn't expected to find evidence that someone else was time traveling—and possibly time tampering. Okay, they were pretty sure someone was tampering—or testing—time. And if that weren't challenging enough, they didn't know if they'd tried this before. This could be the first, second, third, or fifth time they'd tried to do something about the tampering.

She leaned in, studying their map without touching it this time. Despite her caution, she felt the hairs on her arms lift as she got closer.

The picture in the red circle was of an older man with an

unhappy face: Dr. George Merriweather. Was he truly the epicenter of the time event? He didn't look like an epicenter kind of guy. Scientist, widower, father. Why would time care about him? There was only one way to find out. But she still had a question to ask. Mostly because she needed the reassurance. "You think what he was working on was important enough to stop?"

Granger shoved his hands in the pockets of his slacks. "I do."

Of course he did. Did she think his answer was going to change now, when he was so close to getting what he wanted?

"We don't even know it would have worked," Mel felt she had to point out. Again.

Granger's gaze shifted to Jack, then back to Mel. His shrug was slight. Mel knew why. The schematics Granger had found were too far ahead of their time. And they reminded Jack of a young, WWII pilot who'd dreamed of time travel.

The project was either amazing enough to stop, or an irresistible trap for Jack—and her—if they knew about her. That was the other kicker. They didn't know what the other guys or gals knew. And with time travel, knowing could be a moving target as time changed in response to the interference.

"Don't you find it troubling they couldn't get a test pilot?" Mel asked. Unless that record had been erased.

"Testing experimental aircraft was—is risky. Pilots died. I'm sure they had good reasons for not wanting to test this...*Manta Ray*. And there was plenty of competition at the time," Jack added. "Too many planes, not enough pilots."

They only had fragments of information about the plane. No pictures had survived. But it was the engine that interested Granger and Jack, Mel knew.

"Or someone sabotaged them," Granger pointed out. "It wouldn't take much to get a whisper campaign going if someone wanted to make sure it didn't get tested and on any official record."

The explosion and fire certainly supported that contention.

But which had they been after? The plane or its engine? Could have been both, she thought with a silent sigh.

She turned back her board, her gaze very reluctantly finding the small news item no one had wanted to add there. But it was what they did, no matter how bizarre.

"The official record says President Eisenhower had a toothache," she murmured. The headline popped out as if to mock her: *Dateline February 20, 1954. President Dwight Eisenhower Meets With Two Extraterrestrials.* Just looking at it made her eye twitch faster and her head hurt more.

"It does," Granger agreed.

"Whatever happened that night," Jack said, "Merriweather disappeared. His daughter was killed. And most of his research was destroyed."

What had happened that night? Had Merriweather been relocated by the time-tampering time travelers? Or had he run away because of his daughter's death?

"If it had worked—" Mel stopped.

"I only saw preliminary drawings of the engine, but if it did what I think he was trying to do? The space program would look completely different," Granger said. "We might already be on Mars."

She spun around. "But…aliens?"

Both men shrugged. It was Jack who responded. "Someone traveling from the future could easily make themselves appear to be alien."

And they had evidence someone—other than them—was traveling through time, possibly from the future, but they could be from now, since it had been current-to-this-time tech they'd attempted to plant in World War II.

"I don't think the President met with aliens," Granger said, yet again, "but it's an anomalous event within the time frame that is triggering our machines."

She shoved her hands into the pockets of her jeans. An anomalous event? That was classing a rumor up a bit.

"You know that you have to—" Mel began, because she felt he still didn't get it. How could he not get how freaking hard time travel was?

"Jump into a vortex without a parachute," Granger said. A slight, satisfied smile twitched the edges of a mouth that was full and rather sensual. "And if something goes wrong, I could end up lost in time. Or dead."

Yeah, he thought the idea sounded fun until he was looking down that vortex and having to step off the edge into nothing. His confidence made her want to shake her head, but the decision had been made long ago, perhaps even a timeline or two ago. And the clock was ticking. If Granger was right, and if everything went perfectly, they'd be just in time.

She shrugged and sighed. Boys and their time travel aspirations. "Let's do it then," she said.

CHAPTER 2

*I*t was not always a good thing to get what you want. Or to know so much about what could go wrong, Tyson Granger thought a bit wryly. For instance, he wished he didn't know that the human body fell at one hundred and twenty-two miles an hour, and if the time machine failed to form a vortex, that was how fast he'd be going when he hit the ground. He also knew exactly what it would do to his body—in addition to killing him.

There was also the possibility that the vortex would form, that it would work—and send him to the wrong time or place. He could end up nose-to-nose with a dinosaur, he supposed. Crap happened.

And despite knowing these things, here he sat, the engines rumbling through his body, straps holding him in place, as the plane clawed its way to drop altitude. There was a metallic taste in his mouth that he told himself was the oxygen or the mask. Not fear.

Drop altitude. For the falling part.

You know you have to jump into the center of a vortex without a parachute.

Mel had tried to prepare him for this. Or scare him out of doing it. He wasn't sure which. Okay, maybe he was sure. He'd appeared attentive during the briefing, and patiently endured having a computer chip inserted into his posterior. At least Mel hadn't been in the room for that. The chip was his ride home, once his mission was complete. Who didn't want a vortex to grab them by the butt and yank them home? If she'd expected him to comment, she'd been disappointed.

And then they strapped on the perfect-to-period, dead man's watch for his wrist. If something went wrong before his extraction time, or if someone tried to forcibly remove it—say, in the event he was arrested—if would inject him with cyanide. It was a necessary precaution, considering where he was going, what he knew, and the fact he'd be dealing with a military suspicious of spies, not to mention the possible time-traveling enemies. He still wasn't thrilled about it. At least, he had instructions on how to remove it properly, along with a lot of cautions on not doing that unless absolutely necessary.

Because he didn't know he shouldn't take it off.

He'd maintained outward patience, while inside he wanted to shove them all out of his face and get on with it. This was not something he wanted to spend a lot of time thinking about. He was a scientist, so he should want to think, but he also didn't want to wimp out. He'd asked for this and he wanted it. Not as much right now, but still enough to keep going if they'd get it done soon.

He shifted on his seat, but the problem wasn't the seat. Mel, he recalled now, had muttered about the miserable clothes in the past, and now he understood her comments better. The old-fashioned fabrics lacked the comfort and ease of movement. His gaberdine suit and business coat were not warm enough for the temperature in the cargo hold. The shoes were not ideal either. Secured next to him was a to-period duffel containing changes of clothes and gear he'd need to accomplish the mission. Identification papers—to protect his future, his real name had not been used—appropriate money, and a few other critical items were secured to his body with a money belt. Mel claimed she hadn't lost any of the clothes she'd been wearing, so that was good. But he might have the duffel ripped from him by the buffeting of the vortex.

Buffeting.

Mel had said this with relish. While she'd warned him every which way she could, he had a feeling she was glad someone else would know what she was talking about. If he made it back. He glanced at the duffel again. He sincerely hoped the duffel made it. It would not feel right if his first act in the past would be to go shopping.

The plane engines whined as it banked and then began to level off. The techs seated across from him unstrapped and got up, going to the device that would create the time vortex. It was small and looked innocuous, hanging above the hatch he hoped to use for his jump into the past. If it managed to form the vortex. And he managed to stand up and do it.

It had formed before, he reminded himself, if he believed Hamilton and Mel. And he did. He believed them enough to step off the edge of that hatch. At least, he was pretty sure he was going to step off that edge. They just needed to hurry up and let him do it.

"Don't look down," Mel's voice said through his headset.

He met her eyes across the hold and nodded.

"Saying it now because if I say it then, you'll look down," she added.

Granger was pretty sure she grinned behind her oxygen mask.

"Did you look down?" he asked.

"Yeah," she admitted.

"And you jumped," he said.

"Yeah, but I'm certifiable. Ask anyone."

He chuckled then and felt the inner tension ease. Tension he hadn't realized was there.

"I closed my eyes before I stepped off the edge, though."

That seemed like a good idea.

"We're ready, sir."

Granger unstrapped and rose, steadying himself as the plane rocked slightly. Someone handed him his duffel and helped him strap it to his chest. He hugged it, hoping that arms and straps would beat the buffeting. He lifted a hand to remove his face mask and headset, but one of the techs told him to wait. They fiddled some more and then a hum, different from that of the plane, began to build up through the bottom of his feet. The device's lights flashed and then the air between it and the open hatch began to waver and change.

Unease crawled up his back at the sight. It was…unnatural.

With a nod from the other tech, Granger stepped up to the edge and yes, he looked down. There was no view of the land below, just a silver, spinning vortex. He wasn't sure the vortex wasn't worse than what the view would have been without it. At a signal, he removed and held out his oxygen mask and headset, because he couldn't look away from the sight. He gripped the duffel once more, though with a new reason for doing so. It was something to hold on to—like a grown-up teddy bear. He almost grinned at himself. But the cold had numbed his lips. Yeah, the cold.

"Five…four…"

The countdown had begun. He couldn't look away and the vortex continued to build, the roar of it drowning out the voices. The tech must have known because he switched to fingers.

"…three…two…"

Before he could change his mind, he closed his eyes and stepped off the edge.

* * *

An aircraft roared overhead as Alice stood in the narrow hall of their bungalow, smoothing her gloves down over her wrists. The engine note changed, faltered, and she tensed, her gaze going up, even though she couldn't see the aircraft. The roar picked up once more and she relaxed, glancing toward her father.

George Merriweather was a distinguished figure in his gaberdine suit, wings of gray in his dark hair. Some of the other spinsters—her lips twisted a bit wryly—on the base had tried to catch his attention. They'd failed. They didn't know he was a…dead man walking. Her mother's death had taken the heart from him, leaving only the science behind to provide some animation.

They were a sober pair, she with her pencil skirt in almost the same shade of brown as her father's gaberdine. His clipped hair and her equally sober bun. She'd been told she looked like her mother, but she wondered if that were still true. It had been twenty years since…she stole a glance at herself. Maybe if she got glasses. Her mother had worn glasses, very scholarly glasses.

Her father took a last drink from his coffee cup, then set it down on a table that had seen better days, and turned toward her. His heavy-lidded, gray gaze was distant, more so because of his professorial glasses. He straightened his tie, visibly gathering himself to leave the house, to face the day. Every day he shrugged resolve on like the ill-fitting coat he rarely needed living in the high desert of California. Thankfully, temperatures were moderate in February. It was hard enough to begin the day without a wall of heat to push through. At least the holidays were well behind them. Though their problems with the project remained unresolved.

He walked past Alice, pushing open the screen door and then holding it for her with the careful courtesy that was as much a part of him as his eyes and hair and melancholy.

Alice tucked her purse under her arm and followed him, then paused before she pulled the inside door closed to say, "I'm going to Palm Springs with some friends tomorrow."

"Friends?" Mild surprise animated his voice.

"Some of the other"—she looked at him now—"secretaries."

His gaze turned to meet hers for a long moment, before falling away. Walking ahead of him down the walk, her footsteps kicking up small puffs of dirt, she slowed to give their driver time to scramble out and come forward to open the gate. She nodded and murmured thanks, then waited by the car for both men to join her.

They did this every weekday, and had since they'd arrived here two years and six months ago. Their driver had changed a couple of times. And the weather. Or she'd have felt caught in time, reliving the same day over and over again.

After a brief exchange about the weather, the rest of the drive was silent. Alice stared out the side window as the bleak terrain slid past. After some initial resistance, she'd come to a point of fondness for the Joshua trees. Or possibly she felt a kinship with the prickly, twisted, dead-looking trees. And then they'd surprised her by blooming.

Not dead after all.

The desert vista was broken by the base infrastructure and their car pulled to a stop in front of the hangar that contained their workspace. For how much longer? She tamped down this thought. They'd find a pilot. They had to. So much work—

The airman opened the door for her and she slid out. Alice inhaled the cooler—though still dry—air and cast a last look around before she had to go inside. He was there again, waiting by his car.

The man in black—Alice knew his name now—John Phillips, was still a mystery, an enigma. And Alice trusted him as much as she had that first day, which was to say, not at all. He'd been there to see their arrival, then vanished, reappearing six months ago— when their project was nearing testing readiness. In their other life in academia, Phillips' upright, military aspect would have stood out, but here on the base, he was just one in a crowd—

though one not wearing a uniform. This somehow kept him separate from the others. Or perhaps it was his choice to not be of them, to try to blend.

Alice might have understood blending. At thirty-three, she was a spinster, well past dating and marriageable age, consigned to fixture status. This gave her another reason to distrust Phillips. He'd hovered around her when he'd returned, acting interested without ever acting on that so-called interest. He wouldn't be the first man to try to get close to her father through her, but he was the first non-scientist. Because Alice felt uneasy around him, she'd maintained an even strength—a phrase she'd learned from the pilots' wives.

Phillips straightened and crossed the road to her father's side, giving her a brief, somewhat dismissive nod as he passed her.

"Sir," he said, his tone respectful.

His body language did not reflect deference. Her father was on the tall side, but Phillips topped him by several inches. He exuded toughness, in thought and body. Her father had called him a thug during a rare burst of temper, but Alice was not so sure he merited the epithet. There was intelligence in his chilly gaze and Phillips could hold his own in discussions of fuel percentages and aerodynamics. And he was clever. He'd managed to never explain—in her hearing—what his role on the base encompassed. He appeared to support her father's project and claimed to be working on getting them a test pilot. So how was it that, in a test pilot training facility filled with pilots eager to be the fastest men on earth, he'd failed to find a single one willing to fly the *Ray*? And why did he care? The channels that had been there when they arrived had slowly closed, leaving him as the only option for acquiring supplies and other things—like pilots.

There was also more pushback from the other groups. They didn't like the money that had been funneled toward the *Ray* and had a lot of questions about how they'd even managed to get a setup here. Politics, Phillips had said, with an edge of scorn, but the politics had gotten worse since he'd come back.

There were indications that they'd lose their research space if something didn't change soon. Phillips had not appeared discouraged by the setbacks. He managed to say a lot without saying much of anything. Bright—possibly brilliant—persistent and, she suspected, ruthless, she found him as tiring as the desert summer heat had been. That had finally gone away but Phillips hadn't, she thought a bit ruefully, as she watched Phillips and her father go inside.

Was there new purpose in the set of Phillips' shoulders? In his determined stride? What did he want? Or did he finally have a pilot for them?

"Is there anything wrong, ma'am?" the airman asked.

She looked at him and managed a smile of sorts.

"No, thank you." She longed to turn and walk down the long, dry road away from all of it, but, after gathering in her own resolve, she followed them inside.

* * *

PALM SPRINGS, February, 1954

Nothing, no briefing, not the most urgent warning, could have prepared him for the extreme buffeting of the vortex, the sense of falling down its silver length—and then suddenly finding solid ground beneath his feet.

He swayed, took a stumbling step forward, and opened his eyes.

The sense of disorientation from the disconnect was intense. His eyes saw, but the input struggled to reach his brain. Only now did he begin to understand Mel's briefing and her concern about the effects of traveling through time. Had he traveled through time?

He glanced around, worried someone might notice him, but other than a car driving past, he appeared to be alone.

Alone where? Alone when?

The line of palm trees gave him hope he had "integrated" where he was supposed to be.

Granger had not only studied old photos of Palm Springs, but he had also visited the city and walked the streets that had existed in 1954. He drew a shaky breath and turned slowly, the disconnect intensifying. Even the color photographs had not—could not —prepare him for the reality that his eyes saw but his brain rejected as wrong. It was the colors, he decided. They were vibrant instead of faded. Of course they were, but cars and the houses—it was both wrong and so very right.

Palm Springs, he was sure this was where he was. The line of palm trees. Vintage—to him—cars parked next to the curb. The quiet of the street, and how the light fell across it were a possible indication it was early in the day.

What day? What year?

Someone came out wearing a robe and bent to collect a newspaper. He straightened but didn't turn, instead eyeing Granger over the top of the paper. That's when he realized he still clutched the duffel to his chest. He eased off the straps so he could hold it with one hand, smoothed down his vortex-ruffled hair, and strode with apparent purpose down the street toward an intersection. He needed to figure out where—and when—he was. The vortex was brutal, and very imprecise, according to Mel. He could be a few days to a couple of weeks ahead of his targeted arrival. He could be too late…

Having a purpose, moving forward, helped to mitigate the feeling he'd landed in an old movie set. Even as his brain struggled to process the sights, the sounds, and the smells, his eyes continued to process the full, living *real* color. For the first time, he had to confront the part of him that had wondered if it was really possible to travel through time. He hadn't let himself doubt, had pushed through all the resistance to...this.

He was in the past. Okay, he was pretty sure he was in the past.

In the distance, past trees and buildings, the cloud-topped San Bernardino, the Santa Rosa, and the San Jacinto mountains circled the Coachella desert valley where the city nestled—just as they had in the future. So why did they look so different now? It could be that the air was clearer, he decided. The mountains couldn't have changed that much in sixty-five years.

He reached the street sign, but it took him a full minute to absorb what it said and then orient himself on the map he'd memorized. Based on where it was, the sun rising in the high, blue sky, he felt reasonably certain he was in Palm Springs. It felt early, but early when, he wondered once again.

He glanced around and found a sign for a diner. He had to stop himself from touching the hoods of both a '53 Ford and a Buick Super. It was like dropping into the ultimate car show. He had to get it together, but part of him still wondered if this was real or some drug-induced hallucination. All of it felt real, the training, the briefings, the tests, but what if he'd walked into some trap and was currently in a virtual reality chamber? Was he crazy that he believed time travel over anything else?

He pushed open the swing door of the diner—and stepped further back into the past. Checkerboard black and white floor. Red seats, chrome everywhere and a big jukebox against one wall. Only a couple of customers, one seated in a booth, the other seated on a stool at the end of a long counter. A rack of postcards next to a gumball machine.

A waitress looked up from wiping the countertop and said something that could have been a greeting. There was a clock on the wall. It was closing on ten. Ten when?

"Cup of coffee?" he requested, then realized his money was in the belt strapped around his waist. "Bathroom?"

She gave him an odd look, but indicated the direction for him and then turned to the coffee pot. He returned, his wallet now in his back pocket, complete with ID and cash. He noticed a rumpled newspaper on the end of the counter.

"That today's?" he asked, and when she nodded, "May I?"

She nodded again, so he straddled the stool and picked it up, a slight tremble to his hands as he unfolded it. The smell of ink wafted upwards, briefly kicking out the coffee smell. He stared down, trying to keep his breathing even and his shock hidden.

Unless he was in some kind of drugged state, it was there in black and white.

February 13, 1954.

He had time traveled to 1954. He was sitting in the past. Out there somewhere, his dad was a baby, his mom not even a twinkle in his grandparents' eyes yet, but here he was. Sixty-six years away from where he belonged.

In the mirror behind the counter, he saw himself, as poker-faced as always. It could be a dream, he supposed, born of his intense drive to make this trip. He lowered a hand and gripped his leg hard. But the diner didn't fade. And he'd read this issue of the newspaper as part of his briefing. A faded edition copied from microfilm. He set it aside with hands that shook again. He clenched them, then reached for the coffee cup.

"Anything else?" the waitress asked, giving him a hint of a flirty smile.

He returned her smile with just enough warmth to not raise hopes, ordered some breakfast and ate swiftly, with the newspaper folded in half before him. He knew more about this time than the paper's reporters. He pretended to be reading it, but his brain was busy with what to do next.

In his head, there was a map of the city and he was pretty sure he knew where he was, though the sense of disorientation persisted. He knew from his briefing his best chance of connecting with Edwards Air Force Base personnel was at a diner, not this one unfortunately. Dilly's was just off Palm Canyon Drive. If he could hook up with someone, he could hitch a ride, and avoid leaving the wrong kind of paper trail by renting a car. He glanced at his watch, now set to local time, then waited until the waitress had finished pouring a cup for a newcomer. When she noticed him looking, she came to him, the pot hovering over his cup. He shook his head.

"I'm supposed to meet a friend on Palm Canyon Drive. Just want to make sure of my directions."

The waitress's eyes flickered toward the other man at the counter. After a hesitation, he turned toward Granger. He wore a delivery uniform of some kind.

"I gotta cross Palm Canyon," the man said, adding with a hint of warning, "I only cross it—"

"Anywhere on it is fine," Granger said, with an easy smile. "I've got some time to kill before he'll get there."

The man nodded. "Let me finish this cup and we'll go."

"Thanks," Granger said, wondering what his chances were of catching a lift to the base this early. He did not want to have to hang around in Palm Springs for too long. Unlike Mel's adventure in time, where she'd known what she needed to do, he had one short week to figure it all out and then act—or not. He was either just in time or irretrievably late.

He walked over to the rack of postcards, spinning it slowly until he caught sight of one featuring this place. He plucked it out and went back to the counter, handing the waitress the single coin to purchase it. He pulled out a to-period pen and wrote "Having a wonderful time." He added slashing initials and the date, and a predecided-upon address, then pocketed the pen.

"Any chance there is a post office on the way?"

The waitress, with another flirty smile, found him a stamp.

"Thanks," he tossed some more onto her tip. There'd be a post office box somewhere on the way.

"Ready?" the deliveryman asked.

"As I'll ever be," Granger said.

* * *

ALICE WAS sure she'd made a mistake before she climbed into the back seat of the '51 Studebaker Champion rumbling in front of her, its top down. She was, in her way, as stubborn as her father. He'd accepted her kiss on his cheek with a mild, "I hope you know what you're doing," then turned back to his book.

Alice tied a scarf over her hair as Mary put the car in gear. Betty already sat next to her, both wearing scarves, too. Alice was aware that they were dressed similarly, but somehow the two girls' swing dresses were brighter and younger than Alice's version. And Alice's buttoned-down cardigan came off as prim, rather than fashionable. Oh, the joys of being a spinster.

"Helen not coming after all?" Alice inquired as they turned toward the gate. Helen was somewhat closer to Alice in age. They might have had something to talk about.

"She got a better offer," Betty said with a giggle.

It turned out Alice needn't have worried about keeping up an end of the conversation. Betty and Mary were fully capable of keeping up several peoples' ends. So she sat back and enjoyed the rare treat of being off base, even if the view didn't change that much until they started into the mountains. It was here that she realized her spirits were lifting with the altitude and the change in scenery. They made only one comfort stop, where all three of them bought sunglasses. Alice needed a little persuading. These were not the glasses she'd pondered purchasing. But at the sight of herself in the small mirror...

Funny what a difference that made. It was as if the dark glasses gave her a degree of separation from herself, not to mention a hint of glamor that her somber-colored dress did not.

Back in the Studebaker, she began to relax and enjoy the snippets of conversation the wind carried to her. She felt half embarrassed by her almost sprawl but then she thought, why not? Who was here to care?

Betty and Mary seemed to feel it, too, because they lounged in their seats more and their talk got louder and more animated. Betty turned the dial on the radio until she found a station playing recent hits and Frank Sinatra began to croon to them.

"Frances says she saw Frank on Palm Canyon Drive," Mary said with a sigh. "He has a house there now." Her tone was of one 'in the know.'

Alice didn't admit that she only heard hit songs when not around her father. He considered silence essential to the ordered mind. But he'd listened to music before, when her mother was alive. He'd never been given to huge gestures of affection, but she'd seen them exchange a look when certain songs came on. Her mother—but what was the point of knowing her mother wouldn't like what George Merriweather had turned both of their lives into? She was gone. And if either of them disturbed the fragile balance?

It could actually get worse.

She was glad when they rolled into Palm Springs and down the famous—according to her two companions—Palm Canyon Drive. It felt to Alice as if she'd been transported into a place of color and vibrant life—civilian life, she reminded herself. The base was busy, as well, but in a more purposeful and focused way. It was certainly more serious, at least the part Alice interacted with, since life and death were on the line almost every day. But it felt as if even the air smelled different, of flowers and citrus and food and...life.

Mary found a parking spot and they climbed out to do some window shopping. All three of them pulled off their scarves and the two younger women fussed with their hair for a minute or two. It was good they weren't driving, because both girls craned, in hopes of seeing someone famous. It was so outside Alice's experience that she did some craning herself. They paused at a street corner and Alice stared at a flashy convertible cruising slowly past. The driver lowered his sunglasses and gave her a cheeky smile and a wave. Somewhat dazed, Alice returned Frank's wave. At least, she thought it was the famous singer as the car continued down the street. She opened her mouth to tell Mary, then closed it. She wasn't sure, after all. But those blue eyes. She gave a tiny shiver. My word.

With a start, she realized the girls were crossing the street. They attracted some catcalls and whistles. Alice didn't assume any were for her. She glanced at the three of them in a big-paned window as they strolled past. She was definitely the sober older—sister—in the frame. But her figure was still trim and her hair looked nice, pulled back loosely from her face and released from its customary bun. And the glasses, well, she had good reason to believe they imbued her with an air of mystery she did not deserve. Mary must have caught Alice's small smile

"Are you having fun, Alice?" she asked, her tone that of someone speaking to an elderly aunt taken out for the day.

Alice chuckled to her surprise. "I'm having a lovely time, thank you."

Mary and Betty exchanged startled looks, then Betty said, "You have a great smile, Alice."

"I'll bet you could snag a widower if you used it more," Mary agreed.

"I'll try to keep that in mind," Alice said with as much sincerity as she could muster. She glanced at her watch, mostly to take their minds off her smile, and said, "Where is this Dilly's you talked about?"

"Oh, we don't want to be late!" Betty exclaimed. "We might miss people."

"I'm sure you're worried about missing *people*," Mary said with emphasis, but she turned back in the direction of the car so eagerly that Alice was sure Mary had someone she hoped to see, too.

Had she been invited as chaperone? Or was she going to be dumped? No, they wouldn't do that, she decided, but she might be charged with driving the car back to Edwards. It was a good thing she had a good memory and knew how to drive. It had never occurred to either girl to ask her if she could or would. Maybe it was a single girl's code she hadn't heard about.

Alice felt a strange sensation in her throat and realized with a sense of disbelief that it was a giggle. She thought she'd forgotten how. The giggle, or perhaps the lightness of this place, seemed to have filtered into her arms and legs, possibly even her whole body as she climbed out of the Studebaker, now parked in front of Dilly's. She shook out her dress and tucked her clasp purse under her arm. The door to Dilly's opened, and music, sound, and laughter spilled out.

Perry Como's "Don't Let the Stars Get in Your Eyes" was playing inside.

Was it a warning? An invitation? An interesting coincidence?

Either way, she was going in.

* * *

JACK SAW the bunker light activate and went to help with the door. They were alone, so he wrapped his arms around Mel as she entered.

Even after their time together, after all he'd seen her do in the past, he had a hard time reconciling this Mel with one who had starred in *Make Mel Cry Uncle*. It had been available to stream and he'd watched every episode. She had been crazy, he told her. She'd laughed and told him he'd seen it before and her craziness wasn't exactly a news flash. This made both their eyes twitch because "before" was when he'd been an old man. An old man, she liked to point out, who had sent her back in time and into a war.

They were both crazy—crazy in love. He still marveled at the miracle of being with her, of being married to her, of living in this time where he could be with, and work with her. He still felt disconnected at times from his past, from his friends and family, but they'd all lost something in the war. He'd gained so much, he couldn't complain.

What he feared—a fear he hadn't shared with Mel—was that this other time traveler might, by accident or intent, undo all they'd accomplished. And worse, separate he and Mel once more. Would he even remember her if this timeline was undone? It didn't seem possible that could happen, but how could he remember someone he'd never met?

In their attempt to understand time travel better, they'd done only micro-jumps of minutes, or a day or two into the past, since their time smackdown. Jack still had misgivings about sending Granger back, but the window to travel to this particular time wouldn't open again for a year. And Granger had made a compelling case for interference. In a year, untold damage could be done to the future and no one would know it.

His thoughts always circled back to the need to fight this other incursion and who might be doing it. He couldn't consider them benign, not when they'd introduced future—no matter how minor—tech into the past. If the Germans had managed to study the item, it could have changed the course of the war.

His arms tightened on Mel.

"Granger get off okay?" Jack murmured against her hair, inhaling the scent of her and freshness of the outside air she'd brought with her.

"Well, we didn't find him splattered all over Palm Springs."

She pushed back, studying his face with worry creasing her brow. He reached up and smoothed the spot, his hand getting close enough for her to brush her lips against the back. His breath caught and he swept her close again, finding her lips with his.

They were both breathing faster when he lifted his head.

"I like your research technique," she murmured, the light in her eyes one he knew very well now.

He couldn't, he wouldn't lose her. He planted a last kiss on her forehead and then turned them both, still holding her hand, back to the map that filled one whole wall. Would they know if something had changed? They'd hoped the bunker would provide some protection from time's changes, so they could track them and create a response. So far, well, he didn't know how well they were doing.

"How do you think he's doing?" Jack asked, his gaze running over the board. Had anything changed?

Mel was quiet for a minute and Jack knew, without being told, she was thinking about her first few hours in the past.

"He's trying to get over being…boggled," she finally said, with a grin. "But at least he isn't dodging bombs in 1940s London."

"I have apologized for that," Jack pointed out, mostly with kisses that had led to other things.

"It's not like I could forget," Mel said.

Jack often envied her photographic memory, but it could have its downside.

Suddenly her hand tightened on his and she frowned. "But we know, don't we?" she said.

"Know?" Jack shook his head. "How?"

She pointed at the map. "The postcard from Palm Springs." He shook his head and she snagged it, showing him a faded postcard of a diner. She turned it over.

Having a wonderful time. TG, February 13, 1954.

"He made it," she said with wonder in her voice. "I knew it, but I didn't know I knew it until now."

Jack frowned. Did he remember the postcard? There were so

many things on the wall, so many bits of memorabilia. But that—he should remember that. He'd stayed inside for Granger's jump for just this reason. Maybe, just, maybe his time bunker worked.

"I'm happy," Mel said, "and my head hurts."

Jack grinned, but absently. What else might Granger be able to send them from the past?

CHAPTER 3

$\mathcal{F}$red, the delivery guy, had dropped Granger off at the furthest end of Palm Canyon Drive from Dilly's, but he hadn't minded. It gave him a chance to stroll the length. It had also given him time to adjust to bring the outside reality into agreement with his inside reality. When he finally got to Dilly's, it was still early enough for him to secure a spot at the end of the counter. This allowed him to keep an eye on the comings and goings at Dilly's without looking like that's what he was doing. Not that it mattered. Door watching seemed to be a thing in this place. The patrons were probably hoping to spot someone famous, he decided.

Dilly's was much busier than where he'd had breakfast, and maybe a little more high end, but his gray suit still made him stand out among the casual crowd. Early on he'd slipped his jacket off and removed his tie, then loosened the top button of his shirt. He'd tucked the jacket in his duffel, which was now stowed securely at his feet. It made a nice footrest. He'd been nursing a couple of malts—which tasted better than any memory he had of one in the future—and another cup of coffee, for what felt like forever. The staff were all too busy to worry much about him and, looking around, he could tell he wasn't the only one waiting for someone. He was probably the only one waiting for someone he didn't know.

He wasn't as shell shocked as he'd been, but he might be a bit bemused. Dilly's was right out of a 50's bopper movie. Lots of chrome, white and pink. So much pink—including a flamingo painted in bold colors on one wall. So much energy. So many young people. It wasn't that he was the only forty-something there, but the mix was definitely weighted toward the young. He could pick out the pilots, the military support personnel, and the women attached to them. But there were also locals in the mix, he'd guess, mostly girls eyeing the military guys with interest.

The door opened and three women entered, two blondes maybe in their twenties and—

He stiffened, though he wasn't sure why. Maybe she'd been in one of the photos from the briefings? She seemed familiar to him, though he couldn't connect her to anything specific. He was aware she was older than the twenty-somethings, her clothes somehow quieter in a field of bright. She pulled sunglasses off, a half smile edging her mouth as she looked around. With no evidence at all, Granger felt she was as bemused by the place as he'd been. Her hair was long and dark and pulled up and back so that it left her face exposed, with the bulk of her hair tumbling partway down her back like a mane. She gave off an aura of calm in the chaos, though as he watched, the smile faded and her lashes covered her eyes as she followed her companions through the press of people to the counter where he sat.

A strange sense of anticipation filled him at her approach. With even less evidence than before, he thought, *I could like her.*

Follow your gut, your instincts, Mel had told him, but he felt sure this was not the instinct she'd have wanted him to follow. He couldn't afford to get distracted by—his thoughts splintered again when she slid onto the stool next to his and leaned her elbows on the counter, her clean scent finding him despite the myriad of smells already swirling around.

"A chocolate malt," she said, her voice both rich and clear. "That's all for now."

He waited for her gaze to slide his direction, but instead she half turned toward the other two girls. He realized one of them was watching him in open speculation and when his gaze intersected with hers, she smiled with demure invitation. He rejected the idea he might be old enough to be her father, but she was still half child. And he hadn't traveled back in time to get a date. Color heated his face for a moment and he looked down at his half-consumed malt, hoping it would provide a plan for him. It was getting about time he found a ride.

"Oh, there's Jerry," one of the voices said.

Granger slanted a careful look and saw, with relief, that it was his tormentor who'd had slid off the stool and hurried across the room. He wrapped his hands tighter around the malt, welcoming the cold chill of the glass against his palms.

"So what is the actual plan, Mary?" That cool, crystal clear voice had to be hers, amusement adding additional depth.

"Why, Alice—" she protested.

"If you were planning on me driving your father's car back to base, shouldn't you have made sure I can drive?"

Base? Edwards? Granger wasn't sure he should hope. There had been at least two other bases in the area back then—now.

"Alice, don't tell me—" There was clear horror in the young voice.

"I can drive," Alice admitted. Her chuckle sent heat down Granger's spine.

"You're mean!" Mary protested, but there was laughter in her voice, too.

"You'd better give me the key," Alice suggested. "I think I see Henry looking hopefully this way."

"You are the best!" The girl leaned forward and gave her an impulsive hug. "Just leave—"

"I'll leave it in front of my house with the key under the seat?"

"Perfect…"

And then Mary was weaving her way through the press to her young man.

"Well, at least I don't have to be a chaperone," she muttered, turning back to her malt.

Granger had to run a finger around his collar when her lips closed around the straw. He gave himself a mental shake. This woman could be his ticket to Edwards, if that was the base she meant. If. Now how to find out—

"Miss Merriweather," a male voice almost purred. "I didn't expect to see you here."

Granger stiffened—on so many levels—and he almost turned and punched the guy. But he had learned to keep his cool in battle. Merriweather? It felt too much of a coincidence. Was this what Mel meant when she'd said it was half feeling your way and half a kick in the pants from time? Was this Merriweather's daughter? He knew a little about her but his focus had been on her old man.

"Mr. Phillips." The ice in Alice's voice was wholly satisfying. "Why should you expect to see me anywhere?"

Granger angled his body, so he could discreetly study the pair. Phillips was dressed in black, a stark contrast to the rest of the room. Granger's lips almost twitched as he studied the man in black. He definitely gave off danger vibes. He was military, or ex-military, but something else, too.

"I see you were deserted by your companions—" Phillips began.

"I have transport, thank you." She held up the key.

This Phillips guy almost allowed himself to look startled.

Granger had to fight back a chuckle. She was good. Then he frowned. He didn't remember any mention of anyone by the name of Phillips in the materials he'd studied. Maybe he'd try the small, looked-like-it-was-to-period-but-wasn't cuff link camera. He pulled the glasses out of his pocket and put them on—turning them and the small camera in his cuff link, on at the same time. He lifted his arm, first as if studying the time, then turned his wrist so that the camera pointed at Phillips. When he had him centered, he took the shot. He hesitated, then took another. There wasn't room for too many on the device, but his gut told him this one mattered. He lowered his arm, smoothing the sleeve back down over the watch.

Now all he had to do was plant the cuff link in a location that no one would find and hope the timer would trigger the satellite signal in sixty-six years. No wonder Mel said this stuff gave her a headache. He removed the glasses and stuck them back in his pocket, making sure he turned them off. The technology to detect them wasn't available yet, but the battery life was limited.

"I wish you'd learn to trust me, trust I have you and your father's best interests at heart."

"Have I ever said I didn't trust you, Mr. Phillips?"

Phillips did look disconcerted now and decided for some deflection of his own. "You aren't driving back alone—"

Follow your instincts, she'd said.

"She won't be alone," Granger said, turning now to insert himself into their tableau. He held out his hand. "The name's Grayson. Major Tom Grayson."

"You're a pilot." Phillips eyes narrowed and it wasn't a question.

Granger nodded, his danger instinct kicking into higher gear. Why did him being a pilot bother Phillips? "They tell me—" he almost said Edwards, but caught himself in time. They may have changed the name, but base personnel still called it Muroc. "—Muroc is where the action is."

He was close to Alice, though not close enough to touch, but he felt the tension coming off her in waves. None of it showed on her calm cool face. She was not at all what he'd expected, though he hadn't thought about her that much, he conceded. In the few photos they'd found, she was a blurred figure next to her father. Not so anymore. Now she'd become more real than her old man.

The guy part of him wanted to get as far away from her as possible and think about this. Ironic that she was now the one person he needed to stay close to. She was his ticket to Edwards and her old man—if he played this right—and she played along.

Under Phillips' scrutiny, Granger didn't dare glance away from that icy gaze. He felt his hackles rise and slid his arm along the counter. He still wasn't touching the lady, but she was in the circle of his arm. Phillips lips thinned. He gave a sharp nod.

"I'll see you Monday morning then"—there was a short pause, before he finished—"Miss Merriweather."

He'd wanted to call her Alice and hadn't dared. Granger allowed himself a slight, very slight softening of his mouth.

Phillips gaze was hard, but he turned away, his walk betraying his military roots, too. Neither of them moved until Phillips pushed his way out the door. Almost at the same time, they turned back to the counter. In the mirror behind, his gaze met hers. And then, as if that didn't do it for either of them, they both looked at each other.

Her gaze assessed him with a disconcerting, x-ray thoroughness. It was not the first time he'd been drilled by a woman's gaze —Mel came immediately to mind—but it was unexpected in this time and place. Mel had made him watch episodes of *Mad Men* to help prepare him for the culture shock. But the only shock he felt right now was the awareness he felt for and about this woman.

"Well," she said, finally, and turned back to her malt.

Granger didn't turn and finally noted a tinge of color staining her cheeks. She glanced at him again.

"Are you really a pilot?"

"Yes, ma'am."

Her lips twitched. Her gaze slanted up, then down. "You're not in uniform."

"I have it, if I need it." He hesitated. "Can we talk somewhere less public?"

She glanced around. It was true no one seemed to be paying attention to them.

"Is your name really Grayson?"

He hesitated, somehow not able to lie to her. "No, ma'am, but it's better no one knows that."

She was silent for some time, almost absentmindedly drinking her malt. He looked away.

"Do you really expect me to give you a lift to the base?" Without looking at him, she added, "You could be a Soviet spy. Or a murderer."

"I can't prove I'm not either," he admitted. Now it was his turn. "Why did it bother Phillips so much that I'm a pilot?" He turned just in time to meet her once-more drilling gaze. She'd either trust him or she wouldn't. There was nothing he could say to change that. Unless... He lowered his voice. "I understand your father is having trouble finding a pilot."

She blinked. And he knew he had her. She glanced around and a rueful light softened the neutral reserve of her face.

"Well, there are plenty of witnesses—including Mr. Phillips, to testify we were together. You'd have to be crazy to do anything. And you don't look crazy—at least not that kind of crazy."

For the first time, Granger let himself grin. "I'm the right kind of crazy," he assured her.

Her gaze changed, assessing him in a different way.

"You're a big guy. It will be a tight fit."

She wouldn't be the first secretary to know a lot about the boss's business, but there was something in her eyes that made him wonder about Miss Alice Merriweather.

He pushed his malt to the side. "Then I won't finish this."

She laughed then, not a full-on laugh, more as if it had been startled out of her. She pulled it in fast. Granger had a feeling he was seeing an Alice not many people did. And that made her even more dangerous to him.

Follow your instincts, your gut.

How far?

* * *

ALICE ROSE and faced the teeming room, wondering how she'd get her shaking knees to stiffen enough to get her to the door. It was insane. It was dangerously insane. She didn't know him, but the idea of the long drive back to Muroc with Phillips on her bumper—

His hand lightly clasped her elbow and calm flooded through her. Was he a magician? This stranger—only he didn't feel like a stranger. It was more a sense of, oh, there you are. Where have you been? She crushed "all my life" from the end of the question, but it was still there in her mind. He should have been here before. And there was such relief. None of it made any sense, but then not much had since her mother died.

Somehow they were moving and her knees did fine. She saw both Betty and Mary, who looked surprised, then delighted. And then they were outside. The fresh air felt good going into her lungs, but it didn't clear her head, because it wasn't confused. In fact, she felt better than she had for a long time. Now she could smell him, or his aftershave. She wasn't sure. It wasn't familiar to her, which was not a surprise, since she didn't go around smelling men. Phillips wore Old Spice. It followed him around like a cloud. She had liked it until him. She was happy this man didn't wear it. She led him to the Studebaker, pausing only to tie on her head scarf and don the new sunglasses, while he tossed his duffel into the back seat. This time the glasses failed to make her feel like a movie star, though it helped to know no one could see her expression. It felt more like donning protection. Now she could glance at him without being seen, could let her gaze linger on the tall, strong figure moving so confidently beside her.

She realized she kept expecting him to offer to drive, but instead he opened the door for her, waiting until she'd settled behind the wheel before closing the door and going around to the passenger side.

She stared at him as he settled in next to her, half reaching behind his right side, then giving a soft chuckle before pushing his shoulders into the seat and testing the leg room. She half glanced back, but couldn't see anything he might be looking for.

"Anything wrong?" he asked.

"No." She put the key in the ignition and started the car, then lowered the volume of the radio from Betty's setting. Her hands slid up, then down the cool surface, satisfaction filling her at the sense of freedom it gave her, before she put it in gear and backed out. Out of the corner of her eye, she spotted Phillips leaning against his vehicle across the street and her lips tightened. If he followed them—what would she do? she scoffed. She had no power to dislodge him. And he had as much right to be on the road back to Muroc as she did.

Neither of them spoke as she eased the car through streets much more crowded than when they'd arrived. So far there was no sign of Phillips' car behind them, but he knew where they were going. She could allow him space in this car for the whole drive or—she glanced at her companion a couple of times, but he showed no sign of concern about being driven by a woman. Instead he looked around him, his face impassive, but his dark eyes gleaming with interest. Yes, it was much better to enjoy this rare time. He'd probably vanish into the base once he got there. Unless…she bit back the words, the question, and found something else to say. For now.

"My friends are hoping to see Frank Sinatra—or someone famous," Alice said, as she accelerated away from Palm Springs. The car handled fine and it felt good to be driving something.

The wind rushed past her face and the sounds of the wheels on the road meant they'd have to raise their voices to be heard.

"Sinatra?"

Alice nodded. "I think—I saw him. I'm not sure."

He laughed. "Good old Blue Eyes."

She smiled, remembering her small moment with Frank. It had seemed huge then. A real star had looked at her, but now…

"I wonder if it was him?"

"There's no one to say it wasn't," he pointed out.

She laughed. "That's true." She hesitated. "So what is your real name?"

He shifted so that his body was angled toward her. He was big, with powerful shoulders, almost bear-like in his lethality. He had strong brows above eyes that were deep and dark. His features were strong but good. His military-cut dark hair looked crisp and she wondered if it was. His mouth—she decided it was better not to contemplate his mouth. If he was a pilot, and she believed he was, even though he lacked the cockiness of most of the younger pilots, then it was better not to contemplate his mouth.

"I'll tell you when I can," he said, finally, real regret in the deep voice that sent shivers down her backbone, while managing to also induce the strange calm certainty she'd felt from his touch. "You're less likely to slip if you think of me as Tom Grayson, Miss Merriweather."

"Alice," she said, then bit her lip. "When we're alone. If Mr. Phillips—"

"I understand."

And she believed he did.

"What's his beef with you?" Tom asked.

Tom. That wasn't his name and it didn't feel like his name. And he hadn't asked her to use it.

"You can call me Tom or Grayson, whichever is easier for you," he said, as if he'd read her thought.

She flashed him a quick, shy glance and nodded, but then couldn't think of anything to say to use either name.

"You been at Edwards long?" he asked.

Tom? Grayson? Tom, she decided. Interesting he called it Edwards. Most of the personnel called it by its old name of Muroc. "We arrived two and a half years ago," she said. "August."

"August? Wow. And you're still there?"

It was her turn to chuckle. "My father is happy to have a place to test his work." For now. If they could get it tested. Otherwise, for how long would they have space for the *Ray*? Could Tom be the answer to their problem? And did she want him to be? Did she want him to be the first one to test the *Ray*? She knew exactly how many pilots had died testing new craft. She'd seen their graves.

"And Phillips?"

This was the second time he'd asked and she still wasn't sure how to respond. "I don't know. I mean, I saw him briefly when we arrived and then not again until six months ago. I wish I knew —" Why didn't she trust him? He had access to the base, so somebody had vouched for him. Was it right to blame him for their sudden lack of progress? "I don't have a good reason for not trusting him," she said, as much to herself as to Tom.

"You should trust your instincts," Tom said.

She glanced at him. "You don't trust him?"

Tom shrugged. "I've seen his type before, so, no, I don't trust him."

She almost smiled, but had to firmly remind herself she had no reason to trust Tom either—except for those instincts. He could be a Soviet spy, though she had a feeling she spoke more Russian than he did.

As if he sensed she'd backed off some, he switched topics, asking her what life was like on the base. They talked lightly for some miles, then a thought occurred to her. "Do you have a place to stay?"

"I'm hoping I can get into something," he said, not sounding too worried.

If he wasn't expected—she hesitated, then said, "We have a spare room in our quarters. Since you claimed to know us…"

"Thanks." He hesitated. "So, why is the subject of a pilot so touchy?"

She'd have been honest, even if she weren't completely sure of him yet. "We've been experiencing difficulty getting a pilot for our—for my father's craft. It has…some unusual features," she added before he could ask.

"Isn't risk part of being test pilots?" he sounded surprised.

"Most of them are interested in craft that can break records," she admitted. And in not getting killed. She couldn't blame them for that. But it was more than that. Politics and a whisper campaign against the *Ray*? She couldn't prove it, but she felt it.

"I guess I can't ask what makes your father's craft so much more risky."

She bit her lip. "It's not any more dangerous than anything else, at least we—my father believes." She stopped herself. If Tom cleared the gate, well, then others could decide how much to tell him.

"If he'll give me a shot, I'd like to fly it," he said.

"Without even seeing it?" she challenged, even as hope and fear went to war inside her head.

He hesitated. "It's why I came."

"To fly the *Ray*?" She couldn't hide her shock. "But—"

"The people who sent me have…an interest." His mouth twisted in a wry smile. "And no, none of them speak Russian." He glanced around as they closed on a town. "Think we can find something to eat here? I'll buy food and gas as a thank you for the lift."

Alice slowed the Studebaker and flicked on the turn signal, pulling in next to a pump. It was while they were waiting for the attendant to finish filling the tank she saw Phillips' car pass

—slowing for a long moment before speeding up. For a moment she smiled, then it faded. What if he got to her father first?

"I need to make a call," she said.

Instead of questions, Alice saw comprehension in Tom's gaze.

* * *

GRANGER HAD no difficulty finding things to talk to Alice about as they finished the drive to Edwards. Though it felt strange to drive without a seat belt, Alice was a good driver. He didn't mind being able to watch her. He liked it too much, but for the moment he was following orders—by following his gut—which grew tight when he remembered that Alice had—would die in an explosion that would destroy the *Manta Ray* in just a little over a week. They'd been so focused on her father's disappearance, they'd not looked too closely into her death. And now his gut told him that had been a mistake.

His mission brief had not included a test flight, but he wasn't too worried. Nowhere in the events of the week prior to the explosion—or in the other thing—had there been a plane crash, and no pilots had died. Other than a possible visit by aliens, it had been a quiet week at the air base.

It wasn't a surprise when she asked about where he'd served in the war. They'd expected it and planned for it. He'd been in war, just not that one, so he knew how to talk and act. And what not to say. Strange that this lie bothered him the most, even though he had served his country. But the World War II heroes were special. He looked at the bleak landscape until Alice introduced a lighter topic that carried them to the base.

If Phillips had hoped to bar or slow Granger's entrance onto the base, he failed on all counts. There was scrutiny, but his documentation was impeccable. The drive to the Merriweather's bungalow didn't take long in the fading light. Alice removed her sunglasses and stowed them in her small purse, then tucked the keys under the seat and climbed out.

Before they were halfway up the walk, the door opened and Merriweather stepped out.

Granger had come so far to see the man—had traveled through time for this moment—but even with the sunset giving them a last burst of light, it was anticlimactic.

The light was harsh on the man's face. It found the hollows cut deep in his cheeks, revealed every sagging line around his eyes and mouth. The pale skin didn't surprise; he was a scientist, but Merriweather's skin was almost gray. His clothes hung on a frame gaunt to near-corpse point—an impression heightened by his haunted eyes. George Merriweather was not a happy man, though he was somewhat animated—or curious at the moment. He'd looked sad in the photos they'd found, Granger recalled.

Merriweather slanted a quick look at his daughter and for a moment Granger thought he saw fear there.

It was all off, wrong somehow, though how Granger couldn't put a finger on exactly what.

"Did Mr. Phillips come by?" Alice asked. She'd retreated into some place that puzzled Granger, too. There was a flush in her cheeks, and her eyes glowed, but the look in them…well, it was nothing he knew how to read.

He'd felt the connection between Alice and himself, a strange sense of knowing, and this interrupted that enough to make him wonder, once again, if he'd been trusting the wrong instincts. And then she looked at him and the enigmatic look eased, the connection reestablished. Somehow, in some way, she'd made him an ally, but against what? Or was it whom? Phillips?

"He called," Merriweather admitted.

"And?" Alice's voice was too even, too calm to be challenging, but Granger felt it there, in the undercurrents running between the two.

"He said we weren't ready," Merriweather said. "That it was too dangerous."

The sun sent a last flash of red-orange across the scene, putting shadows on both their faces, but Granger had a feeling that neither of their expressions had changed. Then Alice turned abruptly to him.

"Would you like to see it?"

Merriweather might have made a movement. Granger wasn't sure.

"Yes," Granger said simply. He was more interested in the engine, but of course, the craft around it interested him, too. And he was starting to realize just how little time he had to figure out this puzzle. Which was the more critical? The craft or its propulsion?

"We don't—" Merriweather's protest wasn't finished, possibly because he'd seen the car sitting outside their gate.

"Mary won't be by to pick it up for a couple of hours at least," Alice said. There was a pause, then Alice added, "You don't have to come if you don't want to."

Merriweather reached back and closed the door with a small snap.

Granger didn't contest Merriweather for the front seat. After he saw Alice into the driver's seat, he slung a leg over the rear door of the back seat and settled in. This drive felt longer, as anticipation built. There had been so little left of the *Manta Ray* after the fire, just a couple of sketches of the engine, an early tantalizing sketch with a lot left off and one photo of the burned-out wreck. Now he found his curiosity building about the *Manta Ray*. In a few minutes he'd be able to see it, to touch it, to walk around it. Would they let him climb inside? Even better, would he get a look at the design specifications for the engine? That's was why he'd fought so hard to be the one to come. Would either craft or engine live up to his expectations? Was it as remarkable as he'd suspected? As he hoped?

When Alice parked the Studebaker outside a hangar, Granger held the door for her, while Merriweather climbed out and strode to the door. He unlocked it, then turned to watch their approach. Granger took Alice's elbow again, trying to shake off that odd feeling of connection this gave him. Or perhaps he did it to reestablish it. He stayed the gentleman, letting her pass inside first. Merriweather walked ahead, slowly turning on lights. They went down a narrow hall past what might have been a workshop or lab toward the actual hangar.

Anticipation built with each step as Merriweather crossed the dim hangar to a panel, the only sound his footsteps on cement. The plane would tell him something about what Merriweather had intended with the engine design, or so he hoped. The overhead lights flickered once, then again, before steadying. He flinched and blinked, waiting for his eyes to adjust to the bright light.

And there it was.

Merriweather's *Manta Ray*.

Drawn toward it, not against his will, but as if in a dream, he didn't rush. He wondered, had even postulated what it would be like, but he didn't have to now. There it was.

His first impression was how very alien it looked sitting there in the glow of the overhead lights. *Alien.* Was this somehow the key to the strange story about aliens visiting this base back—no, next weekend, he corrected?

Of course they called it *Manta Ray*. There were distinct similarities in its plan form. The nose was not as blunt as a manta ray, but the animal moved through a different medium than the plane. The nose needed to be more aerodynamic. It had trailing and leading edges along both wing spans. The high wing load might be the reason pilots weren't lining up to fly her. It would be tricky.

It was beautiful and unsettling.

Aircraft design had been pushing toward this or something

like it, but it hadn't got there yet in his future, let alone in this past.

He walked to the nose, then slowly traversed the length, circling around to the rear. There were three thrust chambers, two for what looked to be typical jet propulsion and one in the center that was once again alien. The center chamber was high— easily as tall or taller than he was, circular and completely hollow. No turbines or any other obvious source of thrust. He peered inside, trying to pierce the shadow, and thought he saw circular lines cut or marked into the surface.

Could this craft do what he suspected it could? Had the design gone far enough? The schematics he'd seen had held the potential, but there'd been large knowledge gaps. But also some knowledge leaps.

He rested an arm on it and leaned down to study the undercarriage. It had landing gear, which meant they intended it to land and take off in the traditional way.

Alice came around to his side, questions in her eyes he wasn't ready to answer. He walked forward, running his hand along the surface. He glanced back.

"Metal?" It looked right, but felt different under his hand.

She nodded. "It's a composite that we—that my father believes makes it stronger for transit."

Transit? That was an odd way to put it.

He could admit that the addition of the jet propulsion engines had startled him, made him wonder if the engine was what he'd thought it might be. Now he was back to wondering.

"It has an unusual propulsion system for the main engine." She bit her lip. "None of the pilots understand it, which is one reason they don't want to fly it—aside from the inherent risk with any untested craft," she added. "And there are some who are unhappy we got funding when they did not."

Politics. No one was free from it. He studied the plane again. Despite the frizzle of unease running up and down his back—he wanted to try it. It was almost as crazy as traveling through time and potentially a lot more dangerous. He and Jack had wondered if Merriweather had designed a version of a warp engine or even some kind of vortex generator—like the one Jack used to move people through time. But how did the energy from the vortex get turned into propulsion?

"And we can't promise them a record-breaking flight. We just hope…" She sighed.

It depended on the record, Granger thought wryly. But—if this did even some of what he hoped, the government would shove it into a super top-secret category. It had the potential to be a game changer, but without the glory. If he flew it and crashed it, would Mel and Jack see his grave here in the future? Would the chip—triggered by his heart stopping—suck what was left of his body back to his own time? How would that ripple through time? He shouldn't even be thinking about it, but he'd opened the door in his bid to get on the base and close to Merriweather.

It was possible that Phillips would try to delay any testing. It was also possible that Phillips was here to make it happen. Either way, Granger didn't want any help from that guy. His gut warned him every time the guy showed up.

"She's a—thing of beauty," Granger said. His gaze strayed to the woman and he knew he meant both. Alice had a quiet beauty, less flashy than this ship of hers—his thoughts jerked to a halt. He glanced back. Merriweather stood back, not joining them in showing off his ship. How—unless it wasn't his ship? Was it possible? And if it was, how on earth had they pulled it off?

Only when he looked in her eyes, he knew. She had a connection to the *Manta Ray* that Merriweather did not. She lowered her lashes and turned to the ship. The way she touched it, that gave her away, too.

In some ways it made sense. In this time, who would believe a woman could design an aircraft, let alone this one? But he'd studied Merriweather. He'd been designing and inventing when Alice was a little girl. So now, suddenly, the daughter and the father worked together? He needed to think on it when he wasn't looking at Alice, whose restraint was more revealing than if she'd hugged the aircraft. It felt wrong to look, as if he intruded on a private moment.

He crouched to study the undercarriage and located what he thought was the access hatch. Then he rose and found the cockpit, maybe. It wasn't easy to find, blending almost perfectly into the fuselage. That would be another problem. No one liked to fly a plane when they couldn't see out of it very well.

A lot of the aircraft being tested here were taken up and dropped, so they wouldn't have to waste fuel getting to altitude, but the *Manta Ray* was too big.

He frowned. Were those two jet engines powerful enough to get it off the ground? And when it did, what happened then? His mind grappled with the reality of the aircraft and his theories about the main engine, but he knew he needed time to process what he saw now, adjust it against what he'd believed.

He walked along one wing, his hand on the metal, letting his hand sense what his mind processed.

"Will it?" Granger asked. "Take off?" He backed up, trying to see the craft and how it would interact with atmosphere. He could see why pilots might have issues with the design. It looked —his mind came back to alien. He'd studied the aircraft they'd tested here and there'd been some odd ducks, but even those were more variations on a familiar theme.

"It needs a long runway," Alice said, "but it will." Her voice sounded more confident than the look in her eyes.

Which was why Edwards was so perfect for them. Rogers Dry Lake was long and wide. "How does it handle?"

"We—my father sort of adapted a Link Trainer but the pilots don't like it," she admitted, her gaze steady on his. "There are some unique stressors. And there is a lot we won't know until we get some test flights."

His brows arched. No time like the present.

She looked at her father. He hesitated, then extracted keys and went to a door and unlocked it. Alice moved past him and flicked on the lights. Granger walked past her and stopped. He'd seen World War II vintage Link Trainers, used to train pilots for combat and this was one, but it also wasn't. They'd definitely modified it. He walked around it, comparing his memory of the Link Trainer with this one. They'd changed the way the weight was distributed, he decided, but there was no way to really know what it did without trying it.

Alice went forward and lifted the side hatch, then looked back with a frown.

"Someone's been using it." Her gaze moved past Granger to her father.

"Phillips wanted to try it," he admitted.

"Really." Alice was quiet for several seconds. "I don't remember him mentioning he was a pilot."

"Not sure he is," Merriweather admitted. "He seemed to have found it frustrating."

Alice might have smiled. It was tiny and fleeting if she did. Granger grinned. Then his grin faded. If Phillips was a trained pilot, then that made his interest—and the fact that he didn't show up in the historical record—more interesting.

Alice finished making some adjustments inside, then stepped back.

Granger didn't dare hesitate now. He clambered inside and settled in, securing straps and putting on the radio headset. Only then did he check out the various controls. Some of them looked the same, but there were a few he didn't recognize. He pushed some things and it lurched to one side.

He heard Alice's voice in his headset. "What do you think?"

"I don't recognize all the controls," he admitted.

"They don't all work, because we need a test flight," she said. Okay...

* * *

ALICE'S EYES were gritty with exhaustion when Tom finally climbed out of the Link Trainer. He'd tried every configuration and control. Pushed it in every direction the limited Link Trainer could manage. Asked her question after question, but hadn't seemed worried when she told him she didn't know more all the answers. That's why they needed a test. He'd left the Link Trainer and gone inside the *Ray*, then gone back to the Trainer again and again. His reaction had been more curiosity than frustration. At times he'd mutter, "Interesting."

At some point, Alice had realized how late it was getting and asked her father to take Mary's car back to the house and to not forget Tom's duffel in the back seat. He seemed relieved to go. Since her mother's death, he preferred theory to reality.

Alice wasn't sure what time it was when Tom's response to the Trainer began to change. Or maybe it was his questions that changed. She wasn't sure. It didn't matter. At this point her answer was the same.

They needed a test flight for a reason. *She didn't know.* That is where their problems began and ended. And what they didn't know kept them from getting test flight approval—that and the lack of a pilot willing to not know so much before he risked his life. At least, that was part of it, she admitted to herself, but not to Tom. Politics. Money. It wasn't all Phillips. The people who didn't like the money that flowed to their project were pushing back harder now. They weren't "in" here and no one seemed sure how they'd gotten as far as they had. It was ironic it had gotten worse since Phillips came back. She didn't know why, because she felt sure he'd been part of getting them on base. So why hinder them now?

She did know one thing as she and Tom stared at each other in the predawn.

Tom wasn't just a pilot. He was a scientist, but that didn't explain it. That wasn't unusual. Test pilots tended to have more advanced educations or had learned on the job and were extremely smart. But there was something different about Tom's questions and his knowledge base—or she was too tired to be doing this right now.

She opened the lab long enough to get her coat and her father's overcoat for Tom—it would be cold outside now that the sun was long gone—then locked up. Outside, they ran into base security. They checked Tom's papers and then offered them a ride, but after seeing a slight shake of Tom's head, she told them, "We need the walk to clear our heads. Thank you, though."

The fresh air revived her, but there was no question exhaustion had left her feeling oddly lightheaded and happy despite her uncertainty. For a while they walked without speaking, the slow-rising sun a thin tracing of gold along the horizon.

He sighed and she sensed he was ready to talk.

"That's a heck of a plane you've got there, Alice."

She waited, knowing there was more to come.

"I can see why you've had trouble getting a pilot and not just because Phillips is thrusting a spoke in your wheel."

She opened her mouth to protest, then firmed her lips until she was sure she could answer calmly.

"You don't think it will fly."

"I don't know, but if it does fly…" He gave a soft, low whistle, then thrust his hands in the pockets of the overcoat. She realized with a start that he hadn't asked for a cigarette or smoked since she met him. She'd never seen the appeal, but almost everyone she knew smoked. One of the secretaries told her it was something to do with her hands, a reason to break eye contact when she needed it.

"It's not just Phillips, at least I'm not sure, but I don't think so.

Pilots will push the envelope, risk their lives, as you know. I've seen them climb into planes I wouldn't touch." He rubbed his face tiredly. "But there's something, well, your plane has an unusual quality that might be triggering them, in addition to come clever undermining by Phillips."

"How is it triggering?" she asked, curious now.

"They've been pushing the envelope here, trying new designs, new craft, going faster and faster, but your *Ray*"—he stopped, a thinking frown pulling at his brows—"flying is already alien. When you first learn to fly, it's all wrong, but then it gets all right. It gets where you sometimes feel more at home up there than down here." He shook his head. "It's hard to explain."

He didn't have to explain. She'd been sneaking out and taking lessons off and on since she was twenty-one. The hard part was coming up with the cash. Thank goodness her dad was absent-minded and she was good at stretching a dollar.

Of course, the kind of planes she'd had access to were nothing like the *Ray*. But it wasn't alien to her. She knew every inch of it, inside and out.

Then she tensed. He'd called the *Ray* her plane. "My father—"

"We both know your father isn't the brains behind this, Alice." His voice was gentle and possibly a bit awed. "You were born in the wrong time."

The wrong time. She'd felt that, too, had wondered if her mother had… She looked up at him with a half-puzzled frown. He didn't talk to her like the other men in her life. He talked to her as if they were…equal. It was an odd sensation—perhaps a bit like the pilots felt in the presence of her *Ray*?

"Who are you?" she murmured.

"I'm on your side," he said, which wasn't an answer, but still satisfied for some reason.

"If we didn't initiate full—"

"I don't know, but I suspect even a minimal thrust from your…engine…would result in some unexpected outcomes."

"Such as?" She knew, or thought she knew, but did he? Did he really?

"Well, for one thing, protective gear for pilots isn't adequate for what the *Ray* might do. I'm not sure if the flight suits now would provide enough protection for the kind of G-force a pilot might experience."

"We"—his brows arched and she modified it to—"I have designed our own flight suit. It heats, but it also expands to apply pressure for higher altitudes. It also forces air at high altitudes for controlled breathing." She made a face. "But again, without testing…"

"I should have realized you knew." His tone was rueful again. "But you didn't know anyone else would know."

She looked at him and found something in his eyes that made her breathless. "I don't think anyone else realizes how fast it could go," she admitted. "I'm not sure my father realizes."

"Phillips?"

She shook her head. She didn't want to talk about him. She was tired and yet—she'd never felt like this. As if this moment mattered somehow. "I don't know what he knows," she said. "I avoid him." As much as he'd let her. "He's more interested in my father."

"Not as smart as he thinks he is." Tom sounded amused.

That made her smile. "No."

"How did it happen?" He turned then, pulling her arm through his so that they walked close together.

"It began with my mother. I think she protected him, and they always worked together. He was happy. He's, well, he's…"

"Smart, but not a genius," Tom finished for her.

She nodded. "When my mother died, he couldn't—so he used his grief." She half turned. "He was truly brokenhearted. It wasn't an act. But it was also…"

"An out."

She nodded again. "You can't imagine what it was like. I was sixteen and I lived in a house of grief and shadows. Secrets and sorrows. In self-defense, I went into the lab and began reading and learning, I suppose, or adding to what I already knew. My mother had made me part of their research from the time I was little, so it wasn't unfamiliar. But I wasn't trying to become her. It was just a place to escape my reality. To feel alive. Finally I had questions, so I asked, thinking maybe it would help. That if we shared the science maybe he could heal…and we could start living again."

She fell silent remembering the way her father had looked at her. She hadn't known, not until that moment, how much she was like her mother. He hadn't known. Her mother? She'd never know what her mother knew or suspected. She'd taught her daughter, built a foundation for what followed, but what had her mother hoped? She gave herself a shake and they started walking again, only somehow they were closer, their hips and shoulders brushing together with every other step.

"He's really an engineer. I'm not sure how much of the design was his, but I do know the *Ray* is his…passion." The word tasted like dust in her mouth. Her father had no passions of any kind anymore. Had it ever truly been his passion? Or was it always her mother's? She'd taken his and her mother's designs and worked on them, but it was the engine that drove her the most.

"Was his passion," she corrected, feeling a strange need to be honest with this man. She'd been wandering in the desert, a real desert, and he'd appeared. If he weren't a mirage, a creature of her longing and imagination, then perhaps together they could find the oasis, the place of safety she needed more than she needed to be right about her work.

Already it felt as if some of the weight had been shared with his broad, powerful shoulders. She could breathe easier. And she hadn't realized how crushed she'd felt, how alone and…afraid. Afraid of what? She wasn't sure, though it swirled around Phillips. But the threat felt bigger than him. As if a shadow loomed over her, one that—she shivered and realized they were near the cemetery where so many fallen pilots were laid to rest. Would this place, this desert be her final home? She was a scientist, an engineer, but she was also human. And she'd been so alone with ghosts and the past until now. For a second, she could have sworn she saw a headstone with her name on it—

She wasn't sure how it happened, but her hand slid down, or his slid up, and now their fingers twined together. Nowhere, not even the moment she'd realized she felt at home in her parent's lab, had she felt a stronger sense of belonging.

"This is crazy," she said as his hand clenched on hers.

"Yes," he agreed, smiling ruefully down at her. The rising sun topped the mountains, sending light flowing up them both so that she could see his face. His eyes were so deep, she had the strange sense she could fall in if she leaned forward just a bit and the shadow couldn't follow her there. She just needed to get close enough to him.

He stopped and turned to face her. It hadn't even been a whole day since she'd sat down next to him. How was that possible? A stranger who wasn't. She knew him. It wasn't just crazy, it was insane. But when his head bent toward hers, she went up on her toes to meet him. Felt his arms slide around her, pulling her gently but firmly closer.

Science and this man. Her two certainties. And either or both could disappear without warning because of the shadow.

* * *

GRANGER COULD HAVE KISSED Alice for the rest of the day—and possibly into the night—but that wasn't an option. He hadn't traveled through time to kiss a girl, no matter how kissable and brilliant.

His hand might have been shaking a bit when he lifted his head and stroked her hair back off her face. The trust in her eyes and smile shook him to his core. How could he accomplish his mission and save the girl? He had to fight the impulse to tighten his hold on her. Kisses and hugs wouldn't save her life. He needed to think, to figure this out.

It was cold, but Granger felt no desire to return to Alice's bungalow. He didn't trust her father and he wasn't entirely sure Phillips hadn't installed bugs both there and at their hangar. If Phillips believed, as Granger had, that Merriweather was the one with the ideas, had Granger's arrival in this time altered that? Could he have made Alice a target? Even if Phillips wasn't the rogue time traveler—if there was one here—the guy had plans for the aircraft and Merriweather.

And Alice's death? Could it have been an accident? Merriweather had disappeared. If the rogue time travelers had hoped, well, their hopes would be or had been dashed. The old man couldn't deliver, and he could play the grief card again, and there was nothing anyone could do about it.

What had it done to an old man in this time to realize he wasn't the brains in his family? Was Merriweather haunted by more than his lost wife? What would he do to preserve his secret?

"What does Phillips want?" Granger asked, more to himself than Alice.

She stirred in his arms. "He wants us to move our research to Groom Lake in Nevada."

"Area 51?" Granger was startled.

"What?"

Granger shook his head. He needed to be more careful. But... the CIA didn't set up there until '55, or so everyone thought. Was Phillips speaking the truth or trying to lure them away from Edwards? Isolate them from anyone who knew them? Whatever the plan, it would somehow all come to head on the twentieth, seven days from now.

His mission brief didn't involve time travel for anyone but himself. He wasn't approved to alter time except as it related to any time tampering. He was to locate time tampering and attempt to stop it. That was all. He wasn't approved to bring anyone back to the future with him even if she had been born in the wrong time. And he wasn't sure he could. Jack had traveled forward, but there'd been…complications.

He also wasn't approved to save her life on Saturday unless it was the result of time tampering. And he didn't know how to prove that. His arms tightened around her. And whether he liked it or not, the device implanted in his butt was going to suck him back to the future at midnight next Saturday night.

"Your father wants to go?"

She nodded against his chest. "He doesn't like to stay in one place too long."

He was afraid people would start to notice who was the brains of the two.

"I told him I wouldn't go with him this time."

And he couldn't go without her. Impasse.

"Phillips is putting pressure on the wrong person." Despite the challenges of the situation, Granger found he could be amused.

"Yes." She gave a small laugh and then sighed against him.

"It's better he doesn't know," Granger said.

Now she shivered. "Yes."

Tough time for a woman. She had all the brains and none of the power.

"How ironic," she murmured.

"What is?" he wondered if she mirrored his thoughts.

"I can design an engine to propel a cutting-edge aircraft, but I don't know what to do about Phillips or my father." She lifted her head off his chest, leaving the spot cold. "Even if I were to…break with my father…" She sighed again.

This time wasn't devoid of smart women doing smart things, but Granger could admit to not knowing a lot about that. It had not been part of his mission briefing. But he had a feeling that a self-taught female scientist would have a harder time than most proving what she could do with no record to fall back on. Which would leave her vulnerable to Phillips or any time tamperer that happened along.

Death before dishonor? Was that what happened, or would happen next Saturday?

The only thing he could think to do was change the timeline —a little. If Mel was right, this would make his job harder, make the timeline more dynamic, almost fluid. What little he did know might not happen, so he'd be winging it. Well, he was in the right place for that. And it might force the time tamperer out into the open. He thought about the cuff link he'd dropped before they arrived on the base. He sure hadn't wanted it to start broadcasting a signal from inside the base in sixty-six years from now. That would create some hard-to-explain complications.

"We need to go ahead with the test," he told her. She started to protest, but he shook his head. "We go through the motions for now. I'd like a look at your flight suit in any case." If by some miracle it actually worked—he couldn't let himself think about what all of this could have meant to the space program if Alice Merriweather hadn't died. If he wasn't careful, he'd be the time tamperer, which was kind of mind-blowing to consider. But…big changes, according to Mel and Jack, might make time fight back. Whatever else happened here in 1954, he did not want a time ass-kicking.

Alice shivered and eased back. Her smile had worry behind it. "Let's go. I'll fix us some breakfast and we can talk—"

"Not at your place," Granger objected.

Her eyes widened, but she nodded.

* * *

"WE'VE GOT a signal from one of the cuff links," Jack said, over his shoulder. Mel had been staring at their map for at least an hour, trying to tell if anything had changed. Now she spun and hurried to his side, sinking down in her own chair and rolling it close to him.

Jack zoomed in on the location, trying to figure out why Granger had dropped it there.

"That's between the base and Palm Springs," Mel murmured. "Dropped the same day as the postcard maybe?"

"It is far enough from the base to make it unlikely he'd have gone back there, though I suppose anything is possible," Jack finished. Never make assumptions, he reminded himself. He'd made so many the first time. And the second time. And even the third time. And here he was doing it again. "I'm activating the team on the ground to go get it."

"And then we wait," Mel said. "Sixty-six years and some hours."

"Sixty-six years and some hours," he agreed.

CHAPTER 4

*A*lice emerged from the bathroom and came face-to-face with her father. The all-night session with Tom made it harder to control the usual mix of anger, frustration, and love. Looking at him now, it was hard to find the powerful figure of her youth, the man her mother had protected and encouraged her to look up to.

Let's all keep the facade in place, she thought bitterly, and then—as always—guilt washed over her. If anything, her mother had faced bigger challenges than Alice in trying to practice her passion. How many times had her drive to know and understand run into the roadblock of her sex? Alice knew the story of how her parents met and fell in love, but now, with the hindsight of an adult, she wondered. Had her mother sought out George Merriweather? It wouldn't, she reflected wryly, have been hard to get him to fall for her. According to their stories, she was his first and last date. Alice understood, could forgive even. But what had been her mother's plans for Alice? She had to have known Alice shared some of her abilities. Did she plan to fold Alice into the family plan? What other options would she have seen for her daughter? How much easier it would have been if Alice had been a son, she thought bitterly. It would have been natural for her father to work with his son, to share credit.

What would that be like? Standing in the circle with others looking at her the way they did her father—the way Tom looked at her. How had he so easily seen through the facade? She gave an internal sigh. It didn't matter now. Alice had done this to herself. To his credit, her father hadn't wanted to plunge back into academia and research. She'd been crazy to get out and do something, anything. She'd been willing to sacrifice—she'd *thought* she'd do anything for this. The science would be her reward. She'd thought she was so smart when really, she'd just been desperate.

"Good morning," she said, in the cool tone of the secretary. This was her fault, too. They were locked together—and yet apart —and neither knew how to change it.

"Alice—" he seemed to gather himself together, "you were out…late."

"All night," she agreed. "Tom was in the Link Trainer."

"All night?"

Was he trying to be a father? She tried to remember being a daughter and couldn't. But she felt she should make the effort.

"Um, most of it, then we walked back." If Phillips was listening in, he wouldn't get much from this conversation. "I'll fix some breakfast and then we'll head over." She had to bring him with them today or her secret would be exposed.

He opened his mouth, perhaps to protest this rare Sunday visit, but then settled for a brief nod. He knew the risks, too. She headed down the short hall to the kitchen as the bathroom door closed him in. While collecting the breakfast things, she felt an odd sense of irony in the act of assembly when it felt as if this—or their relationship—was beginning to unravel. It wasn't just Phillips, though he seemed to have started it. How badly did her father want to go with Phillips? Was it a desire to leave here? To be somewhere else? Or was he surrendering to a stronger will than his? She felt a flash of shame because she'd been the stronger will more than once. Was he a weak man caught between his daughter and Phillips? There was no win for him in this fight. If he'd ever been excited about the *Ray*, that had died. Did she know when? Was that her real crime? Not noticing when his passion died? Or not realizing he had none?

The lost night's sleep put a haze around her thoughts and she covered her face with her hands, trying to rub clarity into her brain.

"What a mess," she murmured, then glanced around, as if she could see the listening ears of her—enemy. He was, though she couldn't prove it. How long had he been listening? And how ironic was it that there'd been nothing for him to hear that would compromise their secret. They never talked about it. It was as if the act of saying it out loud would bring the edifice of their deceit tumbling down around them. Their sad little comedy would come to a grinding halt.

So much silence. No wonder everyone thought she was his secretary. He would walk around the lab, or the house, making notes that "only she could read." Then she'd type them up—only the words that went into those notes were from the ideas swirling inside her head. Everything that mattered happened out of sight. Only now the silence was broken. The stress had reached, or was close to reaching, maximum.

The storm was coming.

She lowered her hands, pausing to trace the outline of her mouth, remembering a different storm, a welcome inner storm— one that wouldn't last. She felt Tom's conflict even while his strength enfolded her. Whatever had brought him here, he'd not planned on meeting her.

Light streamed in the window, but she stood in shadow wondering what would be left when the dust settled.

* * *

GRANGER STOOD WATCHING Alice from the doorway, his gut tightening as he noted the lines lack of sleep had put in her face. They didn't make her less desirable. His hands curled into fists at his side as he fought the longing to go to her and tell her it was going to be all right.

Because it wasn't.

He was not a guy he'd have said had a lot of clue, but even he had noticed the suffocating silence in this place. He supposed that their secrets were a contributing factor. They hung over them both like a shroud. He didn't know how Phillips had missed it—if he had—but he knew people saw what they expected to see. As a scientist, he'd had to train himself to see past the obvious, to look deeper and further.

And look where that had landed him.

She turned to drop eggs in a sizzling pan and saw him. Her hands suspended over the pan, egg dripping through her fingers. With that look she changed the silence. Charged it, made it hum. She might have made him hum a bit. He knew he wanted to close the distance. One step. That's all it would take, but the sound of the bathroom door opening stopped him. That and the fact he was from the future. She was real and here, but—not for him. He knew it, so why didn't he believe it?

She had an absurdly frilly apron tied around her waist and he realized she'd changed into a somber suit, so trim and straight it made her seem taller. It fitted her disturbingly well, but on a Sunday morning? She caught him looking and gave a slight grimace.

"Dress code."

He glanced down at her low heels. How the—

She shrugged and returned her attention to the eggs.

The silence was different while all three of them ate. Outside, a car and a driver waited for them. She must have called for the car while he was taking a bath. A bath. He hadn't done that for— he realized he didn't know how to count that one backwards and gave it up as a bad job. He missed his shower, though. Mel had told there'd be things like that, that it was the little things he'd miss the most.

Just before climbing into the car, Alice put on her sunglasses, her chin angling some with the action. Granger frowned, wondering why she gave such a simple thing so much significance.

"Ma'am," the airman said, looking at her admiringly as he held the door for her.

Her smile was enigmatic, and both he and the airman enjoyed the brief glimpse of thigh as she slid in. No one spoke during the trip back to the hangar. Granger let the airman open her door. He could afford to be generous. He'd kissed the girl.

"Thank you, Airman," Alice said, giving him another enigmatic smile. She waited until the airman had driven away, then turned back to them.

The sun was still on the morning side of the sky and the air still had a nip to it. Above the fitted suit with its slim skirt, Alice had swept her hair up into some kind of bun thing that would have been prim but the sunglasses stole the prim and made her mysterious instead. Alice looked both ways, but the line was empty. She lowered the glasses.

"Major Grayson thinks that Mr. Phillips might have listening devices in there."

For a few seconds Merriweather looked almost startled. Then his expression softened into something that might have been a smile. Granger wondered if he'd forgotten how to smile.

"He must be profoundly disappointed."

Alice's brows arched, then she smiled. The real deal.

"Well, let's keep on disappointing him."

It must have been a painful process listening in on these two. They'd turned quiet into an art form. Sometime he'd like to get the story—would there be any more of the story when he was back in his own time zone? For a few seconds the horizon seemed to waver and he had to blink a couple of times. He was getting old if a missed night's sleep made him dizzy.

"Why are we here?" Merriweather asked.

"Major Grayson wants to take a look at our flight suits," Alice said.

"Oh. Of course."

Did the old man know about the flight suit? And how did they look at them without giving the game away? Then he halfway shook his head. They'd managed it for at least two years. He'd just follow their lead. Well, Alice's lead.

Merriweather? Granger wasn't sure about him. His admiration for the man had taken a nosedive and now he wasn't sure he trusted him to have Alice's best interests at heart. He wasn't sure he trusted himself to have her best interests at heart. On the other hand, the old man had tried to smile.

As Merriweather unlocked the hangar, Granger took a long look in both directions. He thought he saw a car turning onto the lane, but the light was wrong to get a good look.

"Everything okay?" Alice asked.

"It's all good," Granger said, following her inside.

* * *

SHE WAS NERVOUS, but she'd forgotten how to let it show as she led Tom to the cage where the flight suits were secured. She'd realized early on that none of the flight suits currently being used provided the right protection for the G-forces someone might— she hoped—experience flying the *Ray*. It had been an interesting mental exercise, trying to solve the problem, particularly keeping the pilot breathing productively. She wasn't sure her father remembered giving the instructions or putting in orders for supplies. She'd even managed to work on it herself. Amazing what a pair of coveralls and face protection could do. People, for the most part, saw what they wanted to see.

Which did not explain the puzzle that was Tom Grayson. His eyes saw things differently. His eyes saw her differently. What had the kiss meant to him? Was it sad she could still feel it on her lips? She closed her eyes for a couple of seconds. What mattered now was the *Ray*. They needed that test flight. And this suit needed to be tested, too. If it flew, and flew well, they'd get attention—others' attention—and lessen Phillips' grip on their project. Though flying seemed a distant goal at the moment. First they needed to get approval for a taxi test.

Tom didn't need to be asked to step inside the metal locker.

"Two?" His brows arched.

Alice had to give her father a slight nudge.

"Why yes, the *Ray* can accommodate a pilot and copilot."

Tom reached out, fingering the closest suit. His fingers were long and strong—she knew that from personal experience. She sensed they were capable. Her hands curled into fists at her sides. She wanted to step forward and show him the suit. Instead she had to stand silent while those capable hands felt along the arms, then the legs. He lifted it down, turning it to get access to the inside.

It was going to be a tight fit, especially those shoulders. She moved close, helping him with the fastenings. They weren't simple because they were a weak spot in the suit and had to be able to withstand the G-forces, too.

Tom shrugged out of his jacket and kicked off his shoes. Alice held it for him while he stepped in, then he pulled it up and over his shoulders. She pulled it together and re-secured it. It fit. Barely.

"How does it feel?" she asked. "Can you move?"

He tried different directions of movement. Then he tried some harder movements and finally gave her a thumbs up. Oh, that's right. The possible listening ears.

"There are boots," Merriweather said, crossing to two pairs. "They adjust to fit the user."

She glanced toward the headgear and Tom crossed to lift one off the shelf. He placed it over his head, but she needed to fasten it to the suit for him. Then he pushed his feet into the boots. She used an air compressor to adjust the fit.

She rose and leaned against the wall, crossing her arms to hide the tremble of her hands. None of the pilots who'd expressed any interest in the *Ray* had been willing to don this suit. They'd looked at the *Ray* with much more interest, one calling it "right out of a sci-fi movie." And they'd all faded away. Was the *Ray* the death trap that everyone seemed to think it was? What did Phillips want? Because it wasn't actual tests, at least not here. The move to Groom Lake seemed to indicate a desire to control the project, but it wasn't like there weren't people here, and pilots who knew about the *Ray*. They might not know what it was capable of, but they knew of it. The secret was out. And why would Groom Lake be better than Muroc? They were both desert bases.

Tom moved around the hangar, continuing to test the flexibility of the suit. He moved the arms and legs, did squats and then dropped and did push-ups. The guy was in great shape. He jumped up, then did a handstand and flip, landing solidly on his booted feet. Alice blinked.

"My word," her father said, mildly.

Tom looked at her and she saw he had many questions that he didn't dare ask. Instead, he pointed at the *Ray*. She looked at her father and saw, for the first time in a long time, a stirring of his old interest in the *Ray*. They went forward together and scrambled under the belly so they could activate the hatch. When it had fully lowered, Tom bent and clambered aboard. After a brief hesitation, Alice kicked off her low heels and followed him inside.

She'd been inside on her own, in secret, when everyone had left, through each phase of its construction. They'd built it here. It was unusual and it had created a lot of discussion and dissatisfaction. And it had added another layer of distrust for the pilots. It felt different being inside it with Tom. It was tight. Extra space was limited to a small cargo area behind the cockpit. The tandem copilot seat behind the pilot's was raised because of the tight design of the front of the craft.

She sat on the edge of the hatch and watched Tom studying the interior. What had he looked at in here last night when he was comparing it to the Link Trainer? She had questions and she sensed Tom did, too.

Was Phillips listening? Was there a way to find out? At some point, they would need to talk. But for now, she did not mind the silence. Being here, with him, had changed something about her relationship with the *Ray*. For the first time, she could imagine it in the air. She glanced back and stiffened. There was a gleam in the dimness back by the main engine. She turned and crawled back the short distance.

It was a washer. It wouldn't mean that much, but it hadn't been there the last time she was inside. And there was no reason for anyone to be in here since then.

Someone had been inside recently.

What had they done?

"Dr. Merriweather? I was hoping I'd find you here."

It was Phillips. Alice tensed, meeting Tom's gaze across the small space of the hold.

"I've got a pilot for you."

It was what they'd wanted, so why did it feel like a trap?

* * *

GRANGER FROWNED, his gut twitching with warning. Phillips had suddenly produced a pilot just when it looked like the Merriweathers had him to fly it? There was definitely something wrong here.

"We have a pilot," Merriweather said, "but thank you."

"Doesn't that thing seat two?" Phillips asked, his tone easy but with a thread of determination in it.

That thing? What did Phillips have to gain by putting his pilot on board? And who thought it was a good idea to risk two pilots in an untested craft? Of course, he wasn't risking that much. They had to taxi before they could lift off.

He looked at Alice and saw she held up a washer, then glanced back toward the engine.

Sabotage? But why put his own pilot—Granger tensed. If they were the time-traveling time tamperers, then Phillips' pilot could trigger his recall and disappear, leaving Granger to die in the sabotaged plane.

He gave her a slight nod, to let her know he'd got the message. And he had. Phillips was willing to kill him and destroy the *Ray* to stop this project. If Phillips was from the future, was he here to stop or steal the technology? Or had Granger seen *Terminator* one too many times? According to Mel and Jack, the tampering they'd discovered had been very limited. More like a small pebble dropped in a very large, and already churning, pool.

Okay, taking out his instinctive distrust of Phillips, what if he was here to save Merriweather's life? But then why let the research be destroyed—if it had been—and let his daughter die? Just thinking of that made his gut clench. Was Alice supposed to have died or did they kill her accidentally with their tampering? According to Jack, tinkering with time could cause collateral damage.

She sat in the cramped cargo space of the *Ray*, turning the washer over in her fingers. Her legs were tucked under her. She'd kicked off her shoes, but it was ridiculous for her to be in here in her dress-code suit. And yet, somehow she looked more at home here than at the bungalow where they slept and ate.

His chest tightened. She couldn't die, he—he knew what Mel or Jack would say, but how could he not try to save her?

He turned back to the controls, comparing them with the

Link Trainer controls. He flexed his gloved hands and mimicked using the controls. The suit was good. Flexible and comfortable. Not at all what he'd have expected in 1954. There was also the view. From the outside, the canopy was invisible, but inside the range of vision was great.

Granger scrambled out of the pilot's seat, once more impressed by the flexibility of the flight suit, and joined Alice.

Merriweather had drawn Phillips and the pilot away from the hatch. With Alice's help, Granger got his headgear off.

"Does the *Ray* have any safety features for the pilot?" Were they using ejection devices yet? He kept his voice low.

"The cockpit separates from the ship," she whispered. "It has its own parachutes. Additionally, the seats can eject from the cockpit and deploy parachutes."

He almost whistled. How high was she planning for the *Ray* to go? It sounded like she had a high/low altitude ejection system.

Added to the features of this suit, which sounded like it had something like a CPAP-like oxygen system, she'd done what she could to protect the pilots.

He quirked a brow at her. "Should we go face the man in black? See if we can find out what he's up to?"

Alice made a face. "I'm not sure I can get down without getting charged with indecency."

"I'll go first," Granger said, shifting to the hatch opening and then dropping down. He turned to give her privacy by blocking the others' view of her and, because he was tempted to look, he instead took the opportunity to study the two men with Merri-weather. All three men had turned at the sound of his boots hitting cement. "You need to turn around so Miss Merriweather can get down," he said, with a bland smile.

Phillips shot a look toward the hatch, Granger might have called it a concerned look, then he must have realized he'd have to turn around if he wanted to continue to pretend he was a gentleman. With clear reluctance he rotated so his back was to the *Ray*. With his head somewhat angled, Phillips asked, "What did you think, Major?"

Granger felt Alice's hands on his shoulders as she navigated the ladder, then she was down. They both bent so that they could clear the outer edge of the *Ray*, then Granger turned, his gaze traveling over the *Ray* once again. Now that he'd been inside, he saw her with new eyes. He didn't understand everything yet, but he did know more.

"I don't know why it's been so hard to find a pilot," Granger said, his eyes on Phillips as the man turned to face them. There was nothing to read in the man's eyes, but a muscle by his mouth twitched. His gaze moved to Alice.

"Did you enjoy your day out, Miss Merriweather?" Phillips' tone was carefully respectful, but it still held a note that Granger found condescending. Like an adult to a child.

"Very much, Mr. Phillips." She flicked a mischievous look at Granger. "I saw Frank Sinatra."

"Frank Sinatra?"

Phillips didn't need to sound quite so skeptical.

"It's true what they say about his eyes. I've never seen eyes that blue and"—she gave a breathy sigh—"compelling."

If Granger hadn't known Alice was yanking Phillips chain, her dreamy tone might have annoyed him a bit. But he'd seen the real Alice. He'd kissed the real Alice. The memory of this killed his urge to grin at the look in the blue eyes of the man facing them.

"Yeah, well, that's...interesting." Phillips turned his attention to Alice's father. "So, are we going to see what the *Manta Ray* can do in the air?"

It looked like Merriweather was about to speak, but Alice moved first.

"Father, didn't you say we needed our taxi test first? We could probably get that set up for tomorrow."

Merriweather nodded. "Our Cooper-Harper rating would allow that."

Now why did that annoy Phillips, Granger wondered? He hadn't imagined the flicker of it that passed over the man's face.

"I'm sure I could get us approval to do that right now if you're good to go?" Phillips looked at the other pilot.

"Sure," the man said easily.

Who was this guy? Another time traveler or a dupe Phillips had recruited? How on earth could he get approval for a test on a Sunday?

"It will take time to get a ground crew in," Alice said. Before Phillips could ask, she added, "There's no fuel on board."

"The *Ray* hasn't needed to be fueled since it hasn't left the hangar," Merriweather agreed.

"Tomorrow morning then?" Phillips said.

"I'll start making calls," Alice said.

Her gaze was steady and calm as it met Phillips. Granger wished he felt as calm. Would that give them time to find the sabotage—if there was any? He couldn't help thinking about the explosion that was supposed to happen next week. Had he moved up the date by challenging Phillips?

Pebbles in a very big pool, Mel had said about traveling through time. Had he dropped something in this one just by being here? There had been no record of any test flight involving the *Ray*. Would it taxi tomorrow or would Phillips find a way to stop them?

The horizon seemed to ripple again, and this time he wondered if it were exhaustion or the ripple of the future he was changing?

* * *

NEITHER OF THEM had left the bunker since they got the alert on the cuff link. There had been some changes in the timeline, minor ones. The *Manta Ray* had shown up on a schedule for a taxi test on Monday morning, the fifteenth of February. They'd also found some photographs—not official ones but possibly from ground crew—of the *Manta Ray*.

It was unusual looking, based on what they could see. It had a sci-fi look to it that might have made the pilots of that time uneasy, Jack decided.

"You wish you could fly it," Mel charged him.

Jack grinned wryly. It was challenging to have someone else out there taking the risks and traveling through time…

Jack's computer pinged. He turned, took the two steps and dropped into his seat. It had to be…it was.

"Here's the two photos Granger took," Jack said, opening first one, and then the other.

"Same guy," Mel murmured, leaning on his shoulder.

"Yeah, looks like they are in a diner," Jack muttered. Dillys? Could be. Granger had planned to head there to try for a ride to Edwards. "Who is that off to the side?" Jack blew up that area of the image.

"I think that could be Merriweather's daughter. The one who died in the explosion," Mel said. She pulled her chair over and dropped into it. "It's probably a long shot, but let's run facial recognition on him."

Long shot indeed, Jack thought grimly. If this guy was from the future, good luck finding him in the here and now.

CHAPTER 5

*a*lice was used to being underestimated. She was used to being condescended to by men and women. She was used to being dismissed as stupid by stupid people. Ignored and overlooked. Invisible. Or worse, an object to be groped out of sight of her father.

She was not used to anyone like Tom.

He looked at her like he saw her as a person. He'd kissed her, but he hadn't put his hand on her posterior or asked her to get him a cup of coffee. He hadn't patted her on the head or shoulder, either physically or figuratively. He was confident without being arrogant. He was—

Probably going to break her heart.

She lowered the wrench for a second, processing the idea that she had a heart and that she might have lost it just when she found it. Music filled the hangar from the radio that one of the crewmen had brought with them. It was ironic it was currently playing "Don't Let the Stars Get in Your Eyes." Again. Something in the universe wanted to make sure she got the message not to get stars in her eyes or hope in her heart.

She set the wrench down and lifted a rag to wipe the perspiration from her face, then grabbed a screwdriver. Ostensibly, Tom was helping, but he kept getting distracted by the design of the engine. *Her engine.*

For the first time, she laid mental claim to it. She'd never let herself think it, for fear of letting it slip out at the wrong moment. But it was about more than hiding, she realized. She'd never felt it was hers. But right now, in this place, with this man—

She reached up and laid a hand on the housing. *Hers.* Her gaze strayed toward Tom. *Not hers.*

Her heart rebelled at the thought, but her mind, well, she was an aeronautical designer and a scientist, even if no one knew it but her father and Tom. If she didn't tell herself the truth, she'd cease to be, well, scientific. She'd be…human? Flawed? She'd been that before and would be again. But this felt different.

The guy would fly away. And the *Ray?* It might be lost to her, too, but she'd know she did something amazing. If they could get the an actual test flight, if it worked, then she'd *know* that something that started inside her head flew higher and farther than anything ever had before. Even if she was the only one who knew it, she'd *know* she did that.

It would be nice to know what came after that, but the future was lost to the shadow. She couldn't see past the taxi test at the moment. It wasn't very scientific of her to believe in the shadow, but she knew when it had moved over her.

The day Phillips returned to Edwards.

It felt as if he'd put a foot on her future, as if he'd stamped it out like cigarette in the dirt. She was used to being treated like he'd treated her, but she wasn't used to being…afraid.

"You okay?" Tom asked, breaking into her admittedly dismal thoughts.

She was on the brink of the most amazing moment—second most amazing, she decided, compressing the lips he'd kissed—of her life. She smiled at him, because she couldn't help herself. They were alone. There was no one to know or see.

"Yes." It wasn't a complete lie. When he was there the fear receded some. But she couldn't let herself become too dependent on him. Good thing she'd learned to savor small bites of happiness, to make them last.

"Found anything?"

She turned her attention back to her engine. She knew it like she knew herself. She knew something was wrong but—she shook her head. "Not yet." But she would. Because she had to. If she didn't, then both the plane and the man would be lost. She wouldn't lose them that way.

* * *

ALICE STOPPED to rub her eyes and Granger put a hand over hers, before she could lift the tool again.

"You can't miss another night's sleep," he said. Exhaustion had stolen the color from her face and blurred the clarity of her eyes. She smelled of woman and machine oil. In other words, amazing. And she kept surprising him. Scientist and mechanic. What else had she hidden from the world?

The radio still blared out in the hangar, but they were the only two left. If he was having them watched, Granger wondered what Phillips would make of lights and sound coming from the hangar long after the ground crew had left? And what would the man do if the *Ray* completed the taxi test without incident. Unless he managed to stop it somehow. It all depended on what he wanted. And what he would do to make that happen.

"You're the one who should sleep," she said. "There's a cot in the office you could stretch out on."

"I'm fine," he said. Oddly enough, he was.

She started in again, the only sign of outward tension in the edges of her mouth. She had to be in her thirties, which would mean she was in her 20's in wartime. They'd touched on his "wartime" service, but not hers.

"I suppose you worked with your dad during the war?" He kept his tone casual, but he knew he wanted to know more about her and that's why he'd asked, not just to pass the time.

She glanced at him. "We were in California, oh, not on a base then." She was quiet for several moments, then said, almost casually, "I was almost killed by a Japanese balloon bomb."

He stiffened. Did he know about balloon bombs?

"They kept it quiet. They didn't want people to panic," she said, her hands busy in a contrast to the quiet voice. "I was walking along the beach when it drifted in. It was ugly, but—" She paused.

"Interesting?" he prompted.

She half smiled. "It was that. I started toward it, then, I'm not sure. I just felt like I shouldn't. I backed away because it was still...interesting." Another hint of a smile. "It exploded when it touched down." She paused, her gaze distant. "I felt the heat of it. Was scratched by some shrapnel." She moved her arm. "It was the closest I got to the real thing, but it was shocking, obscene on that quiet beach."

She looked at him then.

"It changed me. Changed what I wanted. As challenging as it sometimes is, I want to help. I still want to...help."

Granger's grin felt crooked. "Helping is good." Good response, he thought scornfully, but she smiled.

They both worked on for another hour, then Alice set down her tool and sagged against the housing. While Tom had found it fascinating seeing the guts of her engine, they both needed to get some sleep before tomorrow's test. She dug the heels of her hands into her tired eyes, as if trying to wake them up by force. When she dropped her hands, she met Tom's gaze.

She'd donned some coveralls and boots she'd had stowed in a

locker and pulled a cap down over her hair so she could blend in with the other crew. Tom wasn't sure how well it worked but he hadn't ever been called out late on a Sunday to prep a plane for a test flight before, so he didn't know how it usually went. In the past. None of them had showed a lot of curiosity. They'd worked as fast as they could, then left to get on with their Sunday rest.

"I'm not sure I can find it in time," she admitted, the droop of her shoulders echoed in her voice.

He eased over next to her. "Maybe you're trying too hard." He was quiet for several seconds, then he shifted so he half faced her. "If you wanted to sabotage the *Ray*, how would you do it?"

She frowned, considering the question. Tom considered it, too. The main engine was unique and didn't use a flammable fuel source, at least he wasn't sure—she stiffened at the same time he did.

"The jet-powered engines!"

The *Ray* didn't have as much fuel on board as a typical aircraft, but it didn't take much if someone used the right match.

"It will still be hard to find," Tom agreed, considering the problem from this new angle. Like her, he'd been focused on the main engine because that was the main event, at least as far as he was concerned. The plane's design was interesting, intriguing even, but the engine. It was the tantalizing bits of its design that had brought him into the past.

"But at least we'll be looking in the right spot." She had hope visible in her tired eyes. She was quiet again. "I don't think— anyone would know how to sabotage anything else."

It was unique. The only thing remotely standard about the *Ray* was the jet engines.

"Let's go hunting," he said.

* * *

THE TIME TREMORS had quieted some, but Mel was unable to take much comfort from it. She turned as Jack came in, closing the heavy door behind him. It was kind of crazy, but they had hoped that the bunker, its contents and occupants, were protected from time changes. They had evidence that the bunker worked, but so far the indications were small. And they wouldn't know if something big had changed until they could see it, track the difference. The problem was, they were hoping to stop big changes, not cause them.

"What you got?" Jack asked, coming over to slide an arm around her waist and drop a kiss on the top of her head.

"Look for yourself," she said, pointing at the computer.

Jack pulled his chair next to hers and sat down, studying the two images. One was from the past—Granger's cuff link. The other image was from the present. A facial recognition hit. "It looks like the same guy," he admitted, skepticism in his tone, however.

He was right to wonder. This guy could be a descendant of Granger's guy. Or it could be some weird coincidence. Odds of him being *the* guy? Mel didn't want to do that math.

"I'm got some people running a background on present guy, just in case," Mel said. She sighed. "How would we know?" And if they did find something out, how did they let Granger know? Was that even possible? This whole thing was weird and seemed to have a few, frustrating rules. One being that even though the past was the past, they were locked into some kind of strange dance with time. While Granger's efforts played out in 1954, they only "saw" them happen with a day's difference either before or after, but still sixty-six years later. That felt—seemed—so wrong. They should be able to "see" everything that had already happened, but wanting it didn't change the reality they dealt with.

"There's something else, too," Mel said, spinning her chair

around and getting up. The map. She was starting to hate that map. It felt alive and kind of mocking. Most of it was still intact as it had been for most of this operation, but the picture of George Merriweather was, well, wavering, as if it were under water or something. She wasn't sure, but she thought the face changed to someone else from time to time.

"What the—" Jack stopped, pushing his free hand through his hair.

"Yeah," Mel agreed.

"Can you tell if anything else has changed?"

Mel studied the map, comparing it with—she hoped—her photographic memory of before Granger had left.

"I don't think so, no, wait." She moved closer. "There's something new here."

She pointed at the map, careful not to touch it, just in case time wanted to give a little kick again.

Jack leaned in. "I don't understand. We knew Merriweather's plane flew once—"

"No, we didn't," Mel interrupted. "Before Granger left, that plane never flew."

"But this says it crashed," Jack objected. "Technically, that's not flying."

"Look closer," Mel said, feeling something like despair. They'd done this.

"It wasn't in the air. It exploded during a taxi test and"—Jack had to stop to catch his breath—"The test pilot, Major Tom Grayson, was killed."

Mel turned, burying her face in his shoulder. "We killed him."

"No, he chose this, Mel, just like he chose to fly that plane."

"But, why? That wasn't in the original timeline," Mel protested.

"As we both know, time crap happens." He stiffened. "Look, Mel."

She looked. Now that article was getting wavy, too. The outcome was still in doubt. "What's the date—tomorrow." They were watching a change happen in…real time. Okay, that sounded all wrong.

"Sixty-five years ago tomorrow," Jack agreed.

CHAPTER 6

*T*hey finished in time to catch a couple of hours of sleep before the time arrived for the *Ray*'s baby steps. It wasn't enough sleep, but Alice pushed that to the side. She could rest later, after the *Ray* successfully taxied down the runway and back. The longing to be in the cockpit curled her hands into fists in the pockets of her coat. Worry was a knot in her stomach. Had they found all the sabotage? They hadn't quit until they'd gone over both lift engines with a fine-tooth comb. But the worry wouldn't go. She'd had to resist the urge to sleep in the *Ray*.

Now she paced back and forth in front of the flight suit locker where Tom was changing. She'd missed something. She felt it in the knot twisting her stomach.

He came out, his headgear under one arm and saw her face.

"What?" He came to her quickly, the concern warming the chill of hangar and worry.

"I missed something," she said.

"We went over the whole—" he began.

She stiffened. "Not everything," she said. "The ejection system. We didn't go over that."

Grim settled over his face. He glanced past her and saw what she already knew. The *Ray* had already been towed out of the hangar. It was on its way to the runway.

"We'll have to postpone," she said.

"If we do, Phillips will know we know about the sabotage."

He didn't add that Phillips would start to suspect her role, too. He didn't have to add it, she could see it in his face. She glanced around and her gaze stopped on the second flight suit. Tom turned, following her gaze. To her surprise, he didn't object.

"We shouldn't need the ejection system for a taxi test," he murmured. "And it's your plane." He stared into the distance for a frowning moment, then turned to her, one brow lifting in a question.

And why not? It was just a taxi test.

"Give me a few minutes," she said, feeling a sudden lightness inside. It took her more than a few to scramble out of her dress-code clothes, into a coverall, and then start on the flight suit.

"Can I help?" Tom said, on the other side of the door.

"Please," she said. He helped secure her suit, then she finished securing his. He stepped back.

"Without the headgear…" He lifted his with one hand. "I'll put on mine if…"

His grin expanded the bubble of light in her stomach. She should be afraid, but she wasn't. What magic hold did this man have over her?

It wasn't typical and it wasn't ideal to wear their headgear out, but they could take them off once they were aboard the *Ray*.

"Let's do it," she said. While they did, she pondered how to get tools aboard.

As if he once again followed her thought processes, he asked, "Can you access what you need to from inside the cockpit?"

She nodded. She'd deliberately created access from inside. Test pilots often worked alongside the techs and knew as much about the planes as the designers—or even more at times. She'd wanted the pilots to have as much operational ability as possible.

As much control over their fate, well, more than she had, she thought wryly. She glanced around. In a few extra minutes, she'd put together two kits that looked like something a pilot might carry. Phillips might smell a rat, but he hadn't shown up yet. Hopefully, they'd already be on the plane before he did.

She confirmed neither Phillips nor his pilot were in sight when they went out and climbed in the jeep that was to take them to the *Ray*. They had a chance if Phillips didn't find a new way to stop them.

For once, the wide, empty desert didn't bother her. They needed that dry lake bed and most of its length to get the *Ray* airborne—when the time came. And it would come, she told herself. This was just the first step. Their taxi test had been approved. Emergency vehicles were on hand and ready to roll.

As was the padre in his crow-black suit. The specter at the feast.

The sun broke free of the mountains and light spilled across the staging area as the *Ray* moved slowly toward the runway. She gleamed so bright, Alice wished she'd brought her sunglasses with her. Wouldn't that have been interesting inside the helmet.

She shifted in her seat so she could look back. No sign of anyone following them. Her father would be monitoring from further back. And probably wondering where she was.

She faced forward once more, but her thoughts went back to the sight of Tom in his uniform this morning, not the fancy dress one, but the working uniform. He'd looked so big and competent and confident. He'd made her heart stop for long enough to worry her. He belonged in the uniform and it belonged on him. He had the bearing, but still that something different that set him apart from the other military men she'd encountered.

When the *Ray* had come out of the hangar, they'd attracted a small audience, enough to drive her back inside to wait for Tom. Taking off and landing wasn't a big deal, but some of the men had not seen the *Ray* before. They'd walked around it with interest, but most shook their heads—while hanging around to see what happened.

Alice didn't blame them. They'd seen some unusual craft arrive on this base. And they'd seen a lot of them crash and burn —or not get off the ground. Alice's main concern was if the lift engines were strong enough to do the job. It had been a tricky balancing act, keeping the *Ray* light enough to lift off and strong enough for what she hoped would come after. One thing she knew for sure, the *Ray* was too heavy to be carried to altitude, like most of the other planes. It had to rise on its own. Only then could the main engine be tested.

But first it had to roll, she reminded herself.

All the way to the runway, Alice kept glancing back in the direction Phillips and his pilot would have to come. Would they even bother for a taxi test? Her father had surprised her by being more animated than she'd seen him a quite a while. Was it hope? Had Tom managed to infuse him with some, too?

She glanced around. It was cold and windy on the flight line early in the morning. The scrub bent under its insistence. Had she ever known it not to be blowing out here? Her flight suit provided pretty decent protection from the chill, but she did wonder...

Tom leaned forward and tapped their driver on the shoulder. "Can you find out about the wind speed for us?"

"Yes, sir!" He grabbed the radio and relayed the question.

After a pause, they got a thumbs up from their driver.

Alice kept waiting for something to come over the radio about her but they pulled to a stop next to the *Ray* and nothing had been said. Alice was careful not to attract any attention from their driver. The crew who had loaded the fuel were about to leave in their own jeep except for the two men who'd been detailed to observe the engines spin up. They had fire extinguishers at the ready, but right now they were shooting the breeze with each other.

She was too far away to tell now if Phillips had arrived. She was happy if he hadn't. He wasn't in charge and if she had her way, he never would be.

The hatch was already down. Tom, carrying one of the tool kits, went up first to relieve the crewman who'd been stationed in the *Ray* until the pilot arrived. Alice waited until that crewman had dropped down. She slung her tool kit over her shoulder and climbed up as he trotted over to the crewman's jeep. The two on fire control duty would leave later, with the driver who had just brought her here with Tom.

She was pleased at how well she could move in the flight suit. It was a pity it wouldn't be getting a workout today, too. *One step at a time, Alice.*

She crawled toward the cockpit where Tom was already seated. He turned to help her out of her headgear, then she started working on the panel that covered the ejection system controls.

"Any sign of Phillips?" she asked, as she removed the last screw and lowered the panel. This panel was close to where Tom sat, so he could direct the beam of a flashlight inside for her.

At first she didn't see it, or didn't realize what she saw. When she did, she took the flashlight from Tom and got it closer to the small device.

"What on earth…." she began.

"I think it's an explosive device," Tom said, his voice icy. "If this panel exploded, what would it do to the ejection system?"

Alice considered the question. "It's so small," she murmured. "It doesn't look like it could do much, but if it damaged the controls…or blew a hole in the side of the plane…"

"It's very localized. I'm guessing it would only do damage right here, though I suppose it could start a fire." He shifted restlessly. "Be careful taking it out, particularly with the wires."

How localized was localized? She handed him the flashlight again and he kept it steady on the object while she detached the wires and lifted it free. Was this why Phillips and his pilot had bailed out on the taxi test? It was suspicious they hadn't shown up, but at the same time, it was a taxi test. If one of the other sabotage attempts had worked, would they have had time to eject? She wasn't sure.

"Can I look at it?" Tom asked.

She handed it to him. His hands were big, but surprisingly deft, even with gloves on, as he studied the device. She saw and felt him stiffen.

"What?" She leaned over, once more directing the light on it. There was a panel on one side with strange numbers.

"I'm not sure, but this could be a timer." His tone was grim. "I can't tell when, but I think it's also radio controlled."

"But…" She frowned. But there could only be one purpose in destroying the ejection system. Ice flowed into her veins. To kill the pilot. "He would have killed that other pilot, too." She looked at Tom, shaking her head. "Why would he do that?"

"He must have decided not to kill both of us," Tom said, his gaze not meeting hers for the first time, but his frown had drawn his brows almost completely together.

What did he know or fear? For whatever crazy reason, she knew this man. And knew he was hiding something from her.

"So, someone could send a signal to this…thing…and it would explode?" she asked. If there was enough explosives in that thing to destroy the panel, then it could blow his hand off. She took it back, though she sensed his resistance. She'd never seen anything like it, though explosives weren't her area of research. This was the closest she'd been to a bomb since that beach in '45.

She'd told Tom about it, which amazed her in a way. She'd never spoken of it since she'd informed the authorities and been sworn to secrecy. So people wouldn't panic. She hadn't panicked, at least not on the outside. She hadn't told them or Tom about the nightmares that followed, dreams of dying in an explosion. Or the one about being trapped by an explosion, but not dying quickly. The nightmares had diminished in regularity, until recently. Until the shadow. She supposed it was the stress that had brought them back.

"I'm guessing," Tom said, giving a frustrated sigh. "We've got to get it off the plane without being seen."

She nodded. "But what's the point? The other sabotage would have killed...a pilot."

"Pilots have survived worse," Tom pointed out. "And your flight suit is unusual for—compared to other flight suits I've seen."

She had designed it to resist fire and G-force pressures, and to keep the pilot breathing in high altitude. It also had a better heating system than those used in the war. All this brought her back to Phillips' apparent desire to murder a pilot. To murder Tom. But this sabotage didn't feel—or look—spur of the moment. Would it have gone off if they hadn't had this test? And when? Like Tom, the numbers told her nothing. She looked at the device again. How easy was it to secure something like this? It looked, she considered, forgetting for a moment how dangerous it was, like something from a science fiction movie.

What had Tom been going to say? Who was this man who'd appeared almost out of nowhere? It was like a movie, the hero riding in out of the sunset to save the—Ray. He'd exposed her secrets and managed to reveal many of his own. What she knew, what she sensed about him, lacked scientific method.

She felt trust. But should she? Could she trust him? How did he know so much? And yet...

"Alice?"

She looked up and saw that now he looked at her. What did he see?

"Now what?" she asked.

* * *

NOW WHAT? Granger stared down at the device like it held the answers to all the questions, when what he was really doing was avoiding Alice's gaze—and the questions in them. Did she know how transparent her eyes were? For a girl who'd hid so much...

He blew out an exasperated sigh. He needed to focus. Because Phillips—or someone—was trying to kill him and destroy the *Ray*. His gut told him Phillips was behind it all. He admitted he was surprised neither he nor his pilot had shown up. It was a lucky break because Alice might be exposed. Of course, she could also die with him if this went wrong.

"Let's do the taxi test," he said, while he tried to think of a way to get the explosive device off the plane without being seen—or blowing anyone up. He'd bet his future salary there were binoculars trained on the *Ray* right now. Was there a backup to the backup plan? He could twist himself into knots worrying about it. *Deal with the problem in front of you.* It had been good advice back in the future. And it was all he had right now.

Her smile might have held an element of relief. Or he was thinking too much. Or hoping too much? That was possible, too. He'd asked for her trust, in so many words, and he might be the last person she should trust.

"What about that thing?"

He looked down at the tools spilling out of the bags they'd brought on board.

"We should probably leave those with the driver," he said.

"But he could get hurt if—" she bit her lips.

Lips he'd tasted. Don't go there, he warned himself. Not right now. He assessed the device. How localized would the blast be? He was pretty sure Phillips would press the button if he got half a chance—or would he wait for the next test? Would there be more questions if there was an explosion during a taxi test?

"The only reason anyone would have for detonating this is if there was an emergency," he said, speaking as he thought it through. "No emergency, no need for ejection."

"So all we have to do is not have an emergency," Alice said.

"Let's get this stuff off and get the hatch closed." They should probably already be on the radio, he realized.

Alice loaded her tools into one of the bags and stowed that in a hatch. She held open the other one so he could drop the device in. He almost objected about the tools, but if she thought she needed them, then they should stay on board.

He crawled over to the hatch and called their driver over. When he came, he handed him the bag and told him to head back. He resisted the urge to tell him to leave it by the side of the road. If it detonated, there'd be a lot of questions.

"Yes, sir." He gave Tom a crisp salute and turned and left.

He closed the hatch, the sound way too final sounding. He needed to get over the feeling that any action he took would result in an explosion.

Alice was waiting with her headgear on and holding his. When both had been latched down, he moved into the pilot's seat, aware Alice settled in the copilot's position directly behind him. He strapped in, feeling calm wash over him as he took the first steps of connecting to this plane. The familiar whine of jet engines spinning up eased his anxieties. It was just a taxi test. If he kept repeating this, maybe his gut would relax. He activated the radio, but his eyes were on his instrument panels. There were all the familiar indicators, gauges, and switches around him. And then there was the special panel, the one that activated and controlled Alice's engine. He didn't let himself dwell on that one. For now, his job was to taxi down the runway, turn this big sucker around and come back. No problem.

"Edwards Tower, this is Tare Fox Roger." He glanced off to his right and saw the jeep trundling across the bleak expanse toward the hangars.

No matter what happened, he was glad Alice was here. She deserved to be here. It was wrong that she couldn't claim her work. It took a sixty-six-year perspective shift to realize how messed up this was.

He didn't know whether to be relieved or worried Phillips and his guy hadn't shown up. Probably both. Interesting there'd been no sign of the guy in any of the photographs they'd found, considering how omnipresent he'd been the last few days. Had his cuff link been found? Was there a picture of the guy back in the future? Would it matter? He needed to survive this test first, he reminded himself. He glanced to the left, but all he saw was desert. He wished the design of the *Ray* allowed Alice to be next to him instead of directly behind him.

"We are ready for your preflight check, Tare Fox Roger," the tower said.

There was no longer a bomb on this plane, Granger reminded himself. And they were pretty sure they'd found all the other sabotage. So he wasn't likely to go up in a ball of fire on engine start. He started his preflight checklist, as a twitch between his shoulders joined with his clenching gut.

Follow your gut.

Good advice, but he didn't know how to get himself and his gut out of this plane without losing face, not just with Alice, but with Phillips. He went over the gauges again. Nothing there to concern him.

He felt a sudden urge to just get it over. He checked the rpms. They were good. He tapped his radio. "This is Tare Fox Roger. Preflight is complete. All systems ready. Am I cleared to go?"

There was a long pause, long enough to start a twitch between his shoulder blades and then…

"You are cleared for your taxi test, Tare Fox Roger."

Well, it was now or never. He leaned forward and started flipping switches. He felt the jet's whine build to a near shriek, felt the increased rpms flow along the length of the plane as he increased pressure on the throttle.

Let's do this, he said to the plane as he eased it forward.

* * *

ALICE FELT and heard the increase in the rpms travel up through her boots and into her body. She couldn't stop herself from bracing for a follow-on explosion. Over the increasing roar, she heard the crackle of the radio through the receiver in her head-gear as Tom talked to the tower. When he got clearance, she felt elation—and terror.

Flying had begun to filter into her nightmares, flying and crashing. And burning. But this was just a taxi test. She repeated that several times.

And she was still glad to be here. Even with fear tightening every muscle in her body, she felt the revolutions of the engines increase. The feel of this was so different from doing the run-up for her flying lessons—as it should be. But the thrill went further. This was *her* plane.

The *Ray* began to move, slowly rolling on the concrete surface below its wheels.

If only they could take off, if they could soar and see how high her engine could take them.

Her hands gripped the rests on her seat to keep them from reaching for the controls. Her hands wanted, no, they itched to feel them, to feel the plane respond to her. Her gaze strayed to the main engine controls for her engine. If only...

Would they work? No one was successful on their first try, at least no one she knew. The worst that could—should happen—was nothing. The engine and the plane did nothing. She'd postu-lated what might result from a misfire or partial fire, but she didn't know. She couldn't know without testing.

If she could fly it herself, then no one else would be at risk. She knew women had and could fly planes. Pancho Barnes, who had owned the Happy Bottom Riding Club, had been a test and stunt pilot. Alice had seen the burned-out remains of the club and wished she could talk to Pancho. But then what would she have said to her?

"I'm not as brave as you but I'd like to be. How did you do it?" How had Pancho fought free of the undertow of the society she'd been born into and the minister she'd married? How had she been so relentlessly brave? And bold?

Alice sighed and kept her hands away from the controls. This was not the moment to be bold. She'd trained in the Link Trainer, but that wasn't close enough to flying this plane.

"Go for it," Granger said.

"Excuse me?" Alice asked.

"Put your hands on the controls. As long as you don't take over," he added. "Feel how it feels."

"Thank you," she said. She hesitated, but it was as if her body recognized it when the *Ray* began to speed up. She dropped her hands lightly on the controls, letting her fingers curl around just enough to get a sense of how it felt.

It had to be her imagination that the smell inside her helmet changed to something less metallic and more…human. Perhaps the warmth coming off her body and her breath? She didn't know. It was all new and yet familiar.

Her position was elevated, giving her sight lines over the pilot's seat, so she could see the ground running away under them as the *Ray* sped up. She realized she was leaning forward, as if to it urge onward and upward. Not good. No flying today. She glanced down and made sure she was only on intra-ship comms. She needed to say it.

"I wish we could lift off," she murmured.

"You and me both," Tom said. "So far she's handling like a dream."

It felt rougher than a dream to Alice. Acceleration pushed her back into her seat. They were moving fast enough the ground began to blur and ahead of them, the line leading toward the mountains shortened. They'd have to decelerate soon.

The radio cracked. "Tare Fox Roger, begin your deceleration."

"I'm trying," Tom said, a sudden grim note to his voice.

Alice stared at the instruments, all going in the wrong direction.

"We're going to have to take off," Tom said.

Alice took care not to interfere with his control of the plane, but she wanted, she needed to feel it. She wanted to know what it felt like.

"Say again, Tare Fox Roger," the tower said.

"I am unable to decelerate. Tare Fox Roger is taking off. Will try to circle around and land."

They'd have to do more than try. There wasn't enough fuel on board for much longer than that.

* * *

GRANGER PULLED BACK on the stick, and the *Ray* rotated up, her nose pointed toward the rising sun.

"Are you declaring an emergency?" the tower asked.

"Roger, that, tower. I am declaring an emergency." Was this part of the plan? Get the plane in the air and then blow the explosive? He sure hoped their driver wasn't sitting next to it.

The main wheels left the runway. The *Ray* was airborne now. He would have kept the landing gear down if an immediate landing were a possibility. It wasn't looking that way. He retracted the landing gear, feeling the thuds as they tucked in. Alice didn't say anything, which was a relief. He sure didn't have answers either. But he felt her thinking behind him.

The *Ray* was ascending fast. Turning might or might not be an option. He heard movement behind him. Then she was beside him, with a couple of tools and the flashlight clutched in her now gloveless hands. Her headgear was gone, too.

That she wasn't strapped in and didn't have her headgear on

was bad on a bunch of levels. But then so was accelerating out of control.

"Do you think you can fix it?"

"That's the plan," she said.

She eased down—it had to be challenging with the suit on—and then maneuvered onto her back, sliding her head under the instrument panel.

If they survived this, he decided grimly, he was going to make sure the future came back to bite Phillips in the butt, too.

* * *

ALICE SHOULD HAVE BEEN SCARED, but she'd already felt she was going to die in this desert. Dying in the *Ray* was an outcome she'd not imagined. She wished, she hoped Tom wouldn't perish with her. But she was also glad it was him in the pilot's seat. The Link Trainer hadn't prepared her for this. But she still felt the shift, the change in the pressure as the *Ray* kept accelerating.

More so than ever, she felt a sense of ownership.

"I think it's the autopilot." She had to raise her voice for him to hear her. If he said anything in response, she couldn't hear now that she off the radio. She wriggled deeper. She knew this space better than she knew her bedroom. She tucked the flashlight in where it could shine on the right spot and went to work, resting the tools she wasn't using on her chest—and hoping the plane didn't turn and slide them off.

Though she was pretty sure Tom wouldn't try a turn until their airspeed was under control.

She got the cover off and then disconnected the autopilot, rather than try to figure out what they'd done to it.

"I've got control again!"

Tom's words sounded distant, so she tapped his knee to let him know she'd heard him. She grabbed her light and tools and started to slide back out. She could already feel the *Ray* responding. They were slowing and leveling off.

She struggled up and grinned at him. He grinned back, then jerked a thumb which she was sure meant that he wanted her strapped back in her seat.

She started back but they hit an air pocket and the plane dropped suddenly. She managed to grab Tom's seat, barely missing a whack to the head on the roof. It dropped her back down and she had to scramble to get her headgear back, since it had also been thrown. She didn't try to find her gloves. She yanked the headgear on without trying to secure it and scrambled into her seat, barely getting one strap across before they hit more rough air. She got the other strap across, hooked up to oxygen and radio, then worked on securing her headgear.

At least now they knew why she was glad she had head protection. She took a relieved breath, then checked their instruments.

"Our fuel," she said, her shock coming through as she was afraid.

"We burned a lot during that climb," Tom agreed. "Going to start our turn. At least it's a big lake bed. We'll land wherever we can."

As long as there was no more sabotage.

* * *

GRANGER HEARD the tower request an update and considered what to tell them. He didn't want Phillips setting off a bomb they hadn't found, but he also didn't want him setting off the one in the jeep.

"I have control and we're returning to base," he said finally, hoping that would be enough. Would this mess with the next test? The *Ray* had taxied and it had flown. With any luck, Phillips would be really frustrated right now.

The *Ray* started the turn but it was less than satisfying.

"You feel this?" he asked Alice. "how the turn is sluggish?"

There was a pause. "Yes. Is that normal?"

It could be typical for the design. "You designed it to fly faster and higher," he reminded her.

"I wish we could try my engine."

"Yeah, except we're probably already in trouble. Let's get on the ground without any more problems."

As he brought the plane around, he tried to figure out what made it feel harder. The wings maybe.

The tower gave them a vector, but he didn't have enough fuel. They were going down on the lake bed. It felt a bit historic. He sure wasn't the first to do it. Probably not even the first to land there with just enough fuel to make it to terra firma.

He got her straight just in time and started their descent. It felt like the ground rushed toward them, probably because he knew they were almost out of fuel. Of course, that was also good. Harder to start a fire without fuel.

"Gonna be a bumpy landing," he told Alice, and he was right. The bumps helped slow them down. He wasn't sure what braking would be like until he tried it. The wheel brakes worked, just not very effectively. But eventually they slowed and finally stopped.

He told the tower they were down and then unplugged from his radio and air supply. There was nothing to do now but wait for their ride. He started to work on his headgear and felt Alice helping him. She should stay strapped in, but it was a relief when his head was clear. He unstrapped and helped her with her headgear and in the dim light found himself staring at her with almost desperate relief.

"Alice." They were alive and the *Ray* had flown. A pity that the seats and head clearance didn't lend themselves to the passionate embrace it felt like the moment deserved. That's how it worked in the movies, anyway.

"Tom." A smile trembled on her lips.

He had to fight back the urge to tell her his real name. And would he also tell her why he was here and where he hailed from? That would go over well. She'd go from trusting him to having him locked up. Somehow his hand held one of hers. Granger couldn't have said Alice clung to him, but it did seem as if she held on pretty hard.

Funny how the silence made it hard to talk. But thinking wasn't working that well for him either. His lips twisted. Mel had told him to watch out for the challenge he didn't see coming because it was the one he couldn't plan for.

He did like to plan, to act and not react, but he'd been in combat and knew that most of combat flying was reacting. He couldn't control what the other guy did, just what he did in response. It made the whole act/react complicated, but if he didn't do it right, he died.

He hadn't died yet.

"How long do you think it will take them to get out here?"

"I'm not sure, probably not that long," Alice said.

He looked around, wondering how to get them both more comfortable. He looked past her toward the small rear section behind the cockpit. It was their seats or the floor.

"There is a seat that pulls down," she said. She turned and found it.

It was just long enough for the two of them. Not that easy on the butt, but Alice was easy on the eyes and that was enough for now.

It's the challenge you don't see coming that's the hardest to plan for.

That was an understatement of massive proportions.

"I wanted to start the main engine," she said, almost conversationally. "If I'd been alone, I might have tried it."

Granger opened his mouth, considered what words to say and then closed it again. Nothing seemed quite right. Finally, he said, "Why?"

"I wonder if we'll get another test. I know I can fix the autopilot, but it will affect our Cooper-Harper scale."

He nodded, thought some more and asked, "I wonder what would have happened?"

She gave a half laugh. "I'm not sure, and that's the problem, isn't it? The *Ray* flies, but so do a lot of other planes. Does it fly better? Not noticeably."

"The main engine is the main event," he said, not as a question. She nodded. "What do you hope it will do?"

"Propel the plane higher, further, faster. Nothing too startling," she added with a chuckle. She sobered. "Except I think, I hope, it will be safer."

"If you tested it here on the ground, what would it do? Would that be safer?"

"We...I did think about it, but I don't think the wheel brakes would be strong enough to hold it in place. I anticipate considerable thrust."

"The lake bed's pretty big," he said. He should know. And that's why the base was here. Lots of room for mistakes.

She leaned back, considering this.

Granger let her think while he did some thinking, too, mostly about logistics. "Would you have to remove the engine from the *Ray* to test it?"

She hesitated. "I have a small prototype." Her face lost even more expression. "I believe one of the men called it a toy."

"As long as it is a toy with teeth..." Granger trailed off with a grin. "Less fanfare, too." He glanced at her and stopped. "You have tried it."

She nodded.

He straightened. "What happened?"

She hesitated. "I'm not sure how to describe it."

"I'd like to see it." Would she agree?

She considered him for what felt like a long time. Then she angled her head to the side.

"They are coming."

Only then did he notice sound of approaching engines. No siren. That was good.

Help was on the way. He'd never wanted it less.

Her smile was crooked, wry. "Thank you for my first flight."

* * *

"HE'S NOT DEAD." Mel sounded relieved, but she didn't look relieved. She looked exhausted.

Jack pulled her close, feeling once again that he should never have opened Pandora's box of time travel. But if he hadn't? He thought of all the things that had gone right, one of them being the right to hold this woman, and he didn't know what he could have, or would have changed.

It is what it is, Mel's grandfather, and his friend, would have said, if he'd been here with them instead of vacationing with Mel's grandmother in Florida. Jack had a sudden desire to be with them. At least, on a vacation in a sunny spot. All alone with Mel. Doing normal couple things.

She flicked a demure glance at him through her lashes, as if she'd picked up on his thoughts, but a sudden flashing alert on the computer screen had them both spinning around.

"What's happened?" Jack stared at the warning symbol.

"Someone's trying to hack into our system," Mel said tersely. She ran to the terminal and called their geeks. There was a confused exchange that was mostly, "Don't bother us now…"

Mel sat back and let the experts do their thing, but she didn't seem able to look away from the battle playing out on her computer screen.

"Why now?" Jack asked, more to himself than to her. He crossed to her, waiting while she shored up their defenses. "What happened just before the attack?"

Mel seemed relieved to do something else. She escaped the

warning, tapped some keys and scrolled through some data. "I think it was caused by our search for the mystery guy." She searched some more. "It was closing in on a location, and then"—she looked up—"Whoever it is, they started fighting back."

"Can you narrow down the area at least," Jack asked, leaning closer, as if the symbols would tell him something.

Mel did some more magic and a map formed. Her gaze narrowed, she studied the map, moving in and out until...

"Look at that," she said, indicating a large structure near the center of the search area. She shook her head. "There's something about that area..." She was silent for a few moments. "No, it's not coming up."

"Can we get an address without attracting attention?"

"We know the general area. It might be safer to send a team in to check it out," Mel said, "rather than any internet search. We've got one less than a day away that we could deploy." She turned in the chair so she could look up at him. "Who...do you think they are?"

Jack frowned, his gaze going from her face to the screen. He didn't want to say the words. What were the odds...

Mel slid her hand into his. "It couldn't be. It couldn't." Her grip tightened. "Could it?"

He half shrugged. He didn't know. If this were their time tampering foes, it was both a huge coincidence and hugely ironic. A pity he wasn't sure how to find out.

CHAPTER 7

"**I** managed to score a jeep," Tom said. His shoulders were broad enough to block the doorway and his grin—it felt like it lit a horizon inside her head. "I thought we could go to the officer's club for dinner."

Alice's father had shut himself in the room that served as a home office for him. He hadn't said anything about her unexpected flight during the taxi test, and he probably wouldn't in front of Tom, but disapproval came off him in waves. Alice didn't want to think it, but she did wonder if it was because she'd risked her life—or their secret? Since she wasn't sure, she angled her chin in mute defiance and she didn't look at the closed door.

"I'd like that." She'd been to the club a couple of times—as a third wheel. It would be a nice change to go there with what would appear to be an actual date. She'd told herself she didn't care what other people thought about her dating prospects, and there was some truth in that assertion. But it was hard to be alone, exposed in public. Most men ignored her, but some were rude or pushy. They acted as if she should be grateful that any man, even a drunk one, noticed her existence. "It won't take me a minute to change," she added, making a dismissive gesture toward her dress-code suit.

"I'm not going anywhere," Tom said, then appeared almost startled at the words.

This time her smile felt a bit stiff, but she said, "We're all going somewhere." She turned away before she had to see his reaction to her words. She could pretend she didn't know the truth. She'd had lots of practice.

In her bedroom, she had more advice for herself. *Enjoy the right now. It could all change tomorrow.* That was one thing she'd learned around test pilots and experimental planes. Change happened. She stared at herself in the mirror and realized some change had already happened. There was color in cheeks that had been pale, even through the heat and sun of summer. And her eyes—she almost couldn't meet her own gaze. It felt like a stranger's with the shy hope and…happiness in there.

"The *Ray* flew today," she told the image, but she and her image knew it wasn't just that.

She turned away, snagging her purse and sweater and heading back into the hall. Tom was where she'd left him. He straightened as soon as he saw her, his approving gaze running over her then tracking back up to meet hers.

"You look…" his grin was crooked, almost wry, before he finished "…amazing."

She didn't, but it was nice that he thought so. He offered his arm. She took it, feeling that strange sense of right sweep over her again. Outside she was glad for the wide skirt as she clambered into the Jeep, a laugh escaping as Tom gave her a boost into the seat. While he went around to the driver's seat, she slipped on the sweater. It was cooling fast as the sun sent the last strands of light across the desert. For the first time, it didn't seem alien and bleak with tips of the scrub lit up. But it wasn't the desert fueling the feeling. She glanced at Tom as he fired the jeep's motor. It was too loud for talking, but that was fine. With his attention on the road, she could watch him.

He'd donned his uniform, since it was the officer's club. It fitted him well enough she could almost see the ripple of muscles as he shifted gears. Her hands curled into fists. It was fine to seize the moment. It was not fine to lose control.

Tom pulled the jeep into a parking spot and came around to lift her down. It was a bit like flying, but the landing happened faster. His hands lingered at her waist and she sensed it when his gaze settled on her mouth. Her lips might have started to part, but the roar of another vehicle yanked his attention away. He gave her a rueful look and stepped back, offering his arm once more. The door to the club opened, spilling light and sound into the semi-murk of the parking lot. Tom led her forward, pausing to make sure she made it safely over a rough spot.

Inside, she had a moment of almost panic as eyes turned their way. In the women's eyes, she saw curiosity and some surprise, but the men glanced at them, then looked away.

To them, they were just a guy and a girl. It helped her to get over that threshold and to a table. If the conversation had faltered, which it probably hadn't, it had resumed with full force. There was music, too, which made conversation more challenging than the jeep. In a strange way, it was a relief. Trying to talk in such a public place…it felt like she'd expose the new Alice. Hiding, she realized wryly, was a habit that was hard to break.

They placed their order and then Tom raised his voice enough to ask, "Dance?"

Her first impulse was to refuse. But the song was slow and… she wanted to dance with him even if she stepped on his toes. She nodded and took the hand he held out to rise from her chair. The music was dreamy and she fought the urge to relax against him. Not only would it be too revealing, it wasn't allowed in a place like this. Leaning happened in private. As did kissing…

His hand rested at her waist, the other clasping the hand that

wasn't on his shoulder. He didn't try anything fancy, thank goodness. They just shifted from one side to the other. She glanced up,
but he wasn't looking down. She had a feeling he wasn't seeing
the room either, that he saw something different. Or far away. As
she stared at him, it felt as if everything around them wavered, a
bit like being under water. She blinked and her vision cleared.

She really needed to get some sleep tonight. She'd almost
thought she saw something...different in this room. Besides, if
they were up early again to fly the model of the *Ray* she'd built—
was she going to do it? Was she going to fly it for Tom? She
almost snorted. Of course she was...

Tom stiffened and stopped moving. Alice turned and found
Phillips standing there, watching them with his intent, dangerous
gaze. The music wound down and the couples around them
moved back toward their tables. Luckily, they were at the edge of
the dance floor, because Alice wasn't sure either of them could
have moved.

"I'm sorry I missed your *taxi test*," he finally said, breaking the
tense silence, his tone suspicious.

Did he think they'd deliberately lifted off? Or was he trying to
divert suspicion from the sabotage? As far as she knew, nothing
had exploded during their unexpected flight, but it wouldn't
have, would it? They hadn't needed to eject.

"What happened?" Tom asked.

"Car trouble." Phillips added, his light tone at odds with the
darkness in his gaze. "You were lucky."

"It's a good plane," Alice spoke this time. She felt the need to
assert...something.

"Someone said you rode along," Phillips said, making Alice
regret calling his attention to herself.

"Yes," she said, the stark answer more challenging than she felt
was safe. "It was just supposed to be a taxi test."

"What happened?" Phillips asked.

"The autopilot malfunctioned for a few minutes." She tried

not to let accusation enter her voice or her gaze. Had he tried to kill Tom? If their emergency had turned into a bail-out situation, would he have pressed the button to discharge the explosive? If he had, there would have been an intense investigation and not in the direction Phillips had planned on. So they both got lucky.

"You've got a test flight on the schedule this Saturday," Phillips said. "Is that wise?"

Alice felt Tom's small jerk of surprise and hoped it covered hers. Had her father done this?

"The *Ray* should be flight-ready by Saturday," Alice said. She glanced at Tom, but his face was a benign mask, the only sign of tension in the set of his mobile lips. The urge to touch her lips, to trace the curve he'd kissed, almost overcame her. Phillips gaze shifted toward her again. It seemed that he considered what to say next, then gave a short, sharp shake of his head and turned left.

If he'd had a tail, he would have swished it.

Tom's grip on her arm tightened slightly, then he said, "Our dinner is arriving."

Alice waited until they were alone again to say, "My father must have added us to the schedule."

Tom nodded. "Can it be ready in time?"

Alice half shrugged.

Tom's smile was tense. "Why Saturday?"

"That was probably the first opening," Alice said. Did it matter? When she looked in his eyes, she saw it did. "You're not superstitious, are you?"

He reached across the table and covered her hand with his. "Maybe I am. We could go to Palm Springs, go...away."

She wanted to say yes so much, the word hurt her throat as it tried to push out. So why did she fight it? So they waited until Monday? Or the next Saturday? Why did her head shake a slow negative without her permission? Inside her, she wanted the day with Tom more than the test flight. Inside, she wanted to run

PAULINE BAIRD JONES

away from the *Ray*, from her father, from this place and—what? Tom offered a day away, not a life away. All the decisions she'd made, both big and small, had brought her to this moment, to this place. And they'd made her who she was. She didn't know how to be anyone else.

Close to Tom, maybe she could be a little bit different, but not enough to miss the test. That didn't mean she wasn't worried about Tom.

"Maybe we should let Phillips' pilot fly?" Let him take the risk this time. If Tom felt the need to be away, she trusted that.

"Aren't you worried he'll do something to mess up the test?" Tom asked, a furrow appearing between his brows.

She was more worried about Tom, she realized. But there was also a strange sense of inevitability about Phillips and the *Ray*. It was Tom who didn't fit, even though he felt so right to her personally. She looked away and felt that odd wavering of the horizon once more. Was it inside or outside? She took a deep breath and looked back, meeting his gaze with an assumed calm.

"I'd rather he mess up the test than…" her lashes slid down. "He planted a bomb on the *Ray*. Let him blow up his own pilot."

"You'll lose the *Ray*," he pointed out.

"We'll lose time…" Funny how the word seemed to echo through her mind. *Time.* How much time did they have here, or ever? How much time did she have with Tom? She should leave with him Saturday, but her father… "I'm not sure how much more my father…" She let the words trail off, not sure what she'd meant to say.

The excitement of the small test had animated her father, but only briefly. He'd looked more drawn and tired when she'd arrived back at the hangar. It was as if the life draining out of him had made him more brittle and breakable. Finally, she met Tom's gaze again.

"He needs this, I think."

Tom nodded as if he understood. "It is what it is."

The words felt more weighted than they should be. As if Tom were implying more than he'd said somehow.

The music started again, playing "Till I Waltz Again With You." The words implied an "until we meet again," but as Tom held out his hand, they felt more like "goodbye."

* * *

GRANGER KEPT the jeep for their early morning trip out into the desert with Alice's model of the *Ray*. Was he surprised she'd mentioned it? Maybe. He'd sensed her withdrawing, pulling back after he'd asked her to see the model fly. At first he thought she'd held back on telling him about the Saturday test date, until he realized she hadn't known, either. Why had they picked Saturday? Of all the days this week, Saturday—the day Alice was supposed to die—was the one they'd landed on? Plus, it was unusual to have a test flight on a Saturday. It didn't feel like Phillips had known either, so who was behind the move?

If he didn't know better, he'd think he'd tried to fight time and time had kicked back. *It is what it is.* He'd heard Mel say those words, not long ago and six decades in the future, and it had sounded sensible. Except he refused to have *what it is* be Alice's death. It was just his feeling that told him this wasn't right. It had to be the result of the time tampering. If a small voice in his head said he might be deluding himself, he ignored it.

He shoved a hand through his hair, took a deep breath and opened his bedroom door. The hallway was silent, still mostly dark this early in the morning. He heard movement, from the kitchen, he thought, and strode forward toward where a band of light showed under the door. He eased the swing door open and saw her standing at the sink filling the coffee pot. She was dressed in pants that hit about mid-calf. Her shirt was tucked into the waistband and she'd pulled her hair back into a ponytail, then tied a scarf around her head. The ends of the scarf hung down below her ponytail. She had what looked like tennis shoes on her feet. She looked a bit teenybopper, he decided, and dangerously cute.

The running water kept her from hearing him, so he stayed by the door until she turned and saw him. She didn't start, though her eyes widened briefly, then her lips moved in a slight smile and he saw awareness of the kiss they'd shared on the front step last night, and something else. Shyness perhaps? Yeah, that was it. He didn't see it as much in his time, or maybe he wasn't looking for it. He'd been so focused on getting here, he hadn't spent much time looking into women's' eyes.

"Are you sure you're up for this?" he asked. She, unlike him, hadn't signed on for any of this. He'd tossed and turned for what was left of the night. He'd thought and thought, but the only way he could see to protect her was for the *Ray* to fly, to be seen in history. He believed—he hoped—that would make it harder to kill her. He had no proof, but his gut told him that she'd been eliminated from the equation. It was small comfort to know they'd grabbed the wrong Merriweather. And the tragedy of it all? In the future, there would have been a place for Alice.

It was the other way to keep her alive, but he couldn't bring himself to betray her to Phillips, not even to save her life, especially not when neither of them trusted the guy. What he wanted to do was tell her the truth and let her choose. She should have the power to, finally, choose her own future—even if she chose to stay here and die.

She nodded, then looked at the table. For the first time, he noticed a box sitting on one of the kitchen chairs. He wasn't sure why, but he'd expected something bigger. Then he saw the plane sitting on the floor by the table. Of course, radio controllers from this time were bulky affairs. He wanted to study the plane, but now was not the time.

"Would you like some breakfast?"

He should, but he didn't want her fixing it. "Let's get some after." There had to be some kind of mess where service people on base could eat.

Alice couldn't quite let them go without food. She made toast for each of them. As he crunched into the bread, he wondered if he tasted anything like it in the future. It was amazing.

He carried the box with the controller outside, while Alice carried her plane. On the step there was a gas can and what he assumed were the pieces for some kind of portable transmitter. They loaded it all into the jeep and climbed in, too. He fired the motor, then looked to her for direction.

"Off the base," she said, her voice raised to be heard over the noise of the jeep and indicated the direction.

He steered toward one of the base's gates, and then the base was lost in their dust trail. They passed what appeared to be some burnt-out buildings. She touched his arm. He braked and gave Alice a questioning look.

"The Happy Bottom Riding Club," she said. "Haven't you heard of it?"

Alice's look told him he should know it, but he hadn't been here before, he reminded himself. He shook his head.

"Pancho Barnes," she continued. "She was a pilot, stunt pilot…" She hesitated, her gaze on the burnt-out buildings. "She was brave and bold. She did what she wanted to do."

She did it in a time when that wasn't popular to do, Granger realized. Should he have heard of Barnes? Since he wasn't sure, he nodded sympathetically.

"This should be far enough," Alice said, when they were a few yards past the remains of the club. "We won't be out of radar range, but we should be clear for long enough."

How had she handled radar inquiries, he wondered, as he clambered out.

"I tell them my father is flying his model plane," Alice said, as if he'd asked. "And I change which direction I go." She glanced around. "This is my first time on this road. Usually I get further from the base."

Was that the real reason she'd avoided this road? Her glance at the burned-out club had been sad.

She jumped down. He strode forward and lifted out the box containing the controller. Alice took out her model plane, then began setting up the portable transmitter.

It was on the crisp side, but the sun was rising fast, its rays bringing down the chill factor. Alice didn't seem to notice the cold, though she wore only a sweater. Her cheeks were flushed pink, though that could be from the excitement that shone from her eyes as she fitted the transmitter into her controller setup.

Now that he could, he studied the plane. It was smaller than he expected, the wingspan barely two feet across. Based on the gas can she'd brought, it had a gas engine. What he assumed was the experimental engine was perched on top of the structure just behind the cockpit and centered between the wings. He couldn't stop the doubtful look.

"It has to be to scale for it to be useful, and if it were larger, I wouldn't be able to manage it on my own," she said. "In addition, the smaller size is less vulnerable to the stress from the engine activation."

The road around the former riding club had been packed fairly well down and this would, he assumed, be their runway. She positioned the plane, checked her controller, and then went back to the plane and started the gas engine. He snagged binoculars from the jeep and almost forgot to get his glasses and camera ready in time. Though he held up binoculars, his own camera—on video this time—gave him a clearer view.

It buzzed loudly as it rolled along the ground, bounced on a bump, and then went airborne.

"The bumps help," she admitted wryly. She checked her control of the plane, taking it in a figure eight, then brought it back so that it was coming in behind them. "I'll fly it directly away to the maximum range of our radio, then bring it back toward us. Right after the turn, I'll activate the experimental engine with this," she indicated a button on her bulky controller.

Granger followed the progress of the small plane as it drew away from them, its bee-like buzz fading, too. He realized that she was counting under her breath and found himself counting along.

"Making turn now."

"Confirm turn," Granger told her. He watched the plane make the turn.

"Pulsing the engine."

She had to do it that way, she'd explained, because the radio signal might not find the plane in time to stop it. Would it do what Granger expected it to do? The air around the small plane appeared to pulse or wrinkle. He wasn't sure which. And then the plane was gone. There followed a small boom, so small he wasn't sure he heard it.

He searched the sky—the sound of the plane's fierce buzz helped him find it again, almost right over his head. It had taken a couple of seconds at most. He followed it while she circled it around and brought it down in a competent—not pretty—landing. It was sputtering as she hurried forward and turned off the small gas engine. Granger stared down at the plane, somehow managing to keep recording long enough to get video of her miniature experimental engine coated with a film of ice. He shut off recording and looked up at Alice.

He searched for words, finally managing one. "Damn," he said.

As if in answer, the horizon shuddered around him, like—but not like—an explosion. An explosion that shook the horizon, but not him. For several seconds, he thought he saw buildings, instead of the burned-out foundations of the riding club.

Alice turned around, her eyes wide and shocked. Had she...

"That's odd." She looked around, pausing for a long time on the burned-out foundation.

The sky was clear and calm, no mushroom clouds or other signs of explosions in any direction.

"Does that always happen?" he asked.

It almost seemed as if she didn't want to look at him now. "The boom?" She nodded, but she looked pale. Once more her gaze strayed toward the remains of the club.

She'd seen it, too.

He spoke with a calm he didn't feel. "You saw it, too, didn't you?"

Her head swiveled around, her gaze meeting his. She opened her mouth, to protest, he guessed, but she didn't.

"What...was it?" She licked her lips, making his thoughts flicker like the horizon had.

He hesitated, then went for it. "If I told you what I thought it was...you wouldn't believe me."

* * *

SINCE THEY'D TAKEN down the transmitter and stowed her model, they'd been sitting in the unmoving jeep for what felt like forever. When Tom had reached out to start it, Alice had put her hand over his and shook her head. To his credit, he'd sat there waiting. Twice, Alice half turned toward Tom to ask, to tell...to something. She didn't know what she'd intended. Because each time she'd stopped herself.

If I told you what I thought it was, you wouldn't believe me.

It was about more than the strange event. Whatever it was, it was at the heart of what made Tom different. It was about why he was here, and possibly about how he knew about the *Ray*. He'd looked shocked, but not surprised, by what the model engine did. Did she want to know? Would she believe him? Because if she didn't, there was no point in asking.

The problem was, she did—or she wanted—to believe him. She wasn't sure which. No, she knew, she conceded. She'd believed him from the first moment they met when he'd inserted himself into the confrontation with Phillips back in Palm Springs. But this, this was bigger than a ride to the base. It was bigger than flying the *Ray*. That thing, whatever it was, she'd seen —she rubbed her eyes—she thought she'd seen the riding club before it had burned down. Which was interesting, because she'd never even seen a photo of it, but it was there where it had been, where the burned-out foundation was now. Even stranger? The brief...vision...had been peopled. Not long enough for her to recognize anyone, but there had been people going in and coming out...

She considered this event, trying to match it with the other times she'd flown the model. She had seen the horizon waver, but she'd thought it was the heat—even when it wasn't that hot, she realized, somewhat wryly. But how could she see a difference between desert before the waver and desert after?

She'd also thought she was hungry, or thirsty and that it was time to go home. Not—her thoughts refused to go all the way there.

Had her engine caused whatever it was? But if it had, why had Tom...

She realized her hands had been tightly fisted for long enough they hurt. Trying not to wince, she flexed her fingers and wet dry lips.

"Did..." It took another try before she managed the question. "Did I do that? Did my engine do that?"

She knew he looked at her, but she stared straight ahead.

"I don't know, Alice. It might have but..." He stopped.

If I told you what I thought it was...

She processed his words, this time hearing the first part. *He didn't know. He thought he knew.* For some reason, this made it easier to ask. "What do you think it was?"

And now she looked at him.

His brow was furrowed, his gaze...kind.

"Are you sure?"

She nodded, even though she wasn't.

"I think...it was a time event."

"A...time event?" She blinked, holding back an instinctive protest. What did that even mean—time? A time event. No, she still wasn't sure what that meant.

He must have known, because he spoke again. "There's this theory...that time fights back...when someone tries to change it."

She blinked several times. It didn't help. "But..." She didn't know what to say next. Someone? Who? "Me? I'm not trying to change time."

Her protest lacked force because she kept seeing the riding club. The past? It had to be...the past. It could be the future, she supposed, though something told her it wasn't. The clothes of the people, perhaps? There was no question it had been different from this...present. She glanced around. Whatever had happened, they were in the present now. That was a fact. A fact to place against the...fantasy.

Tom shook his head. "I think...someone...might have interfered in your...timeline."

She thought he wanted to say more, but stopped himself, as if he knew she needed time to process each statement. She almost laughed. She needed time to understand a time event?

He was right. This was hard to believe and she'd be laughing and having him arrested or something if not for the...event. She'd seen it. She'd felt it. It might defy logic, but science could be like that until one understood it. Was it possible to understand this event? The question she didn't want to ask—or have answered—hung in the air, quivering like the air had around her during the event. She had to answer the belief question first, because if she didn't, if she couldn't, then why ask? In her mind, she replayed their time together. She didn't linger on the kisses, but she didn't avoid them either. Even when she stripped out the emotion, or tried to, she found no...malice in their interactions. Logic might struggle, but...instinct...believed him.

It was instinct that she'd used in her interactions with Phillips.

She either trusted her instincts or...she was lost.

She couldn't trust Phillips.

She couldn't *not* trust Tom.

"Tom..." she began.

"Ty." He interrupted her. "Call me Ty. When we're alone."

She knew, though she didn't know how, that giving her his name was dangerous somehow.

"Ty." This time she felt the rightness of the name. She half smiled, felt the wry that made it feel crooked. "I...believe you."

His eyes widened. "But, I haven't told you yet."

"I believe you," she repeated. She touched her heart. "I believe you here." She lowered her hand to her stomach. "And here." She paused and added, "I saw...something during the event. I think I saw...the past."

"The riding club." He nodded. "I saw it, too."

He said it matter of factly, as if it happened to him all the time. Maybe it did.

"Who are you?" The question was curious, not accusatory.

He didn't speak right away, but she didn't sense worry or fear. It felt more like he was trying to find the right words.

"I am from the future," he finally said, sounding almost resigned.

She had to ride out the wave of protest, perhaps of shock. She'd told him she believed him. She had to find that place again before she could speak.

"The...future." She had questions. Of course she did, but which mattered the most? Suddenly she felt it, felt time, felt an urgency that needed her to focus on what mattered the most. And that wasn't the how, but the... "Why?"

He might have been surprised by that question. His lips

twisted in something like a smile. "You always surprise me, right from the first time…"

He shook his head and his hand moved, as if he wanted to touch her. He didn't and she respected that, though she also regretted it. She felt cold and hot, an inner storm that needed to break—or spawn a tornado.

"I believe someone has been interfering in your timeline. And your father's. At least, I think your father was the target and you were caught in the crossfire of that."

Crossfire. That sounded bad. His gaze met hers with deep reluctance.

"I…died here, didn't I?" She'd sensed it, known it on some deep level.

He nodded.

She fought through it. She was a scientist, even if she was one in shock.

"Saturday." She looked straight ahead. "That's why…"

"Yes."

Four days to live. Maybe she should go to Palm Springs with him. But… "If it's meant, nothing can change that."

"But what if it isn't meant?" Tom, no, Ty, persisted.

"Who?" But she knew. "Phillips."

"I think he is the one tampering with time," Ty agreed. "Though I don't have any proof of that, just my instincts."

Tampering with time. And she'd died. *She would die.* Tampering didn't seem an emphatic enough word for that.

"You were…collateral damage," Ty continued, "which is ironic because you are probably the one they wanted."

"The *Ray?*"

"Or the engine," Ty said.

"So my father…didn't die."

"He disappeared." Ty's voice was gentle.

It felt odd to feel relieved to know that their deception had an end, one way or another, at least for her. She looked at him, not sure what to ask.

"Time is complicated," he said. "What we're doing right now is rippling into the future. I think that's why we felt...that. I didn't know you could feel it. I thought I was the only one who would." He frowned.

"Because you're from the future?" He nodded. In a weird way, interest stirred, the science kind. She was a scientist after all. He'd traveled through time. She might be boggled all of the sudden. Or getting over the shock? Probably both. *Time travel.* She'd read *The Time Machine.* She'd listened to both radio broadcasts of the story. She'd liked the questions and the possibilities the story stirred in her mind. And perhaps she'd believe it might be possible in the future. "Do you have...a machine?"

He looked rueful. "Not with me."

"It's probably better not to," she said, part of her stunned by how calm she sounded and part of her kind of proud of that. "There are so many things I'd like to know but"—she shifted to look at him better—"there isn't time, is there?"

"Four days," he admitted.

"But if you're from the future, then you know..." She stopped when he shook his head.

"I told you, I thought it was your father. I thought I knew what to do, but...I met you." His rueful look deepened. "And I didn't have that much foreknowledge, more a sense that something special had been stopped, a sense the someone was tampering with time. And," he added with some reluctance, "we had what we believe is evidence of that tampering."

We. Of course there was a "we." HG Wells might have traveled alone, but if he didn't have a machine...

She tried to focus. "What do you know?" Other than that she died and her father disappeared, she mentally amended.

"Just tantalizing scraps of data and..." he looked away now.

"There was another anomalous event that may have happened on Saturday."

Did he look embarrassed?

"I don't—I didn't—believe it, you see, but it was something curious," he added.

Her brows rose. Why was he so reluctant to tell her? He'd told her she died. What could be worse than that?

"There's a story that the president met with…aliens," he said.

"First contact? But that's…" She frowned. "You don't believe it? Why not? Don't you have trade with aliens in the future?"

"I keep forgetting how different things are here in this time," he admitted. "No, we don't have contact with aliens or trade with them."

"Well, that's…disappointing," she said. His downcast expression had her adding, "Not that I blame you." His lips twitched and she burst out laughing. She was laughing. It was amazing. Startling. She was going to die and she was laughing. "I feel a bit insane," she admitted.

"Time travel does that to you," Ty admitted, his wry grin back. "Gives you a headache, too."

Time travel. The words echoed inside her head and part of her felt the shock of it once more. *I believe.* It was all she had to hold on to right now. "So, what's the next step?" she asked.

"I was afraid you were going to ask that," Ty admitted. He rubbed his face in frustration, then looked at her and grinned. "Let's go get something to eat."

The seriousness of her face broke up as she matched his smile and maybe raised the heat some.

"Yes, please," she said.

* * *

MEL AND JACK had decided not to leave the bunker for the next few days. It was actually an old missile site that they'd reinforced and then stocked with enough supplies for a month or more. Mel still couldn't decide if it was creepy or cool. This morning it was comforting, she decided, though they still weren't sure it was working the way they'd hoped, even with the modifications they'd made on some of the interior walls.

She'd gone to sleep feeling like they'd poked a snake. If they found the locus of the time tamperers, what would they do in response? Obviously, they'd tried to track them, but with what intention?

Mel rolled over on her cot and looked around, trying to find Jack with a gaze that was still a bit bleary from a restless night's sleep. He stood in front of their tracking wall, his face showing signs his night hadn't been any better than hers. She pushed back the blanket and rolled out, various parts of her body protesting where and how she'd slept. She managed to get on her feet before Jack saw her grimacing and produced a smile, or perhaps half of one.

"How are we doing?"

"Granger's not dead," he said.

Relief flooded through her, though none of them were out of woods yet—or out of the silo. She joined Jack, sliding her arm around his waist as he pulled her close. She leaned into the squeeze, but her eyes were on the board looking for the proof that Granger was still alive. The newspaper clipping about the accident was gone.

"It feels like we've lost some of the information we had on the *Manta Ray*," Mel said, with a frown.

"We have less information," Jack agreed, "and some of the pictures of Merriweather's daughter are gone, too."

"Alice?" Mel's frown deepened to a scowl. "Does she still...die on Saturday?"

"Yeah." Jack rubbed his face with his free hand. "Our team should be closing on that rogue site in an hour or so."

What would happen, Mel wondered. "Can they find out who we are?" It hurt to put words to her fear, but she needed to face it.

"I don't know," Jack admitted. "We've covered our tracks pretty good, but I never figured on parallel time travelers."

The odds against that should have been huge. But it wasn't unknown for ideas to develop separately but in parallel, or almost parallel. It would have been nice if they could have worked together, but how could they trust their intentions when they'd done something specifically to aid the Germans during World War II?

"It's Tuesday morning back then," Mel said. "What do you suppose Granger is doing?"

As if the question did it, the bunker shook hard. It felt like it had been hit with something big. Like a missile or something. Mel would have fallen if Jack hadn't been holding on to her. Nothing registered on seismic but their time sensor was going nuts.

"Was that…an attack?" Mel whispered, her face pressed against Jack's chest.

"I think it was."

They felt another hit, even harder than the first. The structure held, but Mel thought she saw through Jack for several long seconds.

"They are trying to erase us," Mel said, holding on tighter. Would it be enough to hold on if someone was coming at them through time?

CHAPTER 8

*S*o, what's the next step?

Alice had asked him the question, but Granger didn't have an answer. Time travel was not turning out the way he'd expected. He thought he'd come in, follow the events, stop the bad guy or guys, and get yanked home by his ass. Instead...

He looked at Alice, sitting across from him in the mess hall. His heart clenched. He hadn't counted on Alice. He couldn't quite believe he hadn't realized how much she mattered. He hadn't even looked that closely at her photograph. Okay, it was black and white, but still...how had that happened? He was trained to notice and he had almost missed the real story. There she sat, worry clouding her face, but what a face. She wasn't one of those model types, but there was strength and character and a clean beauty that clenched his heart in his chest. He'd gone from "need to save the girl" to "need to save *her.*"

On the face of it, shouldn't be that hard. She died in the hangar when the *Ray* was destroyed, but...what had happened in there that night? He might suspect Phillips, but that was his gut talking, not proof. And all he knew for sure was, there'd been an explosion. And time was complicated, Mel had pointed out multiple times during his training. If he was wrong…was time already pushing back? Were the disturbances about the tampering or because of something he'd changed? He knew so little about what happened before, or why it was covered up so thoroughly. And why the aliens?

How easy would it have been to fool someone in this time into thinking you were an alien? Alice's reaction had surprised him, but should it have? The decade was known for people being crazy for space and rockets. He didn't remember the aliens in the movies being that benign, but Alice was a scientist. He needed to remember that shaped her reactions to everything.

Her lashes lifted and her gaze met his.

Well, almost everything, he decided, as her slight smile made his heart stutter. Nothing had prepared either of them for this, he felt sure. Despite this exchange, Granger knew her question was still there, between them. He needed more information, but Alice couldn't tell him about the future—wait, she could tell him what was *planned* for this week.

"Tell me what you were supposed to be doing this morning," he suggested.

She lowered her sandwich and considered the question, though it didn't take long.

"What we do every day," she said, grimacing.

Had she felt caught? How could she not?

"Tell me," he said again.

"Well, the driver picks us up and takes us to the hangar to work on the *Ray*."

"What does that entail? It looked pretty done to me," Granger said.

She nodded. "It is. We were…stuck…so my father mostly paces around making notes in his book and I…" She stopped. "Sometimes I'd get in the Link Trainer. It helped me think. Usually I…pretend to be transcribing my Father's notes."

"But instead…" he prompted.

"I...think." She leaned back, her hands tapping on the tabletop. "Sometimes I think about the engine, other times I think about other ideas I'd like to work on."

Her eyes changed and he had the sense that she had a sort of mental chalk board she studied. Because it wasn't safe for her to write much down. He reached out and brushed the tips of his fingers against hers in tacit support.

Her eyes changed again and he knew she was back in the moment. Back with him.

"Do you usually go in on Saturday?"

She shook her head. "Only the one time with you." She looked down, then up again. "There is the test flight now, of course."

He nodded grimly. That was scheduled for Saturday morning which was yet another puzzle. He didn't know, of course, but it seemed an odd time for a test flight. But his thoughts circled back to the explosion. What time of day had it happened? There'd been nothing in the stuff he'd seen. His gut tightened. What if they— what if *he'd* changed how the accident played out? It could be event triggered, not date triggered.

"If I hadn't come, if nothing had changed, why would you have gone in on a Saturday?"

She considered this question with a slight frown creasing her forehead. "A problem in the hangar? One of the other hangars had a break-in last month. A couple of airmen got drunk and wanted to fly a plane. It's odd to have a test flight on Saturday." She frowned.

"How could that happen?" he asked. "Does your father have the clout to make that happen?"

She shook her head. "It could be the financier."

Granger felt his gut twitch at this. "Do you know who that is?"

She shook her head again. "It is my father's other secret." She half shrugged. "He's kept better than I have our other one." She was silent for several seconds. "Perhaps he wishes to see the *Ray* fly and Saturday is the only day he can come."

Or someone had pushed up the schedule with the taxi test? Had that test made it into the official record? It frustrated him that he could send messages to the future, or he hoped he was sending them, but he couldn't get feedback on what was working and what wasn't. Speaking of...he needed to get that footage deposited outside the base. Should he tell her about it? What would she think? Oh, I'm time travel guy and I'm sending information about your designs into the future. She'd said she believed him, but how far would that trust extend?

"Are you done?" he asked, pushing his own plate away.

She nodded. When they'd deposited their plates, they went outside and ran into Phillips about to enter. He stopped, for once looking more awkward than dangerous.

"Miss Merriweather." His gaze traveled from Alice to Granger and then back. There was enough lift to his brows to be questioning.

Would Alice say something? Explain? Defensive was never the strongest position.

"Mr. Phillips." She stepped to the side, so that Phillips could enter.

He didn't move. He was in a tough spot. As far as Granger could tell, he had no right to question Alice, particularly about why she was having lunch with him.

"You don't usually eat here," Phillips said.

"No," she agreed.

Granger had to fight back a grin. Stalemate.

"Your father didn't seem to know you weren't...working... today," he finally said.

Alice's brows arched. "Oh?"

The silence was painful for Phillips, and Granger had to fight the impulse to let it play out for longer, but they did have things to do—if only he knew what those things were.

"We should go," he said, slipping his fingers around Alice's elbow. The possessive gesture tightened Phillips' lips, as

Granger knew it would. The guy had had it all his own way for too long. He'd gotten sloppy. *And don't you get sloppy, too,* he reminded himself. *Or cocky.* She trusted him, but should she? Yes, he'd come to stop the time tampering, but part of it was the engine, or rather his hope of what he thought the engine was or could be. He'd wanted to see it and the small demonstration had only increased his interest. If it could be controlled...

His gaze flicked between Alice and Phillips, then she turned and walked beside him toward their borrowed jeep. She trusted him, Granger realized, partly because she didn't trust Phillips. So far Granger hadn't screwed up, but he could. It could kill her or send her careening into a different future, even one controlled by Phillips. He had one foot on the banana peel and one on the ice. And he needed to not ever forget that.

* * *

ALICE FELT Phillips gaze following her as they drove away from the officer's mess hall. Only when they turned a corner out of his sight did Alice find her voice. "Do you think he suspects?"

"That would depend on any personal limitations in his thought processes," Ty said.

Should she keep thinking of him as Tom? She didn't want to make a mistake and put his future at risk.

Was Phillips a time traveler, too? A side-by-side comparison with—Tom—did not provide clarity. She'd felt differences in how Tom interacted with her, but she'd felt more on every level around him. With Phillips, she'd tried to keep her distance as much as possible. He'd never slapped her on the butt. Mostly he'd been a remote presence, casting a shadow over their project. But was he a malign presence trying to...kill her? Or was her death a "regrettable" accident?

If Tom was from the future, if he'd observed this time through the lens of the future, then might Phillips also be here to…adjust events?

Tom halted the jeep in front of the hangar and turned it off.

"Is this your first time?" she asked, her gaze on the hands clasped in her lap.

"As far as I know," he said, after a pause.

It was, she supposed, possible that her death was caused by this clash of agendas. It felt distinctly odd to look at her own demise so dispassionately, but she'd spent so many years looking at everything that way, it was difficult to switch gears. And she probably didn't entirely believe she was going to die on Saturday. Though it was also odd, it was possible to believe Tom, and not believe that.

She slid out just as the door opened. Her father stood in the opening, his careful gaze assessing first her, then Tom. His lips tightened.

"I need to speak with you, Alice." He hesitated, then added, "alone, if you would be so kind, Major."

"Of course, sir," Tom said, his tone respectful, but his gaze wary.

Alice didn't look back at Tom; she suspected her father was looking for that as she followed him inside. He shut the door, appeared to pause, then turned to face her.

"I've…" He had to clear his throat. "I've decided to accept Mr. Phillips research offer. We're…" His gaze slid away from hers now. "We're moving the *Ray* on Sunday. We'll have to move it by truck to the Groom Lake base, since it can't hold enough fuel for a flight of that duration."

Sunday? That was distinctly odd. Was this an attempt to slip the *Ray* off the base? And what about the financier? He had to be aware and agree. Her father wouldn't move without his permission. Was Phillips his man on the scene? But if he was, would he try to sabotage the *Ray*? Trying to sort through it made her head hurt.

"And the test flight on Saturday?" she asked.

Her father hesitated. "Mr. Phillips wants us to cancel it," he admitted.

But he hadn't yet. Did this indicate distrust or hope on her father's part? Or was this a play by the man behind the money?

"I told him we should be able to pack the house and our files here in that time frame."

The "we" was almost amusing, since her father usually left all the packing to her. But it was true it could be done. They tended to travel light. Alice studied him, almost thoughtfully and he shifted uneasily.

"This is the right—"

"I'm not going." She took a steadying breath. "I'm not going to Groom Lake." She'd have to leave the base. It was a terrifying thought. She'd saved some money for herself out of her "secretary's" salary, but...*I'm going to die anyway, so why pretend I'll go?* What happened on Sunday had nothing to do with her.

"Alice, his offer will be beneficial to *both* of us." He paced a few steps away, then turned to face her.

His body language, Alice noticed, was authoritative. Just as it had been when he'd stood at the head of his classes when he'd been teaching. *I am wise. I know the right way.* The problem, of course, was that her father was too weak to bully or intimidate, so he could only sustain the stance for a few minutes.

"I...I believe this is the best choice for both of us."

And there it went, from authoritative to pleading. Alice opened her mouth to blister him, but closed it. If she said no right now, he had four days to work on her. He didn't know she wouldn't be around. *He didn't know.* And there was the memory of her mother, who would not want her to be disrespectful. And if that wasn't enough to close her lips, there was also the ugly reality of what she'd done to create this mess. She was a thirty-year-old woman who had no obvious credentials. She knew what she knew, knew what she could do, but no one else knew that—

except Tom and her father. Neither of them could give her a reference and Tom had not offered her a ride to the future. How could he when he had no time machine?

She studied her father, trying to play out in her mind what would happen if he went to Groom Lake without her. Could he continue the project? He might, she had to concede. If they gave him an assistant, most of the theoretical work was done. Her fingers curled up into her palms. Maybe *she* was the one who had blown up the *Ray* and destroyed all evidence of her work.

At that moment she felt anger blaze up like an engine and in that instant she was angry enough to set it all alight.

"Alice…" the pleading note in her father's voice filled her with equal parts shame and anger.

She half turned away. "I'll…think about it," she said, forcing the words out.

"I…" he began but stopped when she held up her hand.

"I said I'll think about it. Don't…just don't," she said. She yanked open the door and went out, aware her gait was not not the prim secretary walk, but it also wasn't the stalk she felt inside. Her self-control did not fill her with pride. Why couldn't she assert herself? Be a Pancho Barnes? What was wrong with her? Besides everything?

Tom had been leaning against the jeep with his arms crossed, but he straightened at the sight of her. It took what was left of her self-control not to run into his arms. He must have seen something in her eyes, because he waited to help her aboard, then went around to the other side. When they were driving away from the hangar, she expected him to ask, but all he said was, "How about we put some distance between us and this base?"

She nodded, realized she twisted her hands in her lap and made herself stop. As they drove away, she saw Phillips pass in his discreet vehicle, his head swiveling to follow them. Her chin rose and stared straight ahead, but her brain was starting to work again. What had he offered her father? Or had he offered him anything? It could be the financier calling the shots. Either of them could have brought pressure to bear on her father—what if one of them knew their secret? Ice flowed into her veins. It cooled her anger, but did not dispel it.

Had her father chosen his pride over...her freedom? Or had he told himself it was another opportunity for Alice? Probably both.

How could she be angry at her father when she'd used his weakness against him, too? Only this time Phillips—or her father's backer—was the stronger will. And to be fair, Phillips had closed off most of their options here. A test flight might have changed that equation—could it still? Could they make the flight time on Saturday?

Tom drove until they were halfway between the base and the nearest town, then pulled off on a side road and stopped the vehicle and motor. He shifted in his seat so that he could see her but didn't speak. There was, she'd always known, power in not speaking, but this didn't feel like a power play. It felt like... respect.

She licked her dry lips and said, "What if I'm the one who blew up the *Ray*?" She turned to him now. "What if it was me?"

He reached out and caught one flailing hand, clasping it warmly between both of his. "You think you killed yourself?"

For some reason, that shocked her more than the thought of blowing up her life's work. Had she—would she kill herself? It hadn't happened yet, she reminded herself, but today she felt angry enough to destroy her work—but destroy herself? Would she do that? Groom Lake and Phillips or...

She shook her head in instinctive denial, but... "Maybe," she admitted. "If I felt trapped..." Would she? It felt...extreme. Surely she had another option. "With no way out..." she murmured. Was she asking him to fix it? The thought appalled her. She'd tried that solution, looked to a man to solve her problems, and look where it had landed her. She twisted her mouth in what she hoped was a smile. "No." She said the word strongly, but still felt the need to add, "Of course not."

As she said the words, they eased the sense of helplessness, or perhaps it was the fear. She'd never been free to work, so if she had to take a job in a typing pool, what would really change? Her mind would still be free to think and wonder and even hope. She was only powerless if she surrendered her power. She'd made some friends. It had been hard, but she'd made herself respond to overtures of friendship. Had she foreseen a need? Whatever, it was possible one of those friends could help her find work. They all thought she was a secretary, too.

"What happened?" Tom's voice was gentle.

"My father has decided to accept Mr. Phillips' offer to work at Groom Lake. A truck is coming to move the *Ray* on Sunday morning." It hurt to say the words, to know her power did not include the kind that would stop them from taking the *Ray*. Had she been the one to blow it up? Or had something else gone wrong? Would she know how to blow it up? She was a scientist, not a saboteur.

"Sunday," he said the word as if it baffled him, then gave himself a shake. "What did you tell him?"

"I told him I'd think about it." She saw his face change. "It was a stall. We both know it, but he can't pressure me while I'm thinking."

"Would he do that?" Tom's tone was neutral, but she saw revulsion in his eyes.

"He has before," she admitted. He knew her weaknesses, her pressure points, just as she knew his. And they both knew she'd started this. She'd made the bargain back when she didn't realize how much she'd regret it. "I started this." She looked at Tom and her lips quivered before she managed to firm them. "I did this to myself."

"Could he bluff through it on his own if you don't go?"

"Maybe, with a good assistant. Mostly it's the engineering left.

The theory," she'd seen the model fly at least, she reminded herself, "the theory is mostly worked out, at least as far as I could take it without more testing."

"So, you could walk away?" His tone was reflective, not pushy.

She was grateful for that.

"I could walk away from my father, yes."

"You make it sound so final," he pointed out. "Would it be?"

"It depends," she said, "on what pressure Phillips is applying. I think, I suspect it is pressure and not incentives." Money is what she meant. She moved restlessly. "My father is, well, he is what he is, but he is not motivated by money. I'm not even sure pride is the drive, though it would be devastating to him if the truth came out." She rubbed her forehead. "All he has left is who people think he is. If he lost that…" At least she could get a typing job. What could he do? They wouldn't even let him teach if they knew. It felt as if her choices narrowed again.

"Would…" Tom hesitated, as if he was feeling his way forward, too. "Would people in this time believe you were the brains behind the *Ray*?"

"Enough for me to get work in the field?" She wanted to say she could, but the scandal? They'd believe that. That could destroy her father and it might limit her choices even if they believed she'd been the brain behind the *Ray* or the engine. The accusation would be enough to damage both of them. It was a contradiction, but one she had no trouble believing.

Tom frowned—thinking, she assumed. He gave her a rueful look when he noticed her watching him. "This time is more complicated than I realized," he admitted. "Do you think maybe your father was the one who tried to destroy the *Ray*? I can make the case for him doing it as much as you."

She considered the question seriously, though the idea felt strange. Destruction was an act of passion and her father hadn't had any for a very long time. But… "He might," she said, wondering if she believed he could. Perhaps it were to save himself…

Funny how it didn't help to know she could have either driven herself—or her father—to destruction and suicide. But when she tried to imagine driving off with Phillips…it was easier to see her tombstone.

"Whichever one of us might have done it, it seems unlikely it was Phillips," she spoke slowly as she considered the problem, "or it feels less likely now that my father has agreed to his terms."

"He could still be trying to erase the *Ray* and you from the timeline," Tom objected. "We don't know…"

"What I'll do?" She looked at the horizon and thought for several seconds, that it wavered. It reminded her of the last time, but this time there was no location like the riding club to indicate a time event, and her model plane was not around. There'd been scrub there before and scrub was there now. But she wondered, was time in flux waiting for her to decide? How could she matter enough to interest time? Or history? "It's easier to see my death, than to see myself leaving with Phillips."

As Tom opened his mouth to protest, she shook her head and this time she moved to comfort him by laying a hand on his arm.

"I'm not going to kill myself." Again, the words gave her strength and a sense of power. With that option off the table, and a resolve to not go with Phillips, she needed to sound out her friends. See if any jobs were opening up here on base or if they knew someone. "I have to talk to my father and make it clear— but I'm mean enough to want to make him wait."

And she was exhausted by the thought of the recriminations and begging and manipulating that would follow. She didn't think even her mother would blame her for wanting to postpone that. A flare of irritation shook her. How could he not know she wouldn't, that she couldn't go? No matter how this played out, it would damage what remained of their relationship. She gripped her hands together. She was over thirty and seriously thinking of running away from home, though it felt like a long time since she'd felt at home anywhere.

Tom shook his head, then his expression changed. "I'd like to ask your permission to do something."

Was he trying to find a way to save her? He didn't have a time machine, so she didn't see how that was possible. Did she want to be saved?

He freed his hand and pushed back his sleeve, then removed a cuff link. "This contains a tiny camera and storage space. I recorded the flight this morning and I'd like to send it into the future."

She blinked. "A camera?"

"I'll show you." He extracted the glasses he'd worn briefly this morning.

Now, in hindsight, she could see this was somewhat odd. He did something with the frame handles, then handed them to her.

"Look through these."

She slid them on, perhaps a bit dubiously and then flinched in surprise. Through the main part of the lenses, she could see Tom, but there was also a smaller version of him in the upper corners. She moved her head and the view in the corners changed, too. She slipped them off and handed them back. He could be a Soviet spy, but she'd said she believed him. If she stopped believing…

She needed to believe, she decided somewhat with a touch of inner scorn. "So you have video of the model flight this morning. How do you get it to the future?"

"By dropping the cuff link here. In sixty years or so, it will begin emitting a signal that my people will be watching for. They'll pick it up and watch it. And they'll know your engine worked."

Alice considered this. *They'll know your engine worked.* She liked the sound of that. Nowhere in anything her father had said had he used these words. Or indicated that they would test her engine. "I wish…" she stopped.

"What do you wish, Alice?"

"That I could talk to them, but what would I say?" That she existed? That she lived, that she did something that mattered and then she died? Even if she didn't die this week, in sixty years, she'd be in her nineties. She would be an old lady, and Tom? He'd look just like he did right now. "This makes my head hurt," she admitted. "Drop it."

"Are you sure?" he asked.

She nodded. It wouldn't matter to her even if it did go straight to the Russians. It would change nothing in the here and now. She watched him remove the cuff link, hesitate, then he dropped it in the center of a piece of scrub.

The horizon wavered again and it almost felt as if the jeep jerked slightly, but she couldn't see the future from here. Just the same old desert.

* * *

"WE'VE GOT ANOTHER SIGNAL," Jack said. Mel had been quiet since the last attack—or what he assumed was an attack by the other group of time travelers. They were assuming a lot, he knew. They didn't know the group was operating in the here and now. The photograph only proved that the guy—or someone who looked like him—was from now, not that the time travelers were.

Mel turned to her terminal and keyed in the pickup order. "It's close to the last location," she noted. She made a face. "I wish I knew what that meant." She leaned back and rubbed her face. "What we don't know is…seriously huge, my love."

"I opened Pandora's box, didn't I?" He reached out and snagged her hand, lifting it to his lips. "I should be sorry, but…" His grin was crooked. He squeezed her hand, feeling his heart clutch at the thought of missing this, of missing her because time had decreed they live in different generations.

"Even if you hadn't opened the box, someone else did," she

pointed out, returning the pressure of his hand. "We know what they did back in the war and we think they interfered in Korea and Vietnam, but we don't know for sure." She got up and went to their map. "We couldn't, we didn't dare send people into either war. This event was our best shot."

Or so they hoped, Jack amended, but only to himself. Mel knew how much of their operation was based on hope. It bothered the scientist in him how much they were winging it with this operation. The WWII pilot? He'd spent his time in the war literally and figuratively winging it. He frowned, considering their options. He sure didn't like sitting here waiting for another hit. They needed to fight back, but for that they needed information.

"How do we find out about that building—without drawing attention to ourselves?" That had to be what the other side was doing. They were digging into the past and they'd found their location, or something else was sending time after them. What was it they'd found? "We need to move faster than they are." At least, he thought they'd moved fast. Speed was relative with time travel in the mix.

Mel spun around and faced him, but Jack could tell she wasn't seeing him. She was considering his question. "Are you sure they found us?"

She was right, it could be time that found them. It did not like being messed with. It would be ironic if they were doing this to themselves. In the war, it was what they didn't know that always bit them in the butt.

"We've got our best geeks working on protecting us and trying to hack them," she said.

The geeks were in another secure, or hopefully secure, section in the silo. Jack had compartmentalized the various operations in hopes of protecting some or all of them from time changes.

As if thinking about them had triggered something, his comm went off.

"Sir, we've got activity topside." It was Henderson, his security chief.

"Show me," Jack ordered, striding over to his console and finding the right access portal. The view was fuzzy at first, but when it cleared...

They were definitely black ops types. Whose black ops types? Government or a private enterprise? Friendly unfriendlies or unfriendly unfriendlies?

"How long can we hold them off without..." He stopped, but they both knew it might turn ugly. They had to keep the door open for Granger's return or he could be stuck in 1954. And then time might really smack them.

"If they get lethal, we'll have to, too, sir," Henderson said. "It looks like, for now, they just want in."

Knock, knock...and then what?

CHAPTER 9

*A*lice had warned Granger that her father would be polite but chilly to his now unwanted guest, and she'd been right, though chilly might be an understatement. For someone so essentially bland, he managed to emanate a lot of cold in Granger's direction. The only break in the arctic blast was when Alice brought up the test flight. Guilt flickered in the man's pale gaze, but whatever hold Phillips had on him reasserted itself pretty fast. If Alice was the hold, then Granger couldn't blame the man—no, he could blame him. He could end this with the truth. The man could do the right thing for Alice, for his daughter.

Granger had been relieved to retire to his bedroom. He needed the rest, but it took him a while to get to sleep. When he'd dropped the cuff link, it felt like time reacted, and since then he was aware, though he wasn't sure how, that time was in flux. It felt a bit like the flu, but it was all on the surface, like an itchy rash and a sense of almost nausea. He woke early feeling more rested, but still off.

Out in the kitchen, Alice was fixing breakfast. It felt a bit like he'd wandered into an episode of *Father Knows Best*, seeing her with an apron once more tied around her waist so she wouldn't mess up her prim suit. She turned, giving him a brief smile, before turning back to her pan.

"We'll be preparing our files and the *Ray* for transport," she said.

Her neutral tone told him she still feared the place was bugged.

"If I can help…" he said, letting her know he understood. It was probably a good thing he thought Phillips was listening in. He wanted to offer her a ride to the future, to get her out of here. Why couldn't she disappear like her old man? But that ride entailed huge risks, too. And was his desire to help her without bias? He'd become emotionally involved. He'd faced that fact last night. He couldn't pretend on that one. He…liked her a whole lot. The thought of her dying twisted his gut with pain. But men had been taking her choice from her for all of her life. He didn't want, he couldn't be another one of them, just because he cared about her. He couldn't do it *because* he cared about her.

Her father probably told himself the same thing so he could look at himself in the mirror.

What was the right thing for Alice?

It felt obvious that the future would be better for her, giving her a place where she could do her work without restrictions based on her sex. But she'd been born here, been born now. Jack had been pretty frank about the challenges of changing more than his zip code. He wouldn't change his trip to a life in the future, because he loved Mel, but he'd lost his family and his friends. He'd jumped over a huge chunk of life's experiences when he leaped into the future with Mel.

But Alice was going to lose that anyway. She was going to die. Maybe.

If Granger hadn't already changed her future.

He didn't trust Phillips, but he didn't know the guy was the one tampering with time. He didn't know that this move wouldn't turn out to be right for Alice. He didn't know what he didn't know. He was a scientist and he didn't like not knowing. He wasn't...comfortable with all this feeling either. It was messing with his head as much as the time travel was.

Her father entered, his face tightening at the sight of Granger. Then his gaze turned toward Alice and his lashes lowered. He took his seat, carefully placing his cloth napkin in his lap. Granger went to help Alice serve the food, waiting until she'd taken her seat before he took his. The old man might have flushed. It was hard to tell. Whatever excitement Merriweather had felt when the *Ray* flew had faded, leaving his skin waxy and colorless again. He was so close to looking like a corpse, why did the old man even try to keep breathing?

How could Phillips look at the old man, and then look at Alice, and not know who was alive? And who was the brains of the outfit? If he had...

If this wasn't his first time here, he could be trying to correct that mistake. But then why had he tried to sabotage the *Ray*? Granger felt sure it had to be him or one of his flunkies who had done it. There was no one else here who had exhibited interest in the *Ray*.

Unless...Phillips could be the distraction.

Granger had to look at that idea. He could be what he claimed to be. Granger could be the one missing something. He wanted Phillips to be the one because he didn't like him. It was uncomfortable to admit it, but it was the truth. Could it be the money behind the *Ray*? Alice didn't know and her dad wasn't talking. No one in the future could help him either. So that was his job today, he decided. He had to find a way to see further and perhaps with more clarity. And—this thought was extremely reluctant—he also had to look at Alice. She felt pressure from her father and Phillips. She'd told him she could see herself blowing up the *Ray*. His mind wanted to reject those admissions, but he had to consider them. He might...need to believe her. It was hard not to go all *Star Trek* and remember the "The City on the Edge of

Forever." If he stopped her death, or removed her from this time, how would that ripple forward into the future? Had her death served a purpose he couldn't see?

He pushed his plate back and smiled at Alice, feeling as much a traitor as her father. "Thank you. That was delicious."

Color tinged her cheeks and her smile was shy.

"Yes, of course. Most fine," Merriweather said, a touch too heartily.

Granger helped Alice clear the table, while Merriweather stood awkwardly nearby. Was the man supposed to keep them from being alone together? It was possible. And—for the first time he considered Alice's thought that her father might be the saboteur. Was he the in-plain-sight problem that Granger was missing because the forest had no trees? The bland old man could have hidden depths. What had it done to him to have first his wife, then his daughter be smarter than him? In this patriarchal time, had it twisted him inside to that extent?

No surprise his head started to ache. But despite that, he needed to reexamine his assumptions. It wasn't just the life of an extraordinary woman on the line. There was also the future— possibly even his own future. While Granger was looking for the time tamperers? As Mel had pointed out, they'd be looking for him.

"I'll do the dishes tonight," Alice said, her voice as colorless as her father's face. "The car is here."

"I'll follow in the jeep," Granger said, not looking at the old man.

The old man might have made a protesting movement, but Alice nodded, then turned and left the kitchen.

"It would be better," the old man said, "if you would…"

"Leave Alice to you and Phillips?" Granger asked.

The old man had the grace to flush. "You don't understand."

"No," Granger said, "I don't." He left then, because talking to Merriweather wasn't helping with his no-emotion resolve.

Outside, Alice was already seated in the car. He went to the jeep, feeling rejected even though he knew—he thought he knew—she'd rather be with him. He hoped.

He really hoped.

* * *

IT WAS unfair to feel bereft when Tom climbed into the jeep. Her father slid in beside her, but she didn't look at him.

"Alice," he began, when the car began to move forward.

"Don't," she said.

"I'm not..." He was silent for a block of houses. "But Grayson..."

"Don't go there either," she said.

Was she insane to believe a guy who said he'd traveled back in time to stop another time traveler from tampering with their lives? Probably. She and her father had chosen sides and honestly, they were probably both crazy to pick the sides they had.

What would Pancho Barnes do right now? She asked herself the question almost derisively, because she knew what Barnes would do. According to the stories Alice had heard, she'd ridden a horse naked into her husband's church to get him to divorce her. Alice didn't know if it was true or not, but the boldness of her actions had cleared Barnes' path of many obstacles. Alice didn't think it would help her to ride anywhere naked, but if she stood her ground...

As the car carried them inexorably toward the hangar, she considered what ground she had to stand on, though it was more figurative than literal. Because standing would actually mean letting it all go and walking away. Walking away and taking a job as a for-real secretary. She had to choose and she had to do it soon. Her father and Phillips had chosen and would work to box her in. Her father knew how much she loved her work. And Phillips? He would count on a daughter's love for her father, she supposed. And if he knew her secret? Then the *Ray*, and possibly its engine, were part of the pressure.

How much of her life did she surrender for a plane and her father? She'd given them both a lot—and if Tom was right, she only had four days of life left anyway. For some odd reason, this helped center her spin and changed all the questions. No longer was it about taking a job somewhere.

Instead it became, what did she want to do with the last four days of her life? She couldn't see Tom, but she knew he followed them in the jeep. She wanted to look back at him, not for answers or for a fix, but because he was who she wanted to spend those days with.

Phillips was waiting at the hangar when both vehicles pulled up. Dark glasses covered his eyes, but his lips tightened at the sight of Tom, or she supposed it was Tom that annoyed him. He came forward, extending his hand for Alice, but she pretended not to see it, and climbed out on her own. She turned in Tom's direction and waited for him to join her. And then felt shame for it. She'd hid behind her father and now Tom. Which brought her back to: what did she want to do with what remained of her life?

She could start, she thought, almost wryly, by being half as brave as Pancho Barnes.

* * *

ALICE HAD a strange light in her eyes as they entered the hangar that contained the *Ray*. Granger figured her old man had seen it, because he looked uneasy, though that could be because of Phillips walking next to him. Granger slanted a wary glance at her.

She looked the same for the most part. There might be a change in the set of her shoulders and the way her heels hit the concrete floor. There was also a slight compression to the line of her mouth and a faint line between her brows. But there was something more, if he could just put his finger on it.

She paused outside the office, waiting until her father and Phillips were out of earshot, then said, "Thank you for being here, for staying," she said. "I'm glad you're here...for...now."

He reached out and clasped her hand briefly, but hard.

"I'm glad, too, Alice. I'm very glad." He wanted to say more, to promise something, anything, but she wasn't asking for that, he realized. She was calm and there was no fear in her eyes.

Both her old man and Phillips looked back, and half turned as if to rejoin them.

"I'll start on the files," she said, turning from them to twist the doorknob.

Granger bit back a grin at the look in both men's eyes and he thought they'd made the right choice not to tangle with her.

"I'll just"—Tom gestured at the door she'd gone into—"help, Miss Merriweather." He stopped in the doorway to make sure he was welcome and got that reassurance, though there was still that strange, steely light behind the welcome. He was allowed in and he was happy about that. Mostly. He resisted the urge to look back at the other two men because he did have his pride.

Inside with her, her gaze met his and he was struck again by her dangerous calm. She'd decided something.

"Where would they put..." She indicated her ear.

It took him a moment to get it. She wanted to know where they would hide the bugs he suspected were here. He gave her a nod and looked around, considering. The truth was, all his knowledge had been gained from watching spy movies. There was a phone and a desk lamp. He went to the lamp and lifted it up, examining the base, then removed the bulb and looked inside. The air around him wavered as he eyed a micro-device that he was pretty sure didn't belong in this time. He showed it to her, then grabbed a pair of scissors and used the tip to pry it out. He set the small bug on the desk and almost stopped there. But in the movies, there was always more than one. He moved to the rotary phone. So old school. He checked underneath, but wasn't surprised when it yielded nothing. In the movies, the bug was always in the ear or mouthpiece.

Bingo. The mouthpiece for the win.

Was that it? He'd brought a camera into the past with him, so they might have as well. He looked around. There was the overhead light, but it was centered wrong for the desk. The ventilation grill, however, was right behind the desk and probably had a good view of a chalkboard covered with equations he'd have liked to study in more depth.

Granger moved one of the chairs over, climbed on and examined the ventilation grill. The time waver increased in intensity as he peered inside. "You have a screwdriver by any chance?"

One appeared in his hand and he worked on the screws until the grill came loose in his hand. Another bingo and silent hurrah for spy movies. He handed her the grill and reached in, gently extracting the small camera. It appeared to run on a battery and have onboard storage. So maybe, someone wouldn't get footage of him taking it out. He jumped off the chair, his glance alighting on the two bugs. Someone could be listening right now. He picked up both of them, dropped them on the floor and crushed them with his foot.

Alice came close, looking at the device in his hand with something like awe.

"What is it?"

"A camera." He turned it over in his hand. It had a thin layer of dust on it, which seemed to indicate it hadn't been checked recently. "It recorded video of you working, though I'm guessing it mostly picked up who was here and maybe when you worked on your chalkboard."

She shivered and he didn't blame her.

"You haven't changed clothes or anything in here, have you?"

It could be that simple, except the tech was from the future. Didn't mean someone wasn't a creeper, though.

"No." She shook her head, both hands clutching the grill tightly. She looked at her chalk board, then went to it and lifted the eraser but paused. "If you filmed it, or took that camera with you…when you leave, then you'd have it, wouldn't you?"

"Are you sure that's what you want, Alice?"

The time waver was more of a shudder that made the overhead light swing several times. He knew Alice saw it, felt it, but he didn't know why. But she did, or he thought she did.

"I decided," she said. She waited for a response, but he didn't know what to say. "I want you to film it, as much as you can, and take it with you when you leave." She waited again. "Just the data that belongs to me."

This was about more than trust in him, he realized. She'd decided something, though he wasn't quite sure what. And it appeared she didn't plan to explain beyond what she'd already said. She could be hedging her bets—since he was from the future —or she could be winging it.

"All right," he said. He looked at the camera. He could try to take it with him, but if it was found on him—he had to assume that at some point he could be searched—it would be hard to explain. It wasn't supposed to be here. "I'll film with my tech. I think we—I need to destroy this," he said.

She hesitated, then nodded, watching while he stamped on it, too. Then she collected a broom from a small closet, swept up the debris, and dumped it in her trash can.

Once again he was struck by her deliberate calm.

"Someone brought us boxes, it seems," she said, indicating a small pile stacked behind the desk. "And so it begins."

She turned and pulled opened the top drawer of a file cabinet. Someone…Granger picked up a box and set it on the desk, then he pulled out the glasses and adjusted his sleeves.

"You'll want everything in this one," she said.

He nodded, and began—though he took a shot of the chalk-board first. He flipped the pages over, taking time to make sure he'd captured the whole page. At one schematic, he stopped and looked up, meeting her gaze.

"This is the one..." he stopped. But he thought she knew. It was the one schematic that had survived before. She half smiled, and then picked up a pen and carefully inscribed her name on the lower corner above her father's name. She capped the pen and handed it back.

This time, instead of a shudder, it was as if a wind swirled around them, ruffling the edges of the other papers and the strands of Alice's hair that had escaped her careful bun.

For good or ill, she'd changed something. And he had a feeling this was just the beginning.

* * *

IT HAD BEEN a night of time shocks and assaults topside, but with the rising sun, the black ops guys were just...gone. Mel turned the topside camera three times before she accepted it might be true. Or they could only see what their attackers wanted them to see. It was hard to make the case for "real" in any sense after this week.

Jack was still sleeping for once, but he'd stayed up after her. She'd seen him pacing in the glow of the computer screen when she'd pried her lids open around four. She slipped quietly out and completed some necessary ablutions before returning to get updated on the situation. The time monitor and the seismic monitor were both eerily quiet. The seismic monitor had registered the explosions from the black ops team's attempts to break into the silo. Their enemy had learned a lot, but had missed a key point, thank goodness. That entry was not the real way into the silo.

Mel couldn't tell if they'd backed off to regroup, or if something had changed in the timeline. She reran the security footage and still couldn't tell. There'd been some kind of glitch right before they either left or disappeared.

The footage from the last cuff link retrieval was there. She put on headphones so she wouldn't wake up Jack and watched it three times, before leaning back with a silent exclamation. So Granger had been right about what the engine could do. It was just a model, but...

Dang.

Now she turned to their tracking wall, looking for changes there. It was four days and sixty-six years ago since the so-called alien visit. But she went back to the beginning of their research and studied each item pinned there. It had really begun when Granger found the schematic—she stopped. It rippled slightly, and as she watched, a signature appeared in the corner above George Merriweather's name.

Alice Merriweather.

Mel blinked, but it didn't go away. The wavering faded and there it was, both new and faded with time. She walked along the line of documents and photos, but the change hadn't rippled forward yet, that she could see...

She stopped by the news item of Alice's death. It hadn't changed, at least when she'd died hadn't changed. But how she'd died had.

...accidentally shot during an incident on Edwards Air Force Base...

CHAPTER 10

*T*he *Ray* had begun with her mother, and, she hoped, with her father, so Alice was careful to separate those files from those she considered hers. But she also knew that Phillips wasn't going to let her walk out of here with her files. And her father might back him up. As Tom photographed her files—her backup plan to her backup plan—Alice collected her personal belongings from the drawers and around the office. She found a box and did an assessment. If she hid files under her personal belongings, there wouldn't be room for everything—but would the box be searched? She wouldn't put it past Phillips to find a way. She grabbed a box of equal size and cut the bottom off it, leaving a two-inch rim. She tucked the leftover pieces behind the file cabinet, then measured it against the other box. It looked like it would work, but there wasn't a lot of space. She'd need to focus on the critical stuff, the end of her research. It bothered her not to have the foundational stuff in there, but—she was dying anyway.

Four days, she reminded herself.

She still hated to give that to the...enemy. She considered the problem and a slow smile curved her mouth. It felt a bit evil actually. She gathered the preliminary research files and laid them out in a row, then just started to mix it all up. She also removed pages, shuffled them like playing cards, and tore key pages up, though not without a pang.

As if he knew it, Tom paused his work and touched her shoulder, his gaze complicated but comforting. It amazed her that he didn't question anything she did. She was not used to that kind of support from a man. She felt her strength waver. She wanted more time to know him better, to…she wanted more kisses and she wanted more of this…she struggled for the right word… respect. She liked being seen in this way. She recognized attraction in there, but there was so much more.

Four days.

It wasn't enough time, but it was all there was. She sensed that even if she didn't die, the clock was ticking on Tom's time here, too. The scientist in her wondered how he would return to his own time—and the woman…she just wanted him to stay. It was better not to think about what the woman wanted.

She touched his hand to acknowledge his offer of support and turned back to her boxes. Once she'd ascertained that Tom was finished photographing the critical files, she put them in the bottom of her boxes, and fitted her fake bottom over them.

"Good idea," Tom said, with a grin that lightened her mood. She began adding her personal items, but paused when he added, "He'll expect you to hold back some files."

She considered this, then nodded. "We could make a decoy box."

He grabbed an empty box and set it on a chair, while she grabbed a pile of the files she'd mixed up. Over his shoulder she noticed the still-open ventilation shaft and indicated it to Tom.

He grinned wider and once they'd finished filling the box and taped it down, he climbed up, shoved the box in and reattached the grill. There was double satisfaction in doing it. When someone came to retrieve the camera, they'd get a box of semi-useless files. And because the files had been hidden, she hoped it would slowed them down for a while at least.

She turned back to the box for her personal items, adding them in with care that she hoped would look casual. She filled this box so that it couldn't be closed, then turned to the rest of the room. How could she make it harder for them?

She took discarded typing paper and scattered it around, crumpled pages from other files and dumped them in the trash can. It went against the grain, but her goal was to confuse the issue. Anger helped, but when her anger faded there would probably be guilt and regret, even shame at this destruction. She faced it, deplored the necessity, but for now, she felt only a grim pleasure at the chaos. It was her choice, finally, about what to do with her work. Perhaps it would still vanish in time, or be found not relevant in Tom's future world, but here and now, she got to choose.

Once that was as done as they dared, she turned her attention to the drawers of logs. She supposed they would want them to, but before she could start sliding them into a box, Tom stopped her.

"We need to make sure there's not another player," Tom said. He took a logbook and sat on the room's only other chair.

Alice gave him a doubtful look. It was true that the logbooks tracked every stage of the *Ray*'s creation and every person who'd had access to her, but there had been a lot of people. How did they tell which might be the one they were looking for?

"Look for patterns, for people who shouldn't need to be here, anything that looks odd or out of place," Tom suggested.

"You think Phillips had…" She trailed off. Of course, Phillips had to have had help, but had he brought that help with him? If time was aware of her, surely it would notice that. And that she'd just had that thought was…astonishing. Her belief wavered, but she shored it up. She had to believe. She was committed now. Or would soon be, she thought wryly.

"He probably hired, or convinced people to help him," Tom said.

She nodded, still fighting the sudden wavering. How would she feel on Saturday if it all turned out to be false? Would she be glad to be alive? She didn't want to die, but did she want to live knowing she'd been fooled so completely by someone she—cared about? It was sad to realize she wanted to believe, even if it killed her. But when she looked at her past life? That was truly sad.

There came a tentative tap at the office door and after a pause, her father eased the door partially open and peered in. He seemed startled by the sight of so much disorder.

"My dear, was this necessary?"

"Yes," Alice said, glad her personal items were already stowed.

His gaze strayed to that box, of course, probably because it wasn't taped shut.

"Those are my personal items I'm taking back to the house," she told him. House, not home.

He came and looked in it, but all he saw was a sweater, some books, a clock, a potted plant, a picture of her mother on top of everything...he flinched back.

"That's..." He didn't seem to know where to look or what to say, so he retreated, shutting the door quietly behind him.

Alice released a breath she didn't know she'd been holding. She realized her back hurt and they were barely through the first year of logbooks. One thing about her father, he liked to keep meticulous records. Every rivet and bolt, everyone who worked on the *Ray* had been written down—or should have been. She shifted, arching her back. Tom looked up with a wry grin.

"This is...not exciting."

She chuckled. "No." She touched the log in her lap. "It felt more exciting at the time it was all happening." She leaned back, closed her eyes and remembered when she'd been happy here, when it didn't matter if she got credit as the *Ray* took shape in the hangar. "It was busy all day and each night...the baby was bigger than the day before." At night she'd been able to work on her engine, too. She loved thinking through an idea, but seeing it take shape under her hands had been...exhilarating.

"When did it start to change?" Tom asked softly.

She opened her eyes. It was a good question. When had it begun to change? It had been so subtle, like a small, bleeding wound as hope seeped away. She wanted to blame Phillips, but it had started before he came back, she realized now. Small setbacks and accidents that slowed things down. She leaned forward, sorting through the logs until she found the ones dated seven and eight months ago.

"Look through that one," she said handing him the other one. She flipped hers open and looked at the names and where they were assigned. Though she hadn't worked closely with the men, faces—some clearer than others—emerged from her memories of that time. The ones who'd slapped or pinched her bottom, those she remembered, but there were also the quiet, respectful boys. Because most of them had been boys. There had been one...her finger ran down the page and she turned it twice before she found it. He'd spotted a problem and brought it to her because her father was gone at the time.

And the next day he'd been gone...

She verified that, flipping back and forth between pages. So someone was there then, watching...but why? It kept coming back to that. If the project was worth taking to Groom Lake, then why try to sabotage it? All they'd accomplished was to slow it down—she stiffened. Was that it?

She looked at the names with different eyes, looking for places where one name or names would be active and then gone. And she found this over and over. And around each, there would be a slow down or a problem.

"It's not one person," she said, looking up at Tom. "It's a series of them and each time, there is a slowdown, a cluster of small problems, none of them big enough to raise red flags. He—or they—were trying to slow the project down." She leaned back, rubbing her face in frustration. "Why? What is so special about now, this week, your Saturday?"

"I told you all I know," Tom said. He looked tired, too. If he'd slept as well as she had…

"Aliens?" She said the word softly, her glance darting to the closed door.

"Something happened, will happen this Saturday, that's all I know."

"We're missing something," she fretted.

"Let's go back to what we know," Tom suggested. "We found the device in the panel that feeds power to the ejection system. When was that secured?"

Alice considered the question. "It would be in your logbook, check…three months back? There should be notes about it."

Tom flipped through the pages, checking the dates, then he stopped and looked up. "There's a three-day gap here. I can't find anything about work inside the *Ray* or on the panel."

Alice frowned and took the log from him, scanning the pages and confirming his assertion. "It was there," she said. The pages were numbered, and if she looked closely she could see where the pages had been cut out, very close to the binding. No one would notice unless they were looking at those specific dates. She'd bet money that at least one of the men working those days would fit her pattern of there and then gone.

She checked the dates on either side of the missing pages and dug through the debris for her desk calendar, but when she went back—the three days were missing there, too. She leaned back. How did they fight an enemy one step ahead of them? An enemy who knew more than they did, or so it seemed.

"Anything else significant about those three days?" Tom asked.

"I'm not sure," she admitted. She didn't have an eidetic memory, so she kept notes in lots of places. There were her notes at home, meant for her own use. It felt strange to wonder if they were gone, too. Was it paranoia? No one but her could read them, except for perhaps some of the equations, she reminded herself. It was...unsettling...to think of someone going through her things, either here or there, but it felt worse to think of someone at the house going through her things. This was for good or ill a business space, but that house—while no longer her home—it was...personal. Private. Was there a camera there, too? In her bedroom?

"I made personal notes," she told him. "They'll be at the house." Her gaze told him she wondered if they were still there. Even though they'd removed the things Tom called bugs and the camera, she felt watched, or perhaps she felt shadowed. Death felt closer than before, even as she tried to strike blows against her seen and unseen enemies.

Tom's lips thinned and anger flared in his eyes.

"Let's stop for lunch," she said. She didn't usually, but it felt urgent to discover if her personal space had been violated, too. He nodded and rose, holding out a hand to help her up. She needed it. She felt stiff from all the unaccustomed activity, followed by sitting so long. Tom picked up the box of personal things, shifting it to one side so he could open the door for her.

Outside the office, her father and Phillips were standing by the *Ray*, consulting with several men in coveralls. There were also, she realized with shock, but no surprise, security personnel. Armed men.

Both men turned, Phillips first. He stared at her across the space, for once his eyes not hidden behind his dark glasses. An expression that she almost took for grief flickered in his eyes for several seconds, before he blanked his gaze once more. Who was he? Did he know the *Ray* would be destroyed? Was the promise of the truck to transport the plane something to appease or stall, or did he believe it would truly happen?

Phillips, shook his shoulders as if shrugging something off them, then strode toward them, his gaze on the box. "I'm sorry, but you can't remove anything from the hangar, Miss Merri-weather."

He didn't sound sorry.

"You're worried about my plant?" She let scorn color her voice.

He could see the tips of the plant drooping over the side of the box. She'd never been that good with growing things, but she'd tried harder here.

He leaned forward and, without permission, poked through the items. His gaze shot up to hers suddenly, probing, she guessed, but she'd had a lot of practice deflecting...*lying*, she reminded herself. She was a good liar. Four days suddenly felt too long. It would be good to have it over.

Phillips stepped back, with obvious reluctance and signaled to the two men guarding the door. No one stopped them again, but Alice didn't feel safe, even when Tom started the jeep. Could they have planted those bugs on it, too?

They drove in silence to the house. It took all her willpower not to look back, or around them. And the *Ray*? Had they been preparing it for transport or the test flight? Would her father have the strength to fight for the flight? She could stop and ask. There was less chance of being overheard...unless Phillips had a man in flight control, too. The triple coverage in the office had left her feeling...exposed. It felt as if the last safe place was inside her head.

Alice stared at the house as Tom collected her box from the rear of the jeep, wondering if she really wanted to know. With a shake, she made herself jump down. Together they headed up the path. She'd made a choice not to hide but to live and take action, these last few days of her life. She knew Tom still hoped to stop what had happened, but she felt the...inevitability of it.

It was coming.

* * *

GRANGER FOLLOWED Alice up the steps and into the house, but he went into the kitchen and set her box on the table, while she went into her bedroom. Would her personal notes be gone, too? Was he fighting a foe who already knew all the plays? If her notes were gone, then it felt like the answer to that question was yes.

She came out quickly, the color leached from her face. He lifted a finger to his lips and drew her out onto the porch and away from the house.

"They're gone. All of them." Anger simmered behind the shock in her eyes. "Even the ones not related to the *Ray*." She looked away, gazing out toward the desert. "My whole life...they had no right to do that. To come in here."

Her hands were curled into fists at her sides.

They weren't worried about her rights, but Tom didn't say it. She knew it already.

Granger rubbed his face. He wanted to step close and hug her but something almost fey about her kept him back. Her lips twisted.

"I made up my own code. Do you think they'll be able to break it?"

"I don't know, Alice. With enough time...maybe." Probably. "If they find the key..."

"They won't find it. It's in my head." There was satisfaction despite her bleak tone.

She seemed to sway for a moment and Granger took a half step closer, but then she straightened. "I had to write it so I used a lot of shorthand. The typical things they'd look for, they won't find." Her glance his direction was resigned now. "Maybe it will take them a very long time."

"I hope so," he told her. Now, carefully, he took her hand, letting it lie loosely within the clasp of his fingers. The horizon wavered, the house directly across changing into something more modern. What was it about this woman, or this moment in time, that mattered so much?

"I'm going to burn it," she said, returning the clasp of his hand. "There's a trash barrel out back. I'm going to burn the files we brought here. It's the only way—there's no where we can hide them that they won't find them."

His heart clenched. He was a scientist, too, and he still couldn't imagine what this was costing her.

"I…" he wanted to protest, but he couldn't. She was right. There was no place they could hide them. This house had already been searched.

"Just…get them safely to where you're going," she said.

His other hand clenched, as he thought about the images he'd captured on the storage drive of his cuff link. He'd planned to take it back to the future with him, but now he wondered… Should they do the drop today before Phillips had a chance to do anything else? He looked around, wondering if there were eyes on them right now? If they tried to leave the base, would Phillips let them? The armed guards at the hangar had been a surprise. He hadn't seen it coming. Until he walked out of that room, he thought this was a…personal battle with another time traveler. How had Phillips managed to escalate it?

Jack and Mel had tried sending a team back in time for just one day, and time hadn't liked it one bit. The larger the incursion, the more time noticed. Just sending one or two people hadn't attracted time's attention that much.

"Let's do it," he said, though the words felt dry and hard coming out of his mouth. He'd hoped to stop destruction, not aid in it.

They went back through the house. Inside, Alice removed all of the personal items on top of the files. He wasn't surprised that she checked to see if the files were still there, even flipping through the folders to make sure the papers in them hadn't changed. Then she put them back in the box. If anyone was watching, they'd see them burning a box, not files.

She grabbed matches, and Granger took the box. The barrel

was at the rear of the property. There was a small wind, enough they stood with their backs to it and used the inside of the barrel to protect the match she struck against the inside of the barrel. The smell of it wafted up to his nose, carried by the swirling wind that seemed to build as he lowered the box so she could hold the match against a corner. When it had well and truly caught, he lowered it into the barrel.

The flame stayed on the edges for what felt like a long time, and again, he felt or wondered if they were watched. When the flame finally found its way to the first folder, it raced across this thinner material, removing this cover so he could see notes in what he presumed was her careful handwriting.

The time tremor caught them both by surprise. Their hands came together as they braced, the horizon flickering much like the fire, only this flickered through time like an old movie film. For one moment, he thought he saw a plane dive toward the ground, the crash either part of the fire and the tremor—or it felt as if it were.

The tremors eased as the fire dug through all the files, but neither moved until it was completely black ash. Alice looked around, grabbed a fallen tree branch and stirred the ashes.

"It's done," she said, but her voice didn't sound done and her eyes didn't look done. Almost conversationally, she added, "They took the model, too, you know."

"I'm so sorry, Alice, so…sorry." The words were so inadequate, he cursed under his breath. Had he caused this, or was this how it had played out before? There was no way to know. None. But when he looked into her eyes again, he almost stepped back, startled. "What? What are you thinking of doing?"

Her lips curved up and she looked almost…mischievous.

"I was just thinking of Pancho Barnes and what she'd do right now."

* * *

Tom looked worried, so worried that Alice almost laughed, but if he knew more about Pancho Barnes? He'd be even more worried.

She turned in a slow circle, her gaze passing over the house she'd lived in for the last two and half years, and the other houses in the row, across the desert that had made her feel so defeated for so long. There was no going back. There was no going forward. She had nothing to lose but…it wasn't exactly pride. It was more…existential than that, she decided. She'd lose herself, if she didn't at least hit back. Phillips had everything—possibly even time—on his side. He had the guns and the men and even her father.

And she had Tom until Saturday and, her lips twitched, maybe some aliens. But in the end, she had herself. It felt a bit full circle, too. When her mother had died, she'd been in this same situation. She'd made some choices, some of them desperate choices, but looking back, she couldn't regret them. They'd brought her here and in some strange way, they'd brought her Tom. She'd thought the time together was too short, but when she looked at how far she'd come since she met him, it hadn't been short at all. She'd grown and changed more in the past few days than in her whole life up to now.

"Thank you," she said, turning to him. She felt his sorrow and even his guilt, could see it in his eyes. "Thank you for coming. I'm so glad you did."

His hand shook as he reached out and smoothed back the strands the wind blew across her face.

"I…I don't think…"

"No, it was the right thing for me. It was the right thing. Please don't regret this. I don't." Well, except the part where it had to end, but that wasn't yet. She wouldn't think about that now. "I'm grateful for all of it, but…" she took a deep, steadying breath… "but if there is a way for you to go now, you should take it. You should do it."

He frowned. "Why?"

"Because"—she glanced around and lowered her voice, but didn't moderate the determination—"I'm going to fly the *Ray*. I'm going to test my engine."

"Alice..."

She put her hand on his lips and the feel of his mouth against her fingers almost broke her resolve. "Don't. I...it's the only way to..." She didn't know how to explain it to him, so she shook her head and said, "It's the only way."

He stared at her for what felt like a long time and she knew his mind—his scientific mind—raced with other options to offer. Finally his lips twisted in something like a grin, or perhaps a grimace.

"How can I help?"

* * *

SOMETHING HAD CHANGED OVERNIGHT. Jack couldn't put his finger on it, but it was there. It reminded him of being in his bomber over France with Mel. He rolled out of the cot, sparing a moment to study Mel. She'd been up and down all night. Now she had her face burrowed into her pillow, but one hand dangled off the edge of the cot. He resisted the need to touch her hand. It would wake her up and she needed to sleep.

He fought the urge to head straight to the data, and took care of his morning ablutions first. Back in the main control room and munching on an energy bar, he started waking up the computers and other machines, and put off looking at their tracking board. He watched Granger's video of the model plane again, pausing it when Granger took a close-up of the engine. He itched to see more of the schematics and research behind it. Or he itched because time was not happy. Could be either one.

He felt a flutter of cold air—air that reminded him of the

flight line back when. He turned, following the stream and stared at the tracking board, his eyes going wide.

The whole of it wavered and moved, as if a stream of water ran over it, but under the watery surface, elements faded and flared. Some came back, but others…he didn't know what to call the spaces where they'd been. Blank wasn't emphatic enough.

"Mel…" he said, trying to keep his voice calm.

She pushed up, and shoved her hair back with one hand, while the other supported her. She looked at him, then in the direction he indicated.

"Okay then." She struggled out of the bedding and cot, half stumbling to his side.

He caught her to him as the water or waves lapped closer for an endless minute, then faded back to…what it had been? Or was it? There were still blank places where notes and articles had been.

"Things are missing," he said, not sure if he were asking or telling Mel.

"I've been taking pictures at different times of the day," Mel said, "to see if we can get a better handle on how well this bunker is working." She left his side to collect a camera and then returned, tucking herself back in close. She worked on the camera, then held it up so they could see the screen together as she flipped through the images. Seen that way, it was easier to see small changes happened. When she got to the end, she took a shot of the current board.

"I'll get the images uploaded to our offline computer," she said. "Maybe we can figure out what's happening."

As she took the four steps from him to the computer, for an instant it seemed she walked into something else. Or somewhere else. He reached out to pull her back; the image faded.

She was still there.

For now.

CHAPTER 11

Thursday dawned reluctantly, the sky overcast and ominous, as if Mother Nature herself sensed the coming conflict and was providing the backdrop. Granger stood at his rear-facing bedroom window and studied the dreary landscape. The clouds were low enough to hide the mountains and the dead winter scrub looked dystopian. His sense of being out of sync with time had worsened. Even if he believed it was best for him to fly the *Ray* for Alice, he wasn't sure he could when the horizon flickered and wavered at random intervals. There was part of him that wished he could slow these flashes so he could study the things he glimpsed in both the past and the future.

In nothing could he tell if he were influencing or changing the timeline, despite his strong sense that everything was in flux. He felt Alice's fatalism about Saturday and her fate and understood her drive to soar or die in her machine. But understanding did not ease his need to change the outcome, to save her life.

He fingered the cuff link that contained the images of her research notes. He needed to get it outside the base perimeter, but would Phillips let him leave? And if he left, could he get back on base? It felt like he was playing chess blind-folded while his opponent could see the board and predict his moves. But the fact that he was still here, told him one key thing.

Phillips didn't know who he was or where he'd come from.

He might suspect Granger was from the future, though Granger wasn't sure about that either. Phillips had appeared to find him an annoyance to be pushed out of the way. And to be fair, Granger didn't know Phillips was from the future either. He could be working for the time tamperer.

Or they could all be delusional. He could be delusional. Oh, not about traveling through time, but about this event and what it meant. His arrival could be triggering all sorts of problems and sending changes rippling forward through time.

He could be the time tamperer.

He knew much, though he suspected not all, of Mel and Jack's Charlie Foxtrot, despite its mostly happy ending. More than breathing, he wanted to offer Alice a ride out of this place and time, but Jack and Mel had been separated in the time vortex, torn apart by the extreme buffeting. They'd arrived in the mostly same future but still separated by a chunk of time. Luckily for Jack, he'd had somewhere to go until he could find her again. But Alice? What would she do in the future? Lost and alone? With no knowledge of how to function? He could deliver her to a worse future than her present one.

You can die now or get lost in time didn't offer her much choice. And if they'd changed things enough that she wasn't going to die? Then it became even more egregious to risk taking her with him.

The other choice hung out there, waiting for him to notice it.

He could try to stay. Mel and Jack had put protocols in place to stop that. Leaving a team member in the past with his knowledge was dangerous to the future, to their future. And he'd given his sworn word he wouldn't do that. Did he know all the ways they could suck him back to his own time? Probably not, he conceded. They would know more than most the risks, challenges and temptations of traveling into the past. There was a reason the premise kept showing up in movies—though the ones he'd seen never managed to satisfactorily deal with the paradoxes caused by the human heart.

Once again, he was back to the essential question: what was the best thing for Alice?

And how arrogant of him to think he could know that. Had he asked her what she wanted? She'd said what she planned to do, but what did she *want*?

He heard voices in the kitchen, the lower tones of Merriweather, but someone else, someone male.

He went out and hesitated outside the kitchen door.

"You need to cancel the test flight, Miss Merriweather."

It was Phillips, his tone quiet, but intense. Why did he think Alice—a secretary as far as anyone knew—had the power to schedule or reschedule a test flight?

"It's not safe," Phillips added, after a long pause that Granger suspected had involved Alice looking calmly at Phillips without speaking.

"Alice, my dear," her father's voice held a note of hopeless entreaty.

At least he knew that much about his daughter.

"Do you want the test canceled?" Alice finally spoke.

"Of course not, but we can do it when we get to Groom Lake."

"I haven't agreed to go to Groom Lake," Alice said.

"What would you do?" This was her father again.

"Something," Alice said. There was a pause, then she spoke again. "Maybe I'll talk to Pancho Barnes. I'll bet she'd have some ideas for me."

"Pancho..." Phillips voice trailed off. Granger would have given a lot to see his expression. He'd probably bitten back the question of who in the expletive-deleted—because a lady was present—was Pancho Barnes? Granger didn't know enough either, he admitted, but he knew more than Phillips, it sounded like. She was a woman who had been a stunt pilot and a test pilot in a time when that didn't happen. She'd owned that bottom-something riding club where they'd flown the model. Now she'd become Alice's rallying cry.

"The test flight isn't going to happen, sir. You need to cancel it," Phillips said, with a frustrated bark.

Granger had just enough warning to step back into the shadows of the hall before Phillips burst out, stalked down the small hall and out the front door. The kitchen door was still swinging on its hinge when Merriweather spoke again.

"He doesn't know?" Alice asked. "About who is financing the *Ray*?"

Merriweather shook his head.

"Is that who scheduled the test?"

Merriweather's shrug was frustrated. "I don't know who scheduled it." He glanced at her. "I thought maybe you did it my name."

"I'm just the secretary," she pointed out with careful calm.

"We need the *Ray* to be in one piece."

"Why there and not here? They are both deserts. Both military bases. Why there?"

Her father didn't speak.

"I don't trust him."

There was a long silence, then Alice came out, stopping just past the swing of the door. As if she sensed him, she looked at him.

"Let's get out of here."

"I was thinking exactly the same thing," Granger said.

* * *

TOM DROVE TOWARD THE GATE, braking on approach, as if he expected someone to stop them leaving the base, but no one did. Would they—or he—be allowed back on, Alice wondered? Phillips was moving to narrow her choices down to one and she was sure he saw Tom as a hindrance to that plan. It all depended on how much power he actually had.

He could keep her from the *Ray*. She accepted that. She could have stayed on base, but she was willing to risk that for two more days with Tom. She faced it, accepted it. She wasn't sure she totally understood this willingness. She'd known him less than six days and she'd chosen him over her father.

Of course, she knew her father better.

But she'd also chosen him over the *Ray*.

Which she was going to lose anyway…

The grayness of the day should have discouraged her, she supposed. Under lowering skies the scrub looked bleaker than usual. So why did her heart feel lighter? All right, she knew why, but it wasn't just the man. It was getting away from the base, too, away from Phillips and his minions watching her. And listening. She shuddered. She looked around. It would be hard for them to listen out here.

And then she heard something. A helicopter.

"It can't be, can it?" She had to raise her voice to be heard over the jeep's engine.

"Maybe." Tom made a face, then extended his arm toward her. "Take the cuff link and throw it as hard as you can before they get close enough to see."

The images he'd taken of her research, she realized. She pulled up his jacket sleeve and got the cuff link. Such a small thing to carry so much. She looked back. Tom had sped up, so they weren't closing as fast as they'd been. They still might see her. She saw some thick scrub by the side of the road just ahead and twisted so that her body blocked their view, or so she hoped. As they reached the scrub, she hurled it, a wink of gold for an instant, then it was gone.

The whole horizon shook. The Jeep swerved and as she looked back, the helicopter winking in and out of view several times.

"Why?" She looked at Tom, moving her shoulders in frustration.

"I don't know." He appeared baffled, too. He increased his speed as the helicopter began to draw closer again. "What do you want, Alice?"

"What?" She shook her head. What did he mean?

"No one has asked you. Not your father, not Phillips, and not me. What do *you* want?"

He was right. No one had ever asked her that question. It shuddered through her with the force of the time tremor. Or maybe it was part of an inner tremor.

"I want to fly the *Ray*," she said slowly, but that felt not enough. Despite all the setbacks, it felt too small as an answer. Shouldn't she want more? The *Ray* was a machine, essentially cold and indifferent. It didn't care who flew her. She cared for the *Ray*, but the *Ray* was indifferent. She glanced at Tom. He was driving, dividing his attention between the road ahead and the helicopter behind.

So what did she want?

She wanted to live more than three days. She wanted life. She wanted warmth. She wanted laughter. She wanted…love. She wanted all the things that had been missing since her mother died. And she wanted more. She wanted…him. She wanted Tom or Ty or whatever his name was.

Could she love someone she'd known such a short time? Could she, did she, have the right to call it that? There was some data to support love, but under the data was the big, needy, longing hole around her heart. It was embarrassing how big that hole was, how long she'd let it grow and fester. Only now did she begin to understand how angry she was with her father. And how much she didn't want to spend her last few days being angry with him or anyone.

The helicopter reached them—and flew past. Tom slowed and then pulled off, watching it warily.

"I don't want to be angry anymore," she said, in the sudden silence. She looked at him, choking on the words she wanted to say to him. They were words women didn't say first to men, but she had the odd notion that she could to him—if he wasn't from the future and she wasn't from the now. How could she put that burden on him when he had to leave?

"Alice." His voice was husky and his hand trembled as he reached out and cupped her cheek.

She fought against nestling into this warmth and strength.

"I don't have the right, I've never said...to anyone but my mom and dad..."

She found she could smile, though it felt as if it trembled as much as his hand.

"I...love...you..." he said, starting uncertain and ending strong.

Her heart swelled, joy surging in to fill the hole, even at the despair in his voice. They had to part, but he loved her. *He loved her.*

"I don't have the right to say it, but I wanted, I needed you to know."

She wrapped her hand around the strong wrist so close to her face and let him see the happiness in her eyes. Her heart felt as if it unfurled, freeing something inside her. "I love you, too. It feels crazy, but right."

"I don't know how to save you," he said, the words broken and laced with pain.

"You helped me find the courage to save myself," she said. "I'm not afraid of Saturday or Phillips. You...saw m,e and because you saw me, I saw myself." She shook her head in frustration, because the words didn't begin to explain. "Don't be sorry, please. I will be all right."

The pain in his eyes clenched her heart in her chest; it dented the happiness she felt, the lightness, but... "You'll be all right, too. It's good to love, even if you lose it. It...opened me up." She studied him. "And I think it opened you, too? Next time, I hope you won't be as afraid."

"There won't…"

"No, don't say that. You need to take this, take what we both feel and complete…the circle. Please don't turn this into pain. Grieve for me, but heal, Tom—no Ty. Heal, please? Promise me you'll heal." She saw doubt in his eyes. "There's someone in your time who needs you, too." She gripped his wrist, and shook his hand. "Promise me."

The helicopter was coming back now, and this time, she knew, though she didn't know how, it would stop.

"Promise."

He nodded and turned her hand up to place a kiss in the palm. "I promise."

The wind from the helicopter rushed at them as it landed further down the road. An armed MP leapt out and ran toward them.

"Major. Miss Merriweather. You're needed on the base." When Tom gestured at the jeep, he added, "I'll drive that back, sir."

Drawing on the happiness in her heart, Alice nodded and clambered out. Tom came around, took her arm and walked with her toward the helicopter. She glanced back and saw the MP looking in the rear of the jeep. It was too late, she thought, as she ducked under the spinning blades and climbed in the back. It's all gone.

She settled in the seat and pulled the straps across. It was another first, this helicopter ride. A ray of light broke through, but the clouds in the distance showed signs of a big storm coming.

* * *

Jack was sticking close to her, Mel knew, and she understood why. She wanted to cling to him. The attacks or assaults or whatever had been happening, had changed. It felt as if a river of cool time now flowed through the bunker. She was pretty sure she'd seen the airmen, the men who had been here when the silo had been operational.

Even as items appeared and disappeared on their tracking wall, one thing remained consistent. All the changes were related to the Merriweathers, father and daughter—with occasional mentions of a Major Tom Grayson also reappearing and disappearing.

"I think it might be stabilizing," Mel said, almost afraid to say the words out loud. If time was eavesdropping…they were hosed anyway. It did feel as if time were…almost…a sentient force. It wasn't, it couldn't be…but it felt as if it were.

Neither she nor Jack had ventured close to the…all she knew to call it was the timeline…the rippling, water-like section just in front of their tracking wall. But it did seem to be calming down. The board itself was still in a state of flux, but the disturbance region appeared to be shrinking. She had no urge to go put a foot or an arm in that area yet. And she might be feeling a bit of PTSD from her adventures in the past. It was a pity, sort of, that Jack had been with her and not with himself—her eye hurt from this thought—during that time, so they had no way to compare this to what might have happened in the future while she'd been in the past.

Wow. Now her head *really* hurt. Why were they doing this again? She had her guy, her grandfather had been saved. They should have hung it all up then.

Just then, across from her, an image pulsed out from the cluster of photographs around Edwards Air Force Base. It was Alice. Mel knew her now, from the stuff they'd received from Granger. But this picture was new, different from the others. She seemed to gaze at Mel across the room, the eyes alive in a way they really shouldn't be. As if Alice herself looked at her across time.

The steadiness, the courage, and something more, in her eyes…connected them in some strange way. It felt as if time had connected their fates together. Mel drew in a shuddering breath as Alice's image faded back to just a picture on the wall. But the feeling of being connected didn't ease. If anything, it felt stronger. It felt as if they lived—or died—together.

It was just a feeling, she told herself. There was no real way they could be connected. They hadn't met in the past and there was nothing that connected them now. They'd looked, my heavens, how they'd looked.

There was a whisper of sound or air that seemed to say *you missed something.*

And then the room was…normal again, or what passed for it.

She turned to Jack, who was intent on his monitor. "Is there anything, anything at all, that connects you or us to either of the Merriweathers?"

Jack stared at her. "I didn't know them, Mel…" but his tone was slow, thoughtful.

"Maybe you read something, a research paper or…an article…before you got here?"

"The time between?"

She half shrugged. "Maybe." He'd jumped over almost sixty years of his own life, and unlike Mel, he didn't have a photographic memory, but…some things bubbled up in his mind from that time. Things he didn't personally remember happening.

Before Jack could say more, they got an alert for another cuff link. That would be three. He had one left he could send.

"I'll alert the team," Mel said.

"And I'll"—he hesitated—"study my past."

CHAPTER 12

*A*lice was surprised when they returned her and Tom to the house, not to the hangar. There was no sign of a guard inside the house, probably because of the bug things listening. Tom checked all the rooms, then returned to the hall and gave a shrug.

"Are you hungry?" she asked and when he nodded, they headed for the kitchen. He helped her prepare the food, and to clean up when they were done eating. That alone helped her believe he really was from the future. She couldn't remember a time when her father had picked up a cup after he used it. When the water had been running, Tom had leaned close to whisper, "I think they are trying to figure out what you did or took."

This made her chuckle. They hadn't seen that coming.

After they were finished, they went to the living room. It was a sparse, sad place. The furniture had been there when they arrived and seldom used after. They didn't get many guests after the first flurry when they arrived and it slowed quickly. Her father was not...convivial. The couch was against the back wall, so they could see out the open drapes where the storm still turned the skies a sullen gray. They sat there together, at first simply holding hands. All the words they'd both said were there in the air between them, but in a good way. She couldn't think of more to add, which was good since they couldn't speak without being overheard.

However, she wasn't used to sitting and doing nothing. She had books she could read—would it bother her she had unfinished books? She considered her stack by her bed and decided that, right now, she didn't care. She was tired. Weary in a way she'd never been before, but at peace, too. Her head drooped and she jerked.

Tom's arm went around her and he urged her close. "Use my shoulder. It's nice and broad."

She liked hearing the deep rumble of his voice in her ear and was sorry when he fell silent. But his heart beat steady and strong, and his chest rose and fell with reassuring regularity. She didn't know when she slipped into sleep, but a stir in the hall entry brought her out of it with a jerk. The light was muted coming in the front window, and she saw the car that had picked her father up pulling away.

She was upright, but still close to Tom, when the door opened and her father looked in. Disapproval deepened the austerity of his expression. He avoided looking at Tom, however.

"You left quite a mess at the office, Alice."

"Packing is a messy business." She could have added more, but she was learning, and she had learned from her father not to say too much. It lowered the risk of being caught out in a lie. A lie. It would be a relief to be done with that. The truth wanted to come out, so much her chest hurt until she talked herself off that ledge. Truth right now could hurt Tom, too. So she compressed her lips and waited.

He looked around. "You haven't started here."

"No." Did he even know how to pack a suitcase? Pain flickered in his face and she felt... "You're not leaving until Sunday."

Now it was his lips that compressed. How long had it been

since he'd smiled? But she knew exactly how long. He hadn't smiled since her mother died. She straightened and rubbed her face, trying to erase the remnants of sleep. She was getting maudlin and that didn't go well with her new resolve. Self-pity? Out the door. Regrets? Gone, too. Only living until…well…quit thinking and just live. She inhaled deep enough it steadied her again. Restored the calm her father had disturbed.

Her father hesitated, then came forward and sat across from them. His gaze never strayed in Tom's direction.

"The test flight on Saturday," he said. "You need to cancel it."

So he'd tried to cancel it. It took effort not to smile her satisfaction. Whoever had scheduled it had more clout than Phillips.

"I'm just the secretary. I don't have the power to schedule it, or cancel it," she said, yet again. Who had scheduled it, she wondered. She'd have liked to thank them.

"You…we won't get fuel delivery."

"Then why are you worried about the test flight?" she asked. "I don't think your financier friend wants a furor, though. It seems to me it would just be wiser to go ahead with it."

"Alice…" Eyes and tone were pleading.

A year ago, even a week ago, it would have made a difference. But now she knew he pled for himself and he knew—he *knew*—it wasn't for her good. She wasn't sure he had, or could, think along those lines.

What do you want?

Tom was the only person in her life who'd asked her that question without a food choice being involved.

"I don't have the power to do anything and you know it, but if the *Ray* flies on Saturday, I won't mind," she said, speaking to her father and the listening ears.

* * *

THE STORM BROKE JUST before dawn on Friday. Rain lashed the windows with a ferocity that brought Granger out of his restless sleep with a jerk. He fumbled for a light to check the time. Who knew he'd miss his glow-in-the-dark watch? The light stabbed into his eyes, and when they adjusted and he saw the time, he fell back on the pillow with a groan. He closed his eyes, trying to fall back into unconsciousness, but his brain was already in the "on" position.

He kicked the covers back, grabbed his gear, and made his way to the bathroom. For a bath. He'd have given a lot for a shower right then. Once he was dressed, he made his way to the kitchen and started the coffee pot, then he leaned forward and pulled back the curtain, watching the way the rain slapped the glass and then tracked down. It was kind of a relief, the sight. It also blurred the moments when time flickered in and out of view.

He didn't remember reading about a storm, but he hadn't been looking at the weather reports. If he made it back, he needed to amend his process, that was for sure. He heard sounds of movement, doors opening and closing and then the tub being filled. Was it Alice or her old man? The question was answered when Alice slipped in, holding the door so it wouldn't swing, before turning to him. Her gaze tracked past him to the rain-washed window.

"I was going to see if you wanted to go for a walk," she said, smiling wryly.

There'd been no television in their front room, which was not a surprise, given how new they were to the average home. And why would either of them want one? He had a feeling that sitting and staring at anything, for them, meant thinking, not watching.

He crossed to her, eased her gently in his arms and kissed her. It wasn't talking, he told himself, for as long as he was able to think while his lips pressed to hers. Okay, they might hear the heavy breathing, he thought when he lifted his head. He wanted to wrap his arms around her and trigger the recall. He wouldn't let go, he told himself, even as the sounds of her father stirring in his room pushed them apart.

The silence could not be termed comfortable when the old man joined them. It helped Granger to work on breakfast next to Alice, but it also hurt. He could picture this in his place and in his time. She'd made him promise to heal and he had given his word, but he wasn't sure he believed he could. Oh, he knew the pain would get less, but how did anyone get over a woman like Alice?

They cleaned up side-by-side with the storm providing contrast to the pauses in the storm when the silence was broken only by the sound of the clock on the stove ticking out the slow seconds going by, and the click of dishes against each other.

As Alice finished hanging the dish towel over the stove handle, Merriweather cleared his throat. "Mr. Phillips wants… requests your presence at the hangar. He's sending a car."

Granger had a feeling he wasn't included in the…request.

"We're going to get the *Ray* ready for the test," Alice said, serenely.

The old man's lips tightened, but he nodded. "The car is coming at eight."

* * *

THE HANGAR FELT PARTICULARLY dreary to Alice when she shook the rain off her protective hat and shrugged out of her raincoat. She felt chilled, though not as bad as if she'd worn her "dress code" suit. She'd put on the pants and sweater with…intent…she decided, and not just because of the weather. She was working, not pretending today.

There was a light in the office, but she ignored it, heading directly for the *Ray*. Granger walked with her, not ahead or behind, but with her.

One day.

She wondered how many hours she had, but it was pointless

to waste time on that question. She walked up and pressed her palm to the *Ray*, then began to walk its length. She circled the whole plane once, then began a slower, more thorough survey of the exterior. The landing gear concerned her the most. It hadn't collapsed when they went they landed on the dry lake bed. It was supposed to handle jolts, she reminded herself, climbing underneath to look. She saw Tom's legs as he moved around the *Ray*, too. She heard someone approaching. The legs were sheathed in black pants, the shoes a mud-splattered black, too.

The man in black? Tom had called him that, as if the phrase had some other meaning. She crawled out from under and straightened to face him. He wasn't wearing sunglasses. That would be stupid on such a dark day, but it modified his sinister level, reducing him to a man in a suit.

A dark day. And yet she felt as if she stood in the light. She squared her shoulders, planted her feet, and watched him close on her.

There was something in his gaze that was different. An unease perhaps? She didn't know him well enough to know.

"May I speak with you in the office, Miss Merriweather?" His tone was formal and definitely lacked the arrogant edge of his past conversations with her. His gaze tracked past her, probably to Tom. "Alone?"

She waited, feeling the shift of power flickering between them, then gave a brief nod. He stepped back and indicated the way, as if she didn't know. There was no flare of irritation, though. She was in a different place today and had no desire to let him shift her from it.

Inside, she stopped briefly, noting the chaos had changed somewhat from the way she'd left it. At a guess, it had been further searched. She stepped around a stack of boxes to reach the desk, then stood behind it, her hands clasped lightly in front of her.

He pushed the door almost closed, then went to the other side of the desk. He towered over her, but this time that didn't intimidate her and he knew it.

He was silent for at least a minute, trying to shift the balance back, she suspected. She didn't move, just studied him with a new level of dispassion.

He was a good-looking man. Strange, she'd not noticed that before. Strong of body and face, with intense eyes and a firm mouth over a no-nonsense chin. She'd noted the intelligence in his gaze before, but now she added it to the rest and realized that, had she been completely different, she might have been attracted to him. Perhaps if she'd really just been her father's secretary?

"Alice." He finally broke the silence, a huff of frustration in his voice. "Where is it?"

Alice arched her brows and considered rebuking him for using her first name. Instead, she let her eyes and her silence do it.

"Miss Merriweather," he gritted out. He turned and took steps away, but the size of the room didn't allow for pacing. He turned back. "We…should be…dealing better together."

That raised her brows further. What did he mean by that?

He sighed again and asked in a softer tone, "Where are they?"

She considered bluffing—pretending ignorance—but it felt wrong, it felt as if it denied her new understanding of herself and who she was. In some way, it felt as if it denied Tom, too, at least the things she'd learned from him.

"I only took from this place what was mine to take," she said.

His lips twisted. "I'll admit I miscalculated." He looked away and then his gaze came back harder. "According to the contracts your father signed, the research belongs to your backer, who sold their interest to…"

"To?" She inserted into the pause.

"To the people who sent me here. They own it."

But not before Sunday, she guessed or he could have stopped the test flight.

"Taking it is an act of…theft."

He brought the word out reluctantly. She could see that.

"Once the *Ray* has its test flight, I'll tell you where it is." He wouldn't be happy when he found out it was gone—if she lived to tell him. The shadow was still there, but she felt as if she stood in a circle of light. Had her belief she'd die tomorrow wavered? She didn't think so. But she wasn't afraid. Did she want more time? Of course, but she'd received more in the last week than she ever expected. She was grateful for that. It was…enough. It would have to be enough.

"I suppose you want your Major to fly it," he scoffed.

She stared at him. "Your pilot can fly with him. I just want it to fly."

She could tell he considered this, then he gave a rough shake of his head.

"Don't do this," he warned. "You don't know…this will be… bad for *you*. I am trying to help you."

Her lips twisted slightly, as she considered how to respond. This felt as if he knew more, too. Did it make him a time traveler? A time tamperer? She didn't know and she didn't dare let him know she knew what she knew. "I believe you are," she said, surprising him. "But if the *Ray* doesn't fly tomorrow…"

"You could go to jail," he pointed out.

She gestured around her. "Jail?"

He might have started to get it, or perhaps he sensed her resolve.

"So be it," he said. "I wish…" He gave a vague wave of both hands, then turned and left.

She almost felt sorry for him. He was, perhaps, not used to being beaten by a woman. If she had won. She looked at the clock on the wall and figured the hours left in this day. She should not forget that Saturday began at midnight, and Tom didn't know what time of day…

Outside, the storm hit the sides of the hangar with more fury.

She had the oddest urge to tell it—either hangar or storm—that it would be okay. That it would all be over soon.

* * *

GRANGER SAW Phillips storm out of the office, but it lost something to the storm outside. It came off petty rather than powerful. Granger waited until he'd passed from sight before he crossed to the office, pushing the door wide.

Alice stood there in the crappy light, her gaze coming up with a resolve that faded into a smile at the sight of him.

"You okay?"

"I am," she said, looking almost surprised by that. She took a deep breath, then another. "I feel like I can finally...breathe." She glanced around, then her gaze lifted to his. "He said I'll go to jail for theft." She chuckled. "I don't think he's looked closely at this place."

Granger found he could chuckle, then he tensed as time pulsed and he saw...fire licking at this room.

"Are you okay?" she asked, coming round to touch his arm.

She hadn't seen it, or hadn't noticed it in time. He blinked and time settled once more. "Yeah, I'm fine." He glanced around, aware that listening devices could be back. "Let's get some fresh air, oh, I know we can't go outside, but we can stand in the doorway and inhale."

She chuckled. "Okay."

She was quiet as they walked down the short hall. He opened the door, then put his arm around her as cold air accepted the invite to join them.

"It doesn't look as bad," he said. "Storm might be moving off."

"That's good," she said. "Our test flight is scheduled for noon." She hesitated. "Do you know...when..."

Granger hesitated, then said, "Sometime tomorrow night. That's all I know."

Her shoulders rose and fell. She was quiet for several seconds, as the rain splattered against the road. Across from him, he noticed a couple of guys standing just inside the doorway of their hangar, smoking. While he watched, they tossed their butts out into the rain and turned away, closing their door. She shivered.

"You're getting chilled," he said.

"Yes" she admitted. As she turned, she lifted her eyes to his. "Thank you."

He nodded, hugging her briefly before letting her go, and following her back inside.

* * *

THERE WAS no sign of her father, either in the office or around the *Ray*. Alice wasn't quite sure what to make of it. She did know she needed to keep busy. She went to the storage closet and put on her coveralls, lending Tom a pair as well. She found the radio still there and turned it on, turning the dial until she found some music.

As she moved away from the radio, she felt a pang, a longing for it to just be nighttime, a guy and a girl. Her feet wanted to dance. Her hands wanted to rest on his shoulders while they swayed to the sultry crooning. Instead of machine oil and storm, she longed to smell man and aftershave. But after last night, neither of them smelled that great. She almost chuckled at the thought.

"Heart of my Heart" began to play, and she realized—though it had been simmering below the surface—that she couldn't let Tom fly with her. She couldn't let him die with her. It still felt odd to feel the certainty of both living and dying. Perhaps her mind couldn't quite accept death when it wasn't looming over her. But she could see her life going forward from this place, going forward without Tom. Whatever that meant, she couldn't let him take her place. It was easy for her to tell him to move on, get over her and love again. It was easier for men, though he'd denied it. But she knew that she had less chance of finding someone anyway, so why not hold him in her heart as her one, true love if she happened to survive the night?

She stared at the *Ray* now, seeing it with different eyes. How did she make happen what needed to happen? Two pilots might be needed to board—if Phillips had added his guy to the roster—but only she was going to fly it. It did increase the risk, not having a capable backup, but she doubted Phillips' pilot knew much about the *Ray*. He could sabotage the flight and eject, or disrupt something so they were forced to land.

Well, she'd designed both the suits and helped construct the *Ray*. If she couldn't get it to do what she wished, she deserved her fate.

"What's the…plan?" Tom asked, coming to stand at her side as the music moved between them. He kept his voice low, she assumed to make it harder for any listening devices to hear them.

She looked at him, letting her gaze do most of the talking. "I want to check for damage from our landing on the dry bed. It's probably fine, but I'd like to make sure."

He nodded, and once again, they started going over the *Ray*, looking for signs of tampering or issues from the hard landing. She wasn't sure how much time had passed. She did know, as they opened panels and found no signs of tampering, that time… twitched or flickered. Instead of flinching from the signs, she started studying the instances, trying to see through them to… some when? Perhaps, she decided, she looked for clues or signs, so she'd know when. It was probably not wise, but she found she couldn't look away or stop trying to process those moments that had to be the future. The past? It was easy to see and remember what had happened here.

"What do you think you'll find, Alice?" Tom asked.

She blinked and looked away from the panel where Tom had found the device before.

"Trouble," she said, "though I'm not sure why. I'm sure it will find me." And she laughed.

And as if her words had triggered it, she heard the sound of boots outside.

She exchanged a look with Tom, who looked as surprised as she felt and then crawled toward the hatch and dropped down. By the time the boots reached the main hangar, Alice and Tom were waiting by the *Ray* as Phillips and two MPs came into view. Phillips signaled for them to wait, then came forward.

"Last chance, Miss Merriweather," he said.

She held his gaze long enough for hope to filter into his eyes, then held out her wrists in mute surrender. He stared at her hands for long enough for her arms to get tired and then he stepped back.

"Into the office," he ordered. "Don't let them leave or approach the aircraft."

* * *

JACK COULDN'T BELIEVE what Granger had loaded onto the cuff link storage. He stared at Mel, shook his head, then went back to studying the images, flipping through some of them quickly, always slowing down for the schematics.

The time tremors had slowed to almost imperceptible and their board had stopped looking like a river ran over it. It didn't inspire confidence because there was so much energy in the air around them. It felt as if a storm gathered inside this controlled space—which didn't feel that controlled, Jack had to acknowledge rather wryly. He'd been going through his papers and writings from the time between. It was a strange and unsettling experience to read entries, to feel a sense of familiarity but at the same time to not remember writing it.

"How's the headache?" Mel asked with a sly grin.

"I need more meds," he said. He swiveled his chair and took

her hand, trying not to hold on too tight. He loved the feel of her hands. They were strong, capable, but feminine. Those three words summed her up—with a heavy dose of stubborn. She did not give up, which was how she ended up starring in a show about not giving up. Looking at her now, he still couldn't quite believe all the things she'd done, including the one he'd sent her to do. How had he done it? But if he hadn't...

This confusion of thought wasn't logical. It was an emotional reaction from a guy who wasn't supposed to be all about his feelings. Looking at her now, he could still call up the memory of the first time he'd seen her when she walked into that pub in World War II England, well, the first time he remembered seeing her. His old-dude self had seen her before that.

As if she sensed the change in him, she turned and placed her hand over his. She still made his heart stutter with a single touch.

"Is...love...enough?" The words squeezed out of a throat tight with love—and fear.

She was quiet, so quiet he thought he heard his heart thumping. She looked down at their clasped hands.

"If time rips us apart?" She blew out a breath. "I don't know, but from what I've felt and observed...love makes a difference. It alters us. It works with what we were and what we can be and makes us...able to be better." She paused. "So in that sense, yes, love is enough."

"What if we forget?"

"I'd like to think that somewhere inside, we won't ever forget, but—" She sagged forward suddenly, her head against his chest until he could free his hands to hold her close. "But all we can do is hold on to each other and hope."

And there, holding her and being held by her, he remembered. It wasn't the man he'd met but the wife. Or rather, he'd overheard a snatch of conversation...and looked up the man after the war. Or later? He blinked as the headache ramped up... the memory flickered, slipping just out of reach. He'd done something—in that time that hadn't happened—learned something...

And that was when the time attack started up again. It hit the bunker so hard, their chairs skidded several feet before he managed to get his feet braced to stop them slamming into the wall. But that wasn't the worst part. For several seconds, the longest of his life, he felt Mel fade from his arms...

CHAPTER 13

Someone brought them food and eventually another cot. It was, Granger thought, an interesting choice for the time, forcing them to spend the night together. Not that it was in any way conducive to physical contact of an intimate sort. He was certain they'd restored the bugs and this time he made no attempt to remove them. He and Alice had both had their say. The talking was done. The important talking, he amended. He would have liked to chat with her, the lighthearted kind where you learned about favorite books, colors, movies, music...

But the sixty-six years that divided their interests created an impassable divide and not just because someone might be listening. All they really had in common was this single week—and two hearts. He shifted uncomfortably at this thought. It wasn't like him to get lyrical about feelings, though he had been known to get effusive about schematics. He'd even, he recalled wryly, been dangerously enthusiastic about "managing" time travel.

It was always, Jack had warned him, the human factor that will get you. He hadn't elucidated further, but he hadn't needed to. He and Mel were together. But Granger hadn't understood, nor had he expected any human factor. He was a scientist on a scientific endeavor.

He stared up at the ceiling he couldn't see, while listening to Alice's even breathing from the other cot. *Delusional much?* he asked himself scathingly. And still he searched for a better way out. He was a *scientist.* He should be able to think his way to a solution. Because what scientist hadn't been able to think their way to a solution in less than a week?

His brain threw this at him, calling into question his logic. But his heart? It refused to concede defeat.

He could hear the wall clock ticking and he couldn't see it because it didn't glow in the dark—yet another thing to adjust to in his time. He didn't know when the night passed into early Saturday morning, but it felt as if he sensed every second of it. Until finally, thankfully, he slipped into sleep.

* * *

PALE LIGHT FELL across Alice's face, bringing her out of what had been a light and restless sleep. At least, she had slept some. She blinked slowly at the vague shape of the ceiling, wondering how the light had found its way to this windowless room. She hitched herself up on an elbow and saw that the door was standing partially open.

Well, that was creepy. Who had looked in on them while they slept? She looked and found Tom's cot empty. He might have left it open for her, she supposed. Less creepy. She would go with that hypothesis, she decided.

She sat up and swung her legs to the floor, feeling that odd sense of disorientation she'd felt when time went into flux the last few episodes. Or she sat up too fast. She waited for a clearing of whatever it was, then rose and made her way to the lavatory. Phillips had not allowed them any personal items, but she'd spent many a night here and at least had a toothbrush and a comb. It would not be wonderful to spend her last day on earth in the same clothes she'd worn yesterday, but it was what it was.

She'd half expected to find Tom occupying the bathroom, but it was empty. A frisson of unease tracked down her back. Had he left? He hadn't said exactly when he'd return to the future, so it could have happened. But he'd seemed to expect to be here for the flight.

It was possible that Phillips had removed him from play. It was what she'd wanted, just not this soon. Phillips wouldn't know or care about her longings or timing. He'd been working to narrow her choices down to the point of accepting *his* choice. And now he believed he'd succeeded—a belief she'd encouraged, she had to admit. What would it be like to be free to not deceive, to not be constantly on her guard in a battle of wills with only her freedom on the line?

She stared at her pale face in the old mirror. *You've been alone before. And it won't be long this time. If I can just fly...*

She cut off the thought. He might be able to block her from flying. She couldn't engage in pretense. She might die without flying. Well, she wouldn't have to live with it for long. She finished doing what she could and left the bathroom. There was no sign of the MPs who had stood guard by the door last night, and walked them to and from the lavatory—an exercise in embarrassment. She went back to the main hangar and stared at the *Ray*. If it was going to fly, she'd know soon. The ground crew would show up. Or not.

She turned back to the office, intent on getting a chair to sit on for the wait, and heard the low murmur of voices. Outside? She went down the hall and turned the knob, half shocked when it opened. She couldn't decide if she was surprised or not to find Tom out there talking to an airman who was finishing up a cigarette. She caught a whiff of the pungent smoke on a gust of wind and then it was gone. She hadn't realized how much she needed the fresh air against her face and inside her lungs.

The storm was gone, the sun low but climbing fast in the light blue sky. And Tom? He had the shadow of a beard on his face, a look that was not…unpleasing, she decided. As if he sensed her presence, Tom turned and gave her a wide smile.

"Smith here is in charge of your ground crew this morning," he said easily, his gaze complicated.

But there was, she decided, no warning in there. Perhaps he'd hoped the test would be called off. She couldn't blame him. He still had hope.

She went toward the airman and held out her hand. With a short pause, possibly of surprise, Airman Smith tossed his cigarette and took her hand.

"Thank you," she said.

"You're welcome, ma'am." He had a Southern accent and they chatted for a few minutes about his home and how he ended up at Muroc. Finally, with a sigh, Smith glanced around. "Better go check on my crew. Excuse me, ma'am, sir."

"Of course," Alice said, waiting until he was out of sight to look around. "Do you know what happened?"

"I woke up and we were alone. It was very shocking," Tom said with a wicked grin, "leaving you alone with me all night."

She had to smile at him. It was odd.

"I wonder…" she began, but didn't finish. There were many things to wonder. Would Phillips' pilot show up? If he didn't, how did she keep Tom from flying? Would Phillips or her dad come? But Tom knew some, if not all, the wonders and what ifs. There was no need to detail them to him. She glanced down the road and just as she started to turn away, a jeep came around the corner. It accelerated in their direction, then pulled to a stop in front of them. The passenger was the pilot from the other day. He hopped out and sketched a salute.

"Major Grayson?"

Tom tensed, then nodded.

"CO wants to see you." The man jerked his head toward the jeep. "Airman will take you to HQ."

Alice saw Tom's shoulders tense, but there was nothing he could do but go. Even if it was a trick, he had to obey orders.

He touched her hand. "I'll be back," he promised.

Her smile seemed to reassure him because he clambered into the passenger seat of the jeep. His gaze stayed with her until it had made a U-turn and sped away.

Only then did Alice direct her attention to the pilot. "I don't think I caught your name," she said.

"Jones, ma'am," he said, giving her another salute.

Not too informative, though his uniform indicated he was a Captain.

"I'll show you where to suit up," Alice said. He held the door open for her, and then fell in behind her as she led him down the short hall. Back inside the hangar, the doors had been opened and the *Ray* was gone. She caught a glimpse of it being towed toward the flight line.

"Nice-looking craft," Jones said, pausing briefly.

Alice nodded. "Your flight suit is over here." She opened the door and gestured inside. "You'll want to change on your own."

He nodded and went inside, closing the door. Alice bit her lip, glancing over her shoulder at the *Ray*, then looked at her watch.

When the door opened again, he looked rueful. "This is an unusual flight suit, ma'am."

She smiled at him primly, feeling her insides clench. "It is, and my father isn't here yet to help you finish getting ready. He did say, if you had a problem to wait in the office there. He is on his way."

The captain didn't seem surprised. She showed him the way and was careful to close the door, then quietly eased out the keys and locked him in. Biting her lip, she turned and went back to where the other suit still hung. She'd have to hurry.

* * *

Tom was sure it was a diversion, but he couldn't tell his driver that. He was just following orders. The question was, where had those orders come from? Or rather, who had actually issued them? There was nothing he could do but let the jeep take him away from Alice and the *Ray*. Outside HQ, the jeep stopped.

"Just go inside. CO will see you when he's free," his driver said.

"Is that what you were told?"

The airman looked puzzled. "Yes, sir."

Great. It was Saturday and most likely there'd be no secretary. It was possible the CO wasn't there and didn't plan to be there. But he returned the salute and went inside. As expected, the reception area was empty. According to the clock, he had time to get back before the test, but he heard a voice from the next room. What if the CO had summoned him? His name was on the record as the test pilot—he stiffened. He'd assumed it was on the record. But what if it wasn't?

She needed him, he reminded himself. She couldn't get on the *Ray* without his help...could she? A chill flowed across his skin as his thoughts cleared. What Alice could and couldn't do was not what any of them had believed.

* * *

Alice had had more practice donning the headgear than she'd let on to Tom. Had she foreseen this moment? She trusted him but...he was leaving. And he wanted to protect her. And he was leaving.

Alice had to do this herself, just like so many things in her life she'd had to learn to do for herself. Getting buttoned down in her flight gear was not the hardest task awaiting her. She had to get outside without alerting Jones. And then she had to get on the

Ray and get airborne before anyone realized she was on the plane and Jones wasn't.

She walked softly toward the open doors, but there was so sound from the office. Jones wouldn't be worried yet. Why would he when there was at least an hour before their scheduled liftoff.

She gestured to two ground crewmen to close the doors. After a minute, she crossed to a ground vehicle waiting to carry the pilot to the flight line. She used the screech and rumble of metal doors coming together to help disguise her voice. She tried not to tense. Jones had no reason to think that closing the doors was alarming. The crewman started the vehicle and then they didn't need to talk as they headed after the *Ray*. There was still time before Jones might get restive. *Time.* If this was a race, it was the slowest in history, she decided with a twist of her lips.

No sign of Phillips yet, or her father.

The back of her neck tingled but she didn't dare look back. When they reached the flight line, the jet engines were already awake, softly whining. She headed for the already open hatch and climbed inside, feeling better now that she was out of sight. And that no one had yet appeared to try to stop her.

It could still happen. The *Ray*'s engines needed time to spin up.

She waited until the crew was busy and closed the hatch, locking it down so it couldn't be opened. She sagged for a moment in relief, then gave herself a shake. She wasn't off the ground yet. She took a steadying breath and clambered up to the pilot's seat. She'd sat here many times, in the dark of the night, but never before with intent.

Could she get the *Ray* off the ground? She thought she could. She knew how to take off and land with much smaller aircraft. She'd had a chance to feel the *Ray* going airborne with Tom. But that had been a surprise. This would be on purpose.

She started her checklist, the engines spinning up toward enough rpms to ignite. It seemed as if the plane settled into the runway. If she let herself go there, she could ponder all the reasons Tom had offered about why flying fought against human instinct. Even as a scientist, she felt how unnatural it was. She reminded herself that she'd flown smaller aircraft multiple times. And she lived on a base where flying happened all the time. If she panicked now…well, she couldn't. She was in it now. There was no going back.

What did she have to lose that wasn't already on the line? When the choice was death or death, it made the decision less weighty, though not less terrifying now that she was on the flight line, with the runway stretching out in front of her almost endlessly. It shouldn't make a difference that Tom wasn't here, but it did. The plane felt bigger and less welcoming. Maybe the *Ray*, or time, knew the odds against her, too.

She strapped in and hooked up to her oxygen and power supply for her suit. And then she started her instrument check. She didn't want to use the radio, but she needed to know when the balloon went up out there. A crackle when she plugged in told it was live.

She also kept an eye on the area around their hangar for signs of activity. If Tom made it back, or if Phillips realized…she'd need to take off. She checked her rpms. It was close.

She heard the equipment being pulled away and one of the ground crew used the radio to tell her they'd done their part and were leaving. She thanked them, trying to pitch her voice low, though she knew the radio would disguise her voice to some extent. Her tow vehicle had started back as soon as the tow line had been released, so he was already halfway to the hangar. Now the other support vehicles began to trundle back as well. She checked her watch. Once the crew got back to the hangar, someone could start to put things together.

Her window of opportunity had always been small, and now she felt it shrinking with each second that passed. The rising whine of the jet engines was both comforting and terrifying.

With one eye on her rpms, she began entering presets into her own engine's flight control. She needed to make a fast climb to activation altitude and then...

"Flight," her radio crackled. "A Mr. Phillips wants to talk to you."

To Alice? Or Jones? There was no way to know. That was it, then. Time had run out. Thank goodness the engine was ready.

She switched the radio off, took a deep breath and applied easy force to the stick. The *Ray* began to roll forward. It felt different than she'd felt from the copilot's position, though she couldn't put her finger on exactly why.

The familiar whine of the engines helped ease the strangeness of being in control. As the plane began to accelerate, at first the sense of power felt heady and freeing to one who'd been so earth-bound for so long, but she quickly realized that holding the plane steady in the center of the runway was harder than she'd expected. It was very different from the Link Trainer or the small planes she'd flown before.

With equal parts fear and terror, she increased the speed, pushing back thoughts of failure. It would get easier when she was airborne. She hoped.

The rising shriek of the *Ray*'s lift engines was muted by her headgear, but she felt the pressure pushing her back in her seat. Her suit inflated some to accommodate the pressure. At least it knew what it was doing.

"It's gonna get worse," she murmured. She checked her ground speed and increased push on the throttle. The mountains ahead felt like they were rushing toward her. She knew exactly how long the runway was, but it felt too short right now.

Her ground speed was good. Against a sense that the plane was too big for her to make fly, she pulled the stick to bring the nose up off the ground.

It was too big. She was too small. It wasn't going to work—

The feel of the plane changed as the rear wheels left the

ground. The plane still felt heavy and reluctant, but the jostling had stopped. The mountains rushed closer. She watched the airspeed and pulled back on the stick, but not too much. She couldn't afford a stall now.

She flipped the switch to retract the landing gear, heard it grinding up as the wheels tucked up inside, and noted with relief that the three green indicator lights turned red.

There was no need for a turn yet. She just needed to get high as fast as the laws of aerodynamics let her. She monitored her instruments. Brought the nose up some more. She checked her fuel gauges. She could only use her lift engines until half her fuel was gone in case she needed it for landing. She tried not to think about that now.

Her gaze moved back and forth between airspeed, altitude and fuel.

Now.

She shut down her lift engines and paused for a few seconds, stunned by the silence and the emptiness of the skies around her. It felt like she could see forever, but the slowing of her ascent recalled her to what she meant to do next.

She activated her main engine, using the first preset. There was a pause—a long pause—while the engine powered up. Her engine made no sound, so it must be her imagination that it seemed as if the air itself shimmered, sending prickles along the back of her neck. Did she see or just imagine static electricity dancing across the surface of the canopy? She almost reached forward to shut the engine off but—

The force of the engine's thrust smashed her into the seat, blackened the edges of her vision, and tried to force her lungs up and out her throat. She felt the suit adjusting, or trying to adjust, and the pressure on her legs eased. What helped even more was that the brief transit stopped.

Despite the engine shutoff, the pressure on her chest didn't ease. Her suit must be forcing air into her lungs. She'd built it to do that at high altitude. Warmth began to run up her legs, torso and arms. High altitude. How high?

She took several calming breaths and then blinked to clear her vision. She'd preset this transit for four seconds and it had almost knocked her out. She checked her instruments and realized she needed to level off. This let her put off the moment of realization, but she had to look.

The brief transit had taken her to nearly eighty thousand feet.

That was almost too much to process, so she turned her attention to her accelerometer. The glass front of it was shattered. She reached out and tapped it, but it appeared to be dead. Hopefully, she'd be able to tell how many Gs when she accessed the data recorder that was part of the ejectable cockpit. There was also a voice recorder, though it felt like it took enough effort to just breathe. She had no desire to speak yet. Was the recent G-force or the altitude giving her trouble? She'd read papers about both, but she had no way to tell if what she'd just experienced was more or less than others' experiences. She had nothing to compare this suit with other flight suits, but it felt as if it had provided enough protection. At least she hadn't passed out.

She made sure that her data recorder was still working, checked her oxygen supply's flow once more, and then sagged back in her seat, elation pushing back the ache in her head and in her chest.

It worked. *Her engine worked.*

She was eighty thousand feet above the earth.

She gathered her thoughts, and then, trying for a scientific tone, said, "The *Manta Ray* achieved eighty thousand feet with a four-second activation of the experimental engine. G-force was…considerable but short-lived. I can see"—her voice faltered for a moment or two—"I can see the rim of the world and also the remnants of clouds from the storm we experienced yesterday are moving off to the east."

She maintained her heading with slight motions of the stick.

The *Ray* felt sluggish. She studied the wings, noting a thin coating of ice on the wings. That had happened with the model plane, too. But there was no moisture at this altitude. Had she collected it during her transit? Would it affect her ability to control the *Ray*?

"The silence with the lift engines off is...remarkable. I'm going to leave this recorder going for the duration of the flight, in hopes it will be recovered and prove useful as a scientific aid if I don't survive the next transit. The G-forces were intense even with the protection provided by my flight suit and limiting transit time. I am also experiencing difficulty breathing, though my suit has helped me pressure breathe."

Even as she tried for a scientific attitude, the view finally grabbed her, catching words in her throat as she tried to see it all. This high the detail of the terrain was blurred, flattened even. She noted the pattern of the clouds below her. She was on top of the clouds. Ahead, the rim where the Earth curved drew her gaze again. Higher beckoned, tempted...it was almost close enough to touch.

The silence was soothing and yet eerie in this vastly empty space. Momentum carried the *Ray* forward but it felt like world spun below while she sat stationary above it.

It was time to consider her next move. She'd proved her engine worked. She'd flown higher and faster. She could call it good and try to land. *Try.* Could she? Honesty compelled her to admit she wasn't sure she could land the *Ray*. Taking off had taxed her and the thought of aiming this craft at the ground was...daunting. And to attempt it, she had to get the *Ray* back down to landing altitude so she could reengage the lift engines. If she could. She'd heard it was hard to air-start fuel engines. She knew they needed more oxygen than was available at this altitude.

Since she was up and not sure she could get down, she could

test her engine further. In the interests of science, of course. Not because she wanted to postpone the moment of…truth.

Death or death.

She scanned her instruments, aware that the *Ray* would soon lose altitude. She tried small adjustments, attempting to get the feel of the plane, comparing it to the Link Trainer. Mostly, it was not even close. It was too bad she wouldn't get the chance to adjust the Trainer, based on what she was learning now.

So she'd gone higher with four seconds of activation but could she go further faster?

Could the *Ray* handle more Gs?

Could her suit—and could she—handle more Gs?

She'd debated with herself for half the night. What would she do if her engine worked?

She could do a second longer burn toward another airfield where the *Ray* could land—assuming she could land it.

She could try to spiral down toward Muroc, and attempt a landing. She assumed they'd clear their airspace for her, so the risk of a mid-air collision with another plane was lower here.

What she really wanted to do was a longer "burn" and keep going until she ran out of space or fuel. She could point her nose at the North Pole.

She could even point the nose at the Moon.

She could fly anywhere. Or she could figure out how to get back.

It felt good to be so far away from the watching eyes and listening ears of Phillips, and who knew who else. It felt good to be above all the machinations and politics and expectations. It felt good to be alone—except for the part that missed Tom. But Tom was leaving. Tom had to leave, he had to go back to his own time and place.

So what did she have to go back to?

Death or death.

She considered this question and her "options," she hoped, with dispassion and not self-pity.

She knew what she'd done, but did anyone else? In other tests, there were planes deployed to assist in tracking and to verify results. As she'd previously noted, she was alone up here.

The only way to prove the *Ray*'s main engine worked was to get it and its recorded data back to Muroc. Because she was almost certain that even if she survived, and the *Ray* didn't, no one would believe anything she said anyway. Would four seconds of transit be enough to convince anyone of the efficacy of her engine?

She had time to do one more test of her engine before she went back. She'd been airborne about fifteen, maybe twenty minutes. She checked her fuel and oxygen levels. They were still within safe range. There was time…a little before…she almost laughed. She had time to fly before….*Death or death.*

All right then.

* * *

THERE WAS nothing Granger could do. Alice had turned off her radio before she took off. It was something to see the *Ray* rise, smoke marking its track against the blue of the sky. It kept going, the nose slowly tracking up more and more, as if it were a rocket ship on its way to the moon.

Phillips had an almost self-satisfied smirk on his mouth. Didn't he know—no, he didn't know. He still thought his pilot was on board. He thought the *Ray*, and Alice's data, was his. He'd kept the bargain. The *Ray* had flown. The bargain hadn't included the *Ray* returning. Didn't he realize his pilot wouldn't know how to use Alice's engine? Maybe or maybe not, Granger conceded. He didn't know what Phillips knew.

He still had hope she wouldn't use it—he heard the sonic boom and heard the tech say the plane was off scope.

She'd done it.

"Did it explode?" someone asked.

There was no way to tell the difference between a sonic boom and an explosion, so why did he believe it was the *Ray* breaking the sound barrier, not the *Ray*—and Alice—dying? But—and this was almost the harder thought—successful activation of the engine didn't mean the *Ray* or Alice would survive. He recalled the ice that had coated the model plane. How would that affect the plane as it came out of wherever her engine sent the craft. If she got high enough there wouldn't be moisture for icing. But would she know about the other hazards of high-altitude flight, such as pressure breathing?

The chatter around him amped up when they located the pilot of record locked in the office at the hangar and they realized that Alice—a woman—was flying the *Ray*.

If it was still flying.

Next to him, Phillips paced, muttering what Granger assumed to be profanities. Alice's old man stood staring at the empty sky, his expression blank.

Someone asked Merriweather where the plane was. He stared at them for a long moment, then shook his head and directed his attention back at the sky.

He wouldn't be able to see anything. There was nothing to see. If the engine had worked, then she was far away. If not, they wouldn't know until, and unless, someone found debris. Identifiable debris. Would Granger find out what happened when he returned to the future? Alice had changed her future, or so he assumed. She could make it back. The *Ray* could make it back, and both could vanish in a fire sometime tonight, which would be changing her future some, but had she changed it enough? Had this flight been erased from the future he remembered? And could Alice land the *Ray*? Could she have learned enough in the Link Trainer to bring it down?

He'd underestimated her before. He wouldn't do it again, even if his heart and his mind gave her long odds. If she asked for help getting talked down? Still long odds, but slightly better.

Phillips finally quit pacing and indicated somewhat forcefully that Granger should join him apart from the others. Since he felt he could take the guy, he followed him. When Phillips spun to face him, Granger was tense, coiled to act, but it seemed Phillips wanted to talk, not fight.

"Did you know…did you help her?"

Granger shook his head, letting it answer both questions, though he should have realized she'd take advantage of Phillips getting him out of the way. He hesitated, then figured, what the heck? "You helped her do this by getting me out of the way."

"Would you have gone up with her?"

Granger looked up, shading his eyes against the sun, as he considered the question and how best to answer it. "She wasn't going to budge. She had a better chance if I was with her."

It was Phillips' turn to look up now. Granger watched him and decided the guy might be upset about Alice. It made a sort of sense, though it made Granger's gut twist. How could Phillips not feel something for Alice? He'd have to be made out of stone. But that then begged the question, how could he have not known? How could he spend enough time with Alice to care, and still know nothing important about her?

"What can we do?" Phillips finally asked.

"We wait," Granger said. "We wait."

* * *

"I found it," Jack said.

Mel didn't have to ask what "it" was. He hadn't slept for the last twenty-four hours while he searched his past for any sign of a connection to either Merriweather. For all of that time, they'd experienced a variety of time disruptions against their bunker.

"Look." Jack slid his chair over next to hers, one of his diaries extended for her perusal. With a worried glance at his tired face, she took the diary and studied the entry, her gaze drawn first to the name inscribed there: Merriweather.

Only then did she go to the beginning of the entry. It was brief enough to give Jack an excuse for the memory lapse, even if his past weren't complicated by him not having lived a big chunk of it. It actually referenced an article in a scientific magazine that they'd missed in their research. She paused to consider this. Missed, or erased by the time tamperer?

Jack's entry was a notation about finding the article interesting and a hand drawn sketch of something. She looked up.

"I shouldn't have forgotten even without, well, everything," Jack admitted, rubbing his eyes. "It was that article that got me, or old-dude-past me, further along the path to developing my machine."

Mel looked down at the sketch and blinked. "Seriously?" She frowned. "I thought you knew how to do it back, you know, when?" Jack tried to avoid explaining too much to her about his time machine because of her photographic memory. And she hadn't pressed the issue later because she didn't think she could understand it anyway.

"I did, in theory, but the engineering was complicated. Merriweather was an engineer by training. That might have gotten lost in the other stuff. I'm not sure. But he designed the *Manta Ray*..."

Mel opened her mouth to protest, but Jack held up a hand. "We now know that Alice probably designed the engine, but *Manta Ray* was on his drawing board when Alice was still a kid."

That was true, as was the fact that Merriweather was an engineer. But...

"That little drawing was a breakthrough?" She held it up, turning it on its side. It looked...inexplicable, to be honest. A tube with some notes around it and what could have been an equation.

"It wasn't *the* breakthrough," Jack said. "It was a nudge in the direction of the breakthrough. It got me thinking differently.

That led to a series of breakthroughs before the final break-through."

"You? It got *you* thinking differently?"

"Okay, me before. I understand better how hard it was for you when you…rejoined your life. It's weird. I didn't remember this until I read the entry, and then it's, like, of course I remember that." He massaged the back of his neck. "I can see myself making that entry and the sketch. How do you not have a headache all the time?"

The sex definitely helped, but she didn't tell him that. The guy's ego already lived up in the stratosphere. Instead she tapped the page.

"This isn't the plane, this is a bit of an engine, which we now know, well we think we know was Alice's." Okay, now her head was starting to ache as well, or resuming aching.

"Maybe she wrote it and he got the byline," Jack pointed out. "The article was written before they moved to Edwards."

The article could be the reason they got the invite to Edwards. Mel considered the idea. Could such a small thing be making time throw fits? According to Jack, big events could turn on small things. They were learning that the hard way.

She set the diary on her desk and spun around to the face the wall. Had their new knowledge changed anything on their wall of headache-causing events? Out of the corner of her eye, she saw Jack pick up the diary and turn a page further, then flip back several pages. She started to stand and go to the wall, but instead sank back in her chair.

"Jack." She grabbed his arm and shook it without taking her eyes off the wall.

He turned, saw her face and completed his turn, his jaw drop-ping. She realized her jaw was dropped, too, but couldn't do a thing about it. Just like she couldn't do a thing about the…ripple of time…going through their bunker. On the other side of it, their wall flickered in and out of view. But the one thing time did let them see?

Alice Merriweather died in a plane crash.

And Major Tom Grayson was found dead in the desert a week later.

"How"—she couldn't get the question out, but tried again anyway—"how could they find his body in the desert…"

"…when the recall device is supposed to bring him back dead or alive?" Jack finished when she couldn't.

"That," Mel said, her hand finding and gripping Jack's.

"I don't know. It's not supposed to happen unless"—now it was his turn to struggle with getting the words out—"unless someone found it and removed it."

Mel wasn't sure what her expression said, but it couldn't have been good, because Jack pulled her onto his lap and into his arms.

"We'll get through this," he said into her ear.

"Yes," she said and couldn't manage more than that. She clung to him, hoping that told him what she couldn't say. While she wondered what the device might reveal to their enemy about them. Could they hang on tight enough for what might come?

CHAPTER 14

A lice shook her head to clear it as the *Ray* came out of its second main engine activation, and regretted it immediately. The horizon did a dizzy spin for a minute before it settled. Her head ached, too. Altitude? It could be that.

She'd tried just two seconds this time, and level flight. Had she blacked out? She wasn't sure. How much had her specially designed flight suit protected her through both transits? She had no basis for comparison. If she had blacked out, at least she was conscious again. She felt colder, checked her suit's heating settings, then turned it up some more.

She could be experiencing mild shock.

She'd decided to transit west the way she was already going, west away from continental airspace for safety reasons, though she couldn't imagine what craft could share this altitude with her.

Visually, it felt like a good decision. The Pacific Ocean stretched out below her to the rim of the world. Long islands of clouds curved in bands, both thick and thin, ahead of her, and yes, still below. Everything in the sky below her for once, not above.

She could get used to this.

"After a two second activation of my main engine, the *Manta Ray* is out over the Pacific Ocean. I am going to turn back, drop down, and duplicate the activation to return to Muroc."

She sighed at the thought of going back so soon. But if she allowed momentum to carry her forward for too long, it would complicate her calculations for getting back to Muroc. Even a second too much of her engine could shoot her past Muroc, based on what had happened so far.

She started the long, slow turn back the way she'd come. So far her suit was working pretty well. She felt it applying pressure to her legs and pressure from the oxygen going into her lungs. But for some reason the silence made it harder this time. Did she miss the jet engine shriek? Or was this a lot scarier because she was over water? And she was basically gliding through the atmosphere, so turning meant losing altitude.

She kept an eye on her air speed, felt the turn of the *Ray* in the center of her body and kept it coordinated.

Of course, she lost altitude. She had a lot of altitude to lose, but she wanted to stay high for now. A mid-air collusion would be a negative outcome.

As the *Ray* closed on her desired heading, she began to straighten into the course. She prepared to activate the main engine.

The horizon shimmered ahead of her, not unlike the time events on the ground. It couldn't be that, though. It had to be the stress of flying and the Gs maybe.

She scanned her instruments, waiting for the right moment.

She activated her engine once more.

* * *

THE GROUND CREW and the spectators had gradually drifted away as the minutes ticked by. And now only Merriweather and Phillips remained with Granger just outside HQ. Without spoken agreement, they took turns scanning the skies with a set of binoculars that someone had left behind for them. Granger wasn't exactly sure what to look for. Alice's engine didn't use traditional fuel, except during takeoff and landing—assuming she managed to air-start her engines. So what signs in the sky did they look for? And yet still he looked and hoped.

"I didn't mean for this to happen," Phillips said, not looking at Granger or Merriweather.

Granger lowered the binoculars and handed them to Merriweather. "What did you mean to happen?"

To his credit, Phillips didn't flinch away from Granger's hard stare. "You have no idea what's going on here. You come in, and in a few days, think you know it all."

Granger's gaze flicked to the old man, before he said, "I figured out that Alice," he hesitated, then moderated his initial thought—"is an integral part of the team, not just a secretary."

Phillips shot the old man an angry look, but his attention was resolutely focused upwards.

"They kept it very quiet."

"And you wouldn't have believed them if they told you," Granger asserted, not sure it was true to Phillips, even if it was true to the time period.

"How bad is this, Dr. Merriweather?" Phillips moderated his tone with effort. "Miss Merriweather could bail out, could she not?"

"She would only do it as a last resort," Merriweather said, lowering the glasses to direct his pale, haunted stare at Phillips.

Just when Granger thought Phillips wasn't behind the destruction of the *Ray*, the guy made him start to wonder all over again. The other thing he couldn't tell was if Phillips was the time tamperer. There were only three of them there right now, but was that the complete cast of characters? Was someone going to show up tonight? Could tonight be the real time tampering play? Maybe the money man? If not, then one of them was it, one of them was the guy. And yes, he included himself in that group.

"How long," Merriweather brought the words out as if his throat were dry, "has she been aloft?"

At least he still had his optimism, Granger thought ironically. But he understood the question. If the *Ray* worked like the model, it shouldn't take this long. Before he could look at his watch, Phillips beat him to the answer.

"It's been forty minutes, sir."

If her engine did what he thought it could, she could fly to the coast and back by now. Where was she?

* * *

THOUGH THE ACTIVATION had been no longer than the last one, Alice felt this more, or so it seemed. There was another one of those ripples in the horizon that seemed go right through her and the plane.

She was on course, but the light outside didn't look right. It was darker than it should be. The sun behind her was too low for the amount of time that had passed. She checked her instruments, studied the wings, and checked her air speed again. The plane was slowing faster than the last time. She could see it on the instruments. She'd assumed a lot of things in her calculations, she realized. She'd assumed she knew how to adjust for the movement of the larger plane through atmosphere, but did she? She needed help from the ground to get down, but at what point would she be in range of Muroc? She needed to stay above collision altitude until she got a fix on her location. And she needed to get low enough to show up on radar and attempt to restart her fuel-powered engines. And if they didn't start? She needed enough altitude to glide in.

For someone who wasn't sure she wanted to live—or believed

she was going to die—she was trying very hard to live. Or at least, she was trying very hard to get on the ground.

When had she decided to live...until she died?

The human mind was...curious, she decided, as she reached for the radio switch. It was time to start talking to someone.

* * *

"We've got a radio contact!"

The whole day had passed. It had long since become obvious that staring at the sky was pointless. But Granger couldn't give up. He wouldn't go away. Neither did Merriweather.

There was an airman on the radio and another on radar. The excited radioman turned to the small group around him.

Merriweather spun around, and for the first time, Granger saw real emotion in the old man's eyes, though he quickly hid it.

"Is it"—the old man swallowed visibly—"the *Manta Ray?*"

Was he still trying to hide Alice's involvement?

"No ID yet," the radioman said, moving dials in an attempt to get a clearer signal, Granger assumed.

None of them had said Alice's name since they realized that she was flying the *Ray*. He couldn't decide if it was denial or delusional.

"Anything on radar?" Phillips asked.

"I've got nothing—wait," he was quiet, studying the display, then looked puzzled. "It's high, but descending pretty fast."

Granger saw Merriweather's eyes widen in surprise. And maybe elation?

The radio crackled and then a voice came through faint, but clear. "This is the *Manta Ray* test flight requesting landing assistance."

The voice wasn't obviously female, but Granger knew it was Alice as she repeated her request for assistance.

"What assistance do you require, *Manta Ray* flight?" the radioman asked.

Granger heard another voice summoning in the CO.

"Clear traffic for emergency landing."

She sounded matter-of-fact and Granger thought he could see her expression, too. She'd known, she knew the risks, and accepted them as a consequence of her choice.

"Looks like it's coming down on the wrong side of the mountains. They'll need to level out at nine thousand feet."

The radioman passed the message on and got a "roger" in response.

"The rate of descent is too high. He still needs to level out."

The radioman passed on course adjustment instructions and got another "roger" in response.

Had she been able to air-start her engines? Did she have enough fuel to clear the mountains, then descend to Edwards?

And where had she been all day?

ALICE WAS CONCENTRATING SO HARD she almost made a deadly mistake. She'd planned a long, straight descent to Muroc, but she'd forgotten about the mountains. The voice on the radio told her what to do. She leveled out. Then checked the fuel gauge. It read low. If she was lucky, she had just enough to get back to the base.

And that's when she realized something that made no sense. None.

Her head ached just off tempo with her shoulders, arms and legs. The headache, her transits—nothing explained why night loomed ahead of her, coming in to ambush the *Ray*. She'd been airborne for at most an hour of flight time that had begun mid-morning. How could a whole day have elapsed? She couldn't have been unconscious at any point in her transits, or at least not long, or the *Ray* would have crashed. The *Ray*'s repaired autopilot had not been on, and in any event it was only designed to work with the regular jet engines' flight, not her main engine.

She knew where she was, thanks to the voice on the radio and her own eyes. She'd cleared the ragged crest of the mountains and now she could see see the dry lake out there, its long length of runway beckoning with its illusion of safety and rest. But she was still too high to land. She'd have to make a big circling turn to lose the rest of her altitude and land in the opposite direction. For once, there wasn't much wind. It should be easy shouldn't it?

The strain on her shoulders and arms felt out of proportion to her flying time—though if she'd really been flying for eight hours...? Which wasn't possible. Based on her own data, she'd been airborne for considerably less time. It must be an effect of her auxiliary engine transits. Maybe her body just didn't like G-force.

Neither that nor anything else explained her missing day.

Except...she knew the theoretical basis of her engine's operation, equations involving energy, mass, the speed of light, and what Einstein missed in his famous formulation that $E=mc2$, the variable T. For time. The engine theory treated time as an irrational variable, not real. She definitely had to think about that later. If there was a later.

She began her long circling turn to line up for her landing. Her gaze moved between her airspeed, altitude and forward thrust. The altimeter showed a steady rate of descent. Her shoulders ached from tension. She could land. She'd done it before. Okay, she hadn't landed something this big, but she'd had her hands on the controls. She remembered how it felt.

Perhaps it was what she didn't know the last future time—about landing the *Ray*, about the main engine, about time—was what killed her?

She was finishing her turn when the horizon flickered. Was it exhaustion or…a time event? Now? No way. This was not a good time for time to act up. She tried to blink it away.

When she opened her eyes from the blink she saw another aircraft in a turn on a collision course with the *Ray*. It closed with a speed that took her breath away. The *Ray* couldn't maneuver fast enough to avoid a collision. With a split second to spare, she yanked the cockpit ejection handle. The acceleration of the cockpit as it surged up and away from the *Ray* was almost enough to knock her out again, but being strapped into the seat gave her some protection.

The horizon pulsed the other aircraft in and out of view. Incredibly, she saw a pod that looked just like the one she was in, rising from the other plane.

The other plane…looked exactly like the *Ray*. She didn't have time to process that before she realized that the cockpit pods were on a collision course, too.

She released the top of the cockpit pod, and it exploded upward and tumbled out of sight. Now she grabbed the handles of the seat's ejection system. She rose, in a blur of pain and shock. Just below her the pods collided, debris from the collision rising up around her in a kind of slow motion.

She looked around, but couldn't see the other…pilot.

The horizon flickered again, and then her chute deployed. There was a sharp yank. And so much pain…

* * *

"I HAVE TWO CONTACTS!" The radarman's voice tried to maintain calm as the CO strode into the room. "Repeat, I have two contacts…"

"What?" the CO snapped. "Where did the second one come from?"

"I don't know, sir, it's just…there…"

Granger was aware of the radioman shouting a warning, and

then both contacts on the screen disappeared. He stared at the blank screen, then looked up and met Merriweather's horrified gaze in a face turned gray with shock.

"Alert emergency services," the CO snapped. "Let's get the last-known position to them."

Granger turned and stalked to the door, resisting the urge to slam it because he wanted to slam his fist into Phillips' face. He still had the binoculars, but a quick, frantic scan of the sky gave him nothing. Surely there'd be burning debris? It wasn't full dark, but surely there'd be something?

He lowered the glasses, his arms hanging limply by his sides. Following an instinct he couldn't name, he started walking in the direction of the flight line, passing silent hangars, pausing once for a car to pass him.

He'd known she might die; no, he'd known she was going to die, but he hadn't believed it. He'd played with the theory of it, but his brain had refused to believe it could be reality. She was too bright, too alive, too everything, to be dead.

Dark flowed over him as he walked and he welcomed it. He wanted to shake his fists at time, at a world that snuffed out a life like hers so carelessly. He wanted to turn back and shout, "What is wrong with you people?"

He didn't. He reached the flight line and stared up at a sky that reflected his soul. The stars would be out soon, but for now...

Because anger still drove him, he couldn't stand still. He looked back, then turned and walked out to the center of the runway and began to walk on the line in the direction she should have come. There were distant sounds of sirens as the emergency personnel deployed. He looked back. The wink of flashing red faded in and out of view.

Where had the other plane come from?

Slowly the question emerged from the chaos inside his head.

It hadn't been there and then it was. As if the thought brought the event, the horizon pulsed almost angrily in front of him. This was the worst yet. The ground moved beneath his feet, kind of like a small earthquake, and when it subsided…

He glanced around. The emergency lights were gone and it was later—if the position of moon and stars was right. He looked at his watch, but couldn't see the face. He turned back toward the base and thought he saw a dim silhouette of a vehicle at the end of the runway. A truck, no, a car.

There was a hum above his head and suddenly he was bathed in lights directly overhead. The hum changed to a quickly rising buzz.

His chin jerked up and he lifted a hand against the glare. But the sound of it! It drilled into his head, even though he covered his ears. Nothing helped. He dropped to his knees as pain exploded in his head.

* * *

JACK WOKE to the sound of a message incoming. Thankfully, Mel stirred, too, because they were tangled with each other. They hadn't broken contact with each other since the time river showed up. They hadn't undressed, just fallen onto the single cot in exhaustion at some point last night. He twisted to get a look at his watch.

The twentieth. The day when Alice and Granger would die at some point. They'd both done some digging into Alice's accident, hoping it would help them pinpoint when Granger would get in trouble. The details were, as usual, sketchy and to be honest, he couldn't see how knowing would help them. At this point, they didn't have the power to change the past.

Time was still having fits. It had been so constant, he was almost used to it. Though he eyed the river of time as they managed to get upright without either of them hitting the floor, it was touch and go.

"Does it look the same to you?" Mel asked, keeping well clear of it as she headed to their computer station to respond to the call. She glanced back at Jack. "It's on our secure link." She checked again. "It's the team that picked up the cuff link a couple of days ago."

What could they be calling about now? Jack gave the time river a last long look before he turned to Mel. "I can't tell if it's growing or not."

It flowed through, putting a ripple over their whole board, though the two items they could still read where the deaths of Alice and Granger.

"Let's see what they've got to say," Jack said, dropping down next to her and hooking an arm over her shoulder.

She was still here. They were still here. If their enemy was tracking them through Granger's recall device…they hadn't found them yet.

And then he cursed himself for thinking it, as security alarms went off up top. He pulled up the cameras and saw a small fleet of military-looking Humvees approaching their security perimeter.

CHAPTER 15

$\mathcal{A}$lice opened her eyes, blinking at the disjointed view of the desert in front of her. It felt as if she'd wakened from a long dream, except for the fact that she was upright, swaying a bit, but definitely standing on her own two feet. She frowned. It hurt so she stopped but...one couldn't sleep standing. She looked around and the frown came back, despite the ouch.

She was standing in the desert. Wait. She was standing *alone* in the desert.

She glanced around to verify the aloneness. It was troubling. She inhaled shakily. Okay, that hurt. *Rib?* No, her shoulder. She reached up and cautiously probed it. Yeah, it was sore, but she didn't think it was broken. But why—something tickled at the edge of memory. She'd hit something, or wrenched it. She added 'how' to the growing list of questions.

She started to drop her hand and that's when she realized she was wearing flight gloves. And a flight suit with headgear. The faceplate was cracked. That's right. She'd been in the *Ray*.

Flying it...

She'd had to eject. She'd heard it hurt but hadn't expected it to hurt this much. But why?

The collision!

She jerked around, as if she were still at risk, but she was alone. *And don't jerk like that again because, ow.*

A gust of wind rippled across the top of the scrub and she staggered a few steps as it pulled at her parachute. She turned, grabbing at the tangle of lines. How had she stayed on her feet? She released the chute and the wind carried it a few feet before it and the lines tangled in the scrub.

Her heart still pumped adrenalin from the near collision despite her isolated location. On the ground, she reminded herself with some scorn. She'd ejected the cockpit pod, but then she'd had to eject from the pod. After that...

She remembered the yank when her parachute deployed and her shoulder hit something. But she didn't remember anything after that.

She pulled off the gloves—her shoulder didn't much like that — and gingerly worked at the headgear fastenings until she could lift it off. The sting of the fresh air on her temple made her touch the spot. Her hand came away streaked with red. She rubbed the fingers on the leg of her flight suit, looked at the headgear and gloves, and finally stuffed the gloves into the headgear. She didn't want to carry it...somewhere, but it felt wrong to abandon it.

The cool air on her face helped, even though she fought to return her breathing to a more normal rate.

"Where am I?"

The scrub didn't answer.

She frowned. Why couldn't she see or hear any emergency vehicles? And why was it—she checked the sun's position—mid-morning when she'd ejected in the evening?

The scrub didn't have answers for those questions either.

She needed to figure out where she was. Her last clear memory of her position put her west of Muroc. Her view of the surrounding mountains confirmed that position, though of course it didn't pinpoint exactly where she was.

There was no wreckage in sight, either hers or—what plane had she almost hit and where it had come from? She'd been in touch with the tower. They should have seen the plane well before there was a collision risk.

A sound came to her and she looked up, watching the contrail of a craft far above her until it had passed. It was too high to be headed for Muroc, but she watched it anyway. With some reluctance, she lowered her gaze to the bleak terrain that surrounded her. It did no good to wonder how she got here. It felt as if she were stranded in a brown sea of scrub. There was no sight or sound of help or habitation in any direction.

She closed her eyes and crossed her arms, the one with the damage on top of the less damaged one, the headgear dangling from her hand. There had to be a way. The mountains. She'd stared at them almost every day since they'd arrived. Mountains didn't change. She opened her eyes. Okay, that direction was east, easy enough with the sun helping out. West was that way and north...

The horizon shivered in front of her.

She took a half step back. The last time that happened, things had not gone well for her. She looked left, then right of the shimmer. It appeared to be directly in front of her. She half turned to look back. No shimmer there.

Only in front of her.

As she stared, it almost seemed to stabilize in some odd way, giving her a view through. It reminded her of when she'd seen the riding club in the past. Only this time...was that the road?

She rubbed her eyes. This could be a hallucination, but it wasn't as if she had a lot of options. She could see no indication that anyone was looking for her. And she would only get weaker. She headed for the shimmer, her heart pounding in her chest. The shimmer seemed to like it. It almost felt as if it reached out to her, then closed around her. The view twisted strangely in front of her and she stumbled, but managed to stay upright. She pressed forward, watching her feet more carefully. That helped with the disorientation, too.

She walked for a while, only glancing up to make sure the road was still ahead. The pain in her shoulder began to ease, though she knew she was getting weaker. She had to stop and regather her strength, her willpower, to keep going. She faced the fact she might not make it, that she could be walking away from the road and any chance of getting help. She'd hit her head—she reached up to touch the spot and stopped, surprised. It didn't hurt. Her shoulder felt much better, too, though the pain wasn't gone.

She was losing touch with reality, she decided. She was probably lying somewhere, injured and dying—because she was supposed to be dead—and this was the way her mind had taken to cope. She should sit down and let it happen, but, she glanced around. Even in this delusion, there was no comfortable place to sit. It was probably ironic. It was definitely annoying. But at least she wasn't in as much pain. Was it normal to be hungry and thirsty? Feeling tired, she expected that.

The shimmer seemed to grow brighter suddenly and she threw up a hand to protect her eyes. When it faded, she was standing next to the road to the base. Was it? Based on the position of the mountains, it was the base road. Something was different about it. Almost hesitantly, she walked out into the middle and turned in a slow circle.

She'd driven this road to Palm Springs, and again with Tom when the helicopter had stopped them. She gave a half chuckle and was surprised to hear the sound. This almost looked like the spot where she threw the cuff link. Okay, that was delusional. There was no way she could tell one patch of scrub from another out here. And it felt like the same because she was delusional.

She said the words aloud because it seemed she needed convincing. Again, the sound of her voice surprised her. It sounded real. She felt the words in her chest, felt and heard them emerge from her mouth.

She looked around, then stamped her foot against the road, and realized what was different about this road. It was paved. It hadn't been paved the other day, had it?

This seemed to increase the chances she was hallucinating, so why did its solidity under her feet make it feel more real? Was this what dead felt like? Tom hadn't told her how she was supposed to die. She hadn't, she admitted, wanted to know that or expected to find herself so alone, dead or alive.

If she were dead, was there somewhere she was supposed to go? She looked right, then left. The road stretched in straight line of empty in both directions. Across from her there was that thick patch of scrub—the horizon shimmered again—and she thought she caught a glimmer of gold in the heart of it.

Without pausing to think, she crossed the road, stepping off into the dirt, and then picked her way toward the glimmer. She didn't think it was actually there, but then she brushed against a clump and the light moved, catching the glint once more. She bent and eased branches aside. It was crusted with dirt, but it had caught on a branch, which was probably why it hadn't been buried deeper in the dirt. She scraped away what dirt there was and picked it up, holding it at eye level.

A cuff link.

She blinked more than once as she studied it.

Was it the one Tom had told her to take off and throw? She'd been in such a hurry, she couldn't be sure, but she had thrown it away in a place like this one and now it was out here in the desert with her. It all felt both real and crazy. A crazy dream, perhaps?

And then she heard the sound of a vehicle. She jerked back toward the road, toward the sound. It was approaching from the west, so not from the base, the lowering sun behind it. Wait? What? How had the sun gotten over there? Had she walked all day?

As panic started to rise, she focused on the car. It was a dark speck at first, but its approach helped to settle her. Okay. How long had she walked? It felt long, but not hours and hours long. Or perhaps this was still part of her crazy dream, or maybe God had sent someone to pick her up.

Her fingers curled around the cuff link protectively, for reasons she couldn't define.

The vehicle, as it drew closer, was unlike anything she'd ever seen before. Dark and boxy, it had huge wheels. It kind of reminded her of an oversized jeep, but this was a closed-in vehicle and the windows were all darkened, so she couldn't see the driver. It pulled to the side of the road, stopping almost in front of her. It took all her resolve not to step back as the driver and passenger doors of the vehicle opened and two men jumped out.

They didn't look like God's messengers or anyone she'd dream about.

Their clothing went with the vehicle, being vaguely military but not obvious about it. Not really uniforms, at least they were dressed the same in dark slacks, shirts, and caps. She couldn't tell if they were armed, but they both looked and moved similarly to the military types she'd interacted with. Dark sunglasses covered their eyes so she couldn't tell if they were as startled as she was, but she sensed they were.

What she could see of the interior of the vehicle increased her sense of unease.

"Ma'am?" One of the men lifted the brim of his cap in a respectful way that was, she suspected, meant to put her at ease. "Do you need help?"

She considered this, but there was only one honest answer.

"I...yes," she said. She became aware of how disheveled she must look and tried to smooth her hair down. It might have been the greatest act of futility in her life, and she had many to choose from.

Both men took a half step closer but stopped when she flinched back. She wanted to apologize, but she was a woman alone with two strangers, she reminded herself.

"Are you hurt?" His gaze flicked down and perhaps her flight suit prompted the next question. "You're from the base? Had to bail out?" He looked up as if he expected to see her plane still falling.

She nodded and now he looked in the direction of the base, as if he expected to see transport coming.

The two men exchanged a look and one of them shrugged. "I'm sorry that we can't take you to the base, but we could drop you at the hospital in the next town." He flushed slightly, inexplicably, "I'm sorry we can't call someone for you. It's complicated."

She glanced around. What was complicated about not being close to a phone booth?

The other man lifted something, a small device that emitted beeping sounds. He pointed it past her and then slowly moved it, centering it on her as the beeping sounds increased.

She braced, not sure what she expected.

"Did you find something, ma'am?" The first man asked her this almost as if he expected her to deny it.

It would emit a tracking signal in the future, Tom had told her. If these men were with Tom's team, but no, that wasn't possible. The tracking signal would be in the future. Still, she found her hand opening to expose the cuff link. Their expressions didn't change, but they both tensed and then looked at each other, as if for guidance about what to do next. She studied the vehicle again. It was like nothing she'd ever seen.

"It was in the scrub," she said, stalling in hopes of understanding what was happening.

"We need it, ma'am," the man with device said. "It's...important to..." His words trailed off and he gave a half shrug.

"This sounds crazy, I know," she said, "but what day is it?" It should be Sunday. They should say Sunday and then she'd know…maybe she'd know something.

"It's Tuesday, ma'am," The first man said. "How long have you been out here?" He looked around again, as if he expected searchers to emerge from the scrub.

"Saturday night," she murmured, as much to herself as to them, "it was Saturday night, the twentieth."

"The twentieth is in two days," the second man said. "Did you hit your head?"

Ice seemed to flow into her cells. It was her cells because she felt it so acutely. They didn't seem surprised she'd flown or bailed out, she realized. They were interested in the cuff link, not her. "What..year is it?"

Neither man tried to look dispassionate this time. "It's two thousand twenty, ma'am. February eighteenth," he added. "Must have been quite a bad drop."

He was trying to be kind she realized, as she rocked back in denial. But…she'd seen the past when she was with Tom; she looked into the time event and seen the past.

"Two thousand and twenty." *You were born in the wrong time*, Tom had told her. *Tom*. Was he here somewhere? Had he come home? She swayed again and one of the men jumped close, catching her arm, steadying her.

"Let me take that," he said, easing her headgear out of her hand. To her relief, he didn't try to take the cuff link, though he could have easily overpowered her. "Why don't you sit down." He looked around, then gestured to the other man. "Get her some water."

This man moved to the rear of the vehicle and touched something and the back lifted up, while the other led her toward the vehicle. He opened the door behind the driver's seat and tossed her headgear onto the seat bench. It was so high off the ground, the man knelt, offering his cupped hands, as if he knew she didn't want to be lifted by a stranger. She accepted the boost, settling on the edge, not on the seat. She couldn't get inside. Not yet.

The other man came around, holding out a bottle. It said water on the label, but she'd never seen anything like it.

That's because…but her mind refused to acknowledge why. Reason, even logic said it was so, but reason also warred with logic on the issue. Her headache returned.

She must have looked confused or something, because the man twisted off the lid and extended it to her once more. Her fingers wrapped around the bottle, glistening with condensation, the cool of it almost reassuring. Could she feel this if she were unconscious or dead? She lifted the bottle, letting the water run down a throat that she realized now was parched and dry. She longed to gulp it down, but that wasn't proper. She sipped again, then again and again until half the bottle was gone.

Take it logically, she told herself. It had been Thursday, February eighteenth when she had thrown the cuff link out of the Jeep. Sixty-six years ago, if this were real and not some fevered, pre-death dream. The logic began to break down again.

She opened her hand, staring down at the cuff link. Was it the same one? She looked up and saw both men looking at it, their hands curled at their sides.

"What kind of injuries do you have, ma'am?" Neither man had offered their names, but then neither had she. He'd been the driver. He was taller, a bit bulkier than his passenger.

"I think I hurt my shoulder," she admitted, though she was moving easier, which was another oddity in a long list of odd. "From the ejection."

One of the men's eyebrows arched above his sunglasses. That disbelief felt familiar.

The two men exchanged glances, or at least looked at each other, then the passenger cleared his throat and said almost diffidently, as if he didn't want to attach too much importance to it, "That thing you picked up?"

"The cuff link," she said, looking down at it.

"Yeah, the cuff link." He exchanged looks with the driver. "We kind of need it."

She considered him carefully, as she sipped some more water. It tasted quite wonderful. It was so cold and clean tasting. When had she last had cold water this wonderful? She moved on to considering the two men.

They kind of reminded her of Tom. There was a cleanness to their faces, and they lacked the threatening aspect that had made her wary of Phillips. Could she judge them well enough in this…isolated spot? Tom had feared a time tamperer. That made her fingers twitch to hide the cuff link once more. But if they took it from her by force, she could end up under the bush instead. She had to trust them because, she glanced around, they were the only ones here. And they'd come straight for the cuff link.

And she didn't feel afraid of them. At last logic and reason meshed into acceptance. However unbelievable it seemed, she'd traveled to the future. It was time to deal with what was.

"The data belongs to me," she said. "I…belong with this." At least she hadn't asked them to take her to their leader. Yet.

* * *

GRANGER CAME SLOWLY awake with the strong sense that something was very wrong. His head throbbed, his ears hurt, and his eyes…he opened them but this didn't help. It was still dark.

He blinked. Were those stars overhead? A small gust of cool air brought him the smell of sand and scrub and fuel. That was definitely fuel. He rolled to his side, holding back a groan. He needed some situational awareness before he got too vocal.

His situation appeared to be that he was lying on a runway. The Edwards flight line? Yeah, he'd been out there thinking about…Alice. He'd been thinking about Alice. He'd had two, maybe three hours until his recall triggered and sucked him back to the future.

It could have triggered, he supposed. According to Mel, he'd re-integrate back into his life. This didn't feel like integrating. If he was still on base at Edwards in the future, it could get awkward really fast. His ID was out of date, as was his uniform.

He rolled into a crouch and looked around. The dark buildings in the distance looked like Edwards, so the question then became, *when* was he?

There'd been a light, he suddenly recalled, and that sound. He looked around, but it looked quiet for as far as he could see. He couldn't see that far. The night was moonless, most of the stars hiding behind some cloud cover.

He angled his head, listening and realized he heard one, possibly two sets of footsteps. Sounded like they were heading his way. Acting on impulse, still keeping low, he scrambled for the scrub next to the runway, dropping down into what was admittedly low cover. If it had been daylight, he'd have had no chance.

He peered through the all-too-spare branches as two figures emerged from the gloom. Interesting they weren't using flashlights. They stopped just short of even with Granger and paused to look back the way they'd come.

"I thought it was about here," a voice said.

Granger didn't recognize the voice. But something about it made him frown.

"Maybe he woke up." This was Phillips. "Went back to the professor's place."

"I doubt he'd make it that far." There was a pause. "They've increased security."

Granger frowned. Why—the president? In the story about the so-called alien meeting, there'd been a press report that Eisenhower had died. That had been followed by "oops, he was at the dentist" reports and the official report agreed. The president had a toothache. But the story persisted on the internet that he'd been here. What if something else had happened? Something that wasn't aliens, but an assassination attempt, with alien contact as the bait?

Alice had been interested, not shocked when he'd mentioned the aliens. She'd assumed that someone from the future would already have had contact with aliens.

For a moment he toyed with the idea that aliens had arrived, though the notion that Ike could accept a treaty that allowed for the abduction of citizens...he couldn't wrap his mind around that. But that bright light and the sound—and the mixed-up news reports seemed to indicate a time event rather than an alien event.

He might admit to being...disappointed by his own logic. Had there been some part of him hoping...he'd have shaken his head at himself, if the movement wouldn't have risked exposure.

"We'll find him," Phillips said, with a note of deference.

So Phillips had a boss? That's the guy Granger needed to see. This had to be the time tamperer.

Then the question for him became, was this the trap? Did they hope to hang the assassination on him? Or just use it to lure him out and follow him back to the future?

He needed to see that guy and he needed to see the time. How much time did he have until his recall device triggered?

The two men turned and headed back the way they'd come. Granger made himself count to twenty before he rose from the scrub and started after them. He kept to the far edge of the runway, so he could drop back out of sight if necessary.

A sound built slowly, resolving into the *thup, thup* of an approaching helicopter. The two men began to run, so Granger did, too, though still careful to keep close to the scrub.

Then a circle of lights once again broke the darkness, though this time from the ground. A landing circle had been formed, by jeep lights, he decided, slowing. He needed to get close enough to use some of that light to see the time.

And maybe see the time tamperer? He could only hope.

* * *

"WE HAVE A SITUATION," the team commander said, using video. He gave the hand signal for keeping names and any other critical data on the down low.

This was unusual enough for Mel to exchange a quick, puzzled look with Jack, who was focused on the problem up top.

"Go ahead," Mel said. At least the video wasn't required on her end. She looked and felt like about thirty miles of bad road—after a natural disaster.

"So we're at our designated location to acquire the device and we ran into a...complication."

Device? What device? They hadn't received a signal from the last of Granger's cuff links. This caught Jack's attention long enough for her to mouth the question. Had he picked up a signal? He shook his head.

"Can you verify that location?" Mel responded.

He rattled off the code and she blinked. That was the location they'd been at two days ago. Surely Granger wouldn't use the same drop site two times in a row. Which also didn't answer the question of how or why they hadn't received a signal? Maybe it was the guys up top? That's all she could think of.

"What's the complication?"

"It's easier if I show you, ma'am," he said. The view shifted slowly to one side and Mel saw someone in a flight suit sitting on the edge of the door frame of the Humvee. "She says her name is Alice. Alice Merriweather." He waited a couple of seconds. "Texting you a close-up picture of her—which kind of freaked her out when we took it."

Alice Merriweather? What the—

231

The computer pinged. Not enough time to process this, Mel wanted to object. *You need to slow down*, but she felt it, felt time speeding up around them.

She pulled up the picture and almost wet her pants. Seriously, she hadn't done that since, well no reason to remember that. Alice—if it was Alice and it sure looked like Alice from the photographs they had—looked pretty hammered. She wore some kind of flight suit and her hair was a bedraggled tangle. Was that dried blood on her face?

"Jack," she murmured.

He looked, did a double take and then huffed out a breath. "Because things are bat crap crazy enough already."

"Okay, I see your problem," Mel said, her tone only slightly strangled.

"She says the data on the item is hers," their guy went on. "She says she banged up her shoulder when she ejected from a plane."

His tone was so neutral, Mel wondered if he was trying to warn them or what? Seriously, some of these guys overdid the poker face thing.

"Do we still have the data?" Mel murmured to Jack.

It only took a few seconds for him to pull it up. He turned his screen so she could see it. It looked the same.

"So you can't transmit?" she asked carefully.

"She currently holds the item. And she seems...confused."

"How did you locate her?" Jack asked.

"She was here when we arrived."

Mel considered this.

"How did she seem?"

"Confused," he repeated. "She asked what date it was," he added, almost as an afterthought. "I'm not sure how long she's been out here. She thought it was Saturday. Or maybe Sunday."

"What date did you tell her?" Mel asked, wincing. It was the only way she knew to ask it, but wow.

There was a pause. "I told her it was the eighteenth, ma'am," he said, as if he couldn't quite believe she'd asked. "I told her it was February eighteenth and the year." His tone said, please don't you ask me what year it is.

Mel sagged back, expelling a lot of air. "At least we know this bunker kind of works." She straightened and looked at Jack with almost hope. "Maybe she knows something about…"

* * *

THE DRIVER of the vehicle approached her where she sat, partially inside their peculiar vehicle. Other than this vehicle, the future looked much the same as the past, at least from where she sat facing more desert. Though the two men had treated her courteously, the kind of courtesy she'd experienced from Tom. They'd even given her more water and something they called an energy bar. And when she'd rubbed her aching temple, they'd handed her two tablets they'd called ty-something. She hadn't hesitated long before taking the pills. If they had hostile intent, she was doomed anyway. After a bit, the ache eased, though she still struggled to remain calm in the face of time travel.

Time travel. The future. How was it possible for her to arrive in *his* future?

The driver held out the small device he'd used to take her picture. She'd been both skeptical and reluctant, then amazed and horrified when she'd seen it could take photographs. It hadn't been fun seeing how awful she looked either.

She took it somewhat cautiously and gave him a baffled look.

"It's a cellphone, too. Listen and talk into it," he said.

Cellphone. Phone. That was why he'd apologized for being unable to call for help? She studied the two men's faces, well, as much as she could see of them, and wished she had her sunglasses, too. The sun was bright and she was tired of keeping her back straight. It was also unnerving to be the only one whose name was being used.

"Alice? Miss Merriweather?" The voice, a female voice, came out of the small device.

"Alice is fine," she said. "Who am I speaking with?"

There was a pause.

"Please don't be offended if I don't say. There are…people… trying to find us."

The time tamperers. She recalled Ty's caution against using his name.

"Is…Tom with you? Is he all right?"

There was another pause.

"That's actually what I wanted to talk to you about. Tom… might be in trouble."

She inhaled sharply and wished she hadn't. There were parts of her that still hurt. Apparently sixty-six years wasn't long enough to heal them.

"He was well when…" she trailed off. Sixty-six years ago. Whatever had happened was already done. "What happened?"

"We're not sure." Another long pause. "He somehow ended up in the desert, not that far from where you are right now, but…"

Alice considered this information, her thoughts returning again and again to the time events she'd experienced. She wanted to ask how this could happen. He'd seemed certain he would go home, though he had not told her how. But apparently her ability to ask questions was limited.

"We'd like to understand how you ended up there," the voice continued. "And we're trying to figure out how to get you from there to…here—"

"No," the negative came from instinct. She had no desire to sit by the side of the road, but if Tom were here…here sixty plus years ago…could the same forces that brought her here help Tom? "Could we, could these men take me there? Where Tom got in trouble?" Alice noticed this woman hadn't said Tom had died, but what other trouble would keep him from going home?

While the woman considered this, Alice had to think about it, too. There was risk in this. The time events could take her back to die, but she didn't want to be here without Tom. He'd saved her in ways he couldn't understand. He'd saved who she was, who she'd wanted to become. She knew he'd felt as if he hadn't because he couldn't save her life, but he had, even if she died, he'd saved her. He'd helped her find herself, find her courage, and yes, her hope. She'd left him knowing she'd been loved, truly loved by someone, and more, she'd left him knowing he'd respected her mind, her ability. He'd seen her in a way no one else had. She would trade this present for his life because of who'd she become from knowing him.

It seemed as if she could feel this female voice thinking, considering...perhaps consulting with someone else? Tom had indicated he had a team.

"You're injured," the woman finally said, but Alice thought she heard a desire to be convinced in the voice.

"I am well enough," she told her. "My injuries are the result of the ejection, not...the other. And they are...better."

"Interesting..." the voice said.

How so, Alice wondered. Was it wrong to hope she met this person? To hope she might be able to stay? Hope. She stared at the desert and thought about the blooming Joshua trees...

"Let me talk to...one of my guys there, please," the voice said.

Alice knew, or hoped she knew, that she'd won this round. She handed the phone to the guy who had given it to her.

Phone. She watched him turn away, lifting the device to his ear. The future was interesting.

CHAPTER 16

*G*ranger stopped well clear of the ring of lights and tried to let his senses feel the space. There had to also be a defensive perimeter beyond the light circle.

With the light as backdrop, some things faded into deep shadow and others popped out of the darkness. He saw the two men he'd been following had also stopped, as if waiting for something or someone.

Granger crouched again, feeling in his pockets for the glasses. He had one cuff link left. All he needed was a picture of the guy with Phillips.

And time.

How much time did he have?

The chopper was making enough noise, so Granger moved back into the scrub off to the side and started working his way forward again, stopping often to scan his surroundings.

He almost ran straight into a picket, but the guy was looking up and Granger was able to fade back and pass him.

The closer he came to the lights, the lower he took his profile, until he was basically crawling through the scrub on his stomach.

The chopper circled twice, then came slowly down. Its spotlight flared for a few seconds, long enough for Granger to see his watch.

He had fifteen minutes before midnight.

Phillips and his companion were also using the chopper's distraction to close in. If this wasn't their party...

Granger adjusted the glasses, trying to focus in on the two men. For just a second, Phillips' companion looked in Granger's direction. He snapped the pictures, hoping that future computer enhancement would bring out the face. He dropped his head when he heard the crunch of footsteps behind him. Someone didn't need to hide. Probably another picket.

The man passed him without seeing him, but too close for comfort. If someone stepped on him...

The door opened on the chopper and what had to be secret service guys jumped out, forming a defensive circle for...

Ike. Eisenhower.

Granger felt a thrill, a sense of awe, at the sight of him. This was the guy who'd turned the tide in World War II. And wrested the presidency from Truman. He half expected a military band to start playing "Hail to the Chief," but this was a covert arrival. For what purpose? Eisenhower wouldn't be here for a toothache.

He probably needed to get clear of the area. According to Mel, the vortex that would suck him back to his own time had a way of announcing itself. Not a good idea with so much firepower around to protect the president.

He looked around, once again helped by the light circle. His eyes adjusted enough to find a lone jeep waiting in the shadows. He didn't see anyone around it. If it just had keys, he could drive out into the desert until—

"Get up slowly," a low voice said behind him. "We don't want to alarm anyone, do we?"

Granger's gaze went to where he'd last seen Phillips, but he was gone.

Granger pushed himself upright and turned to face the voice, his hands raised. There was no reason to get shot when he'd be leaving soon.

There was enough light to get a general outline of a male figure, armed with a handgun, for sure. The face was still in shadow, but Granger reached for his glasses, managing to trigger a picture before the figure uttered a short, sharp command.

"Just straightening my glasses," he said, easily and low. "Sorry." He hesitated. It was worth a try. "I was just out for a walk and realized I might have accidentally wandered into a secure area. Was trying to figure out how to get out—"

"Shut up and turn around. I'll tell you when to stop walking."

Granger turned, making sure his raised hands were still clearly visible. The guy was going to march him right past the jeep. Could he make his move? If the keys weren't hanging in the ignition, he was a dead man, but if a vortex sucked him into the sky in front of this guy...

The guy closed in, jabbing him in the back with the gun. Granger didn't mind keeping him close. He'd been trained for close combat.

* * *

ONE OF THE men helped Alice fasten what he called the "seat belt," reminding her of Tom, when he got in the car in Palm Springs. Was it this thing he'd looked for? How strange her world must have seemed to him. This small part of his world certainly felt odd to her.

"You control the temperature for you here," the man explained, showing her some knobs and then pointing to a vent. "Open or close, warmer or cooler with this knob here."

He also pulled down a ring that was the perfect size to hold another bottle of water he'd secured for her. Alice might have enjoyed this, were it not for her concern for Tom.

The woman hadn't told her what happened to Tom, but Alice

assumed something had gone terribly wrong, or the driver of his large and strange vehicle wouldn't have turned off the road and started heading across the desert, following a course marked on an even stranger device they'd called a SAT. It was affixed to the dashboard—which also made her blink with all its many dials. It appeared more complicated that the instrument panel of the *Ray*.

She felt a pang as she thought of her aircraft. It had flown well and had not deserved its fiery finish. Though she did not want to, her mind replayed that moment before the collision.

As they jolted through dips and rises covered in scrub, she tried not to see what her mind told her she'd seen.

That the *Ray* had collided with...itself. The *Ray* had been climbing. Had she run into her earlier self? Had she almost collided with herself in the pod? Had she both lived and died?

Tom must have believed she'd died. He couldn't believe anything else. But he'd known it would happen. She'd believed it would, and now here she was in his future trying to find out what had happened to him in her past.

She stared out the side window, because the seat in front blocked her view forward. She almost didn't notice that the horizon shimmered. The hairs on her arm rose in response. She leaned forward, saying urgently, "You need to turn left!"

"Left, ma'am?" The man in the passenger side half turned toward her, but a voice—the woman's voice came out of a speaker or something, right from the car itself, it seemed.

"Do as she says."

"Can't you see it?" Alice asked. It was right there.

"See what, ma'am?"

Now she recalled Tom's surprise that she'd seen the time event. It was only as the vehicle made the turn that she felt a chill of fear that it was taking her back into the past, but it was the right move. She felt this in her middle.

Her hands clenched as the time event closed around them. Then, odd in a sea of odd, a pulsing sound filled the tense silence.

"We've got a signal, ma'am."

"We hear it, too," the woman said. "It appears you're on an intercept course."

That they could hear the woman reassured Alice she was still in the future, but the waver of the horizon seemed to deepen around them.

"I've got two bogeys closing on our location," the man not driving said. "A couple of choppers."

"From Edwards?" the driver asked.

"No, sir, from the west." He put on a headset. "No challenge from Edwards. It's like they don't see them."

The speed of the vehicle increased. To Alice at times it seemed to fly between the hillocks.

There was a sound over the connection with the woman.

"We've got some bogeys at our location, too. I'm afraid you're on your own for now."

There was a whistle and the ground exploded ahead and to the right of them. They swerved, then swerved again.

"The..." the driver bit back something that was probably profane, "are firing on us!"

"We're taking fire here, too," the woman said, her voice the calm in the sudden storm.

Alice hung on as the vehicle swerved in what she assumed were tactical maneuvers. She saw the shimmer, though this was more like a hole, one where it was darker.

"Go right!" This time the driver responded promptly. "A little more..."

And suddenly night engulfed them. The driver might have cursed and flipped on the headlights.

"You need to stop!" Alice cried and the vehicle skidded so hard it turned to the side.

"Our bogeys?" the driver snapped.

"No sign of them yet."

The woman didn't speak. Was that troubling, Alice wondered?

She fumbled with the seat belt, then somehow managed to get the door open, noting as she dropped to the ground that her shoulder hurt worse again.

"Look," she said, pointing skyward where there was a flash of bright, white light.

"Our bogeys are back. A little off course, but I'm sure they'll adjust." He sounded like he wanted to swear. He looked at his partner. "Get on the gun."

Alice blinked. "Can you hold them off?" She glanced toward the still-pulsing horizon and then back and found him holding out a handgun, butt end first.

"Can you use this, ma'am?"

She took it, checked the weight, then looked up. "Safety here?" He nodded and might have looked surprised. "I was taught to use handguns during the war." She almost added which war, but stopped herself. If they knew, what was the point, and if they didn't? It might cause them additional stress. "Thank you."

She turned toward the waiting horizon. She might have prayed, but for what she was not sure. No, she did know. She prayed for Tom.

* * *

"They've breached the first hatch," Jack said, unable to look away, though what he thought watching would accomplish...

It was irrational to think that if he looked away things would get worse.

"It's getting more unstable in here, too," Mel murmured.

Jack wanted to look back, but couldn't. They each had a train wreck to track.

"How is our team doing?" Would it help or make things work?

"They keep going in and out of tracking. It's a bit disturbing," Mel admitted.

Jack spared a quick glance for her, tightening his grip on her hand. Would Alice and their team's actions make a difference if the timeline unraveled?

"How is..." he jerked a chin toward the time river that was impacting their research wall.

"Getting bigger, wider," she said, after a quick look. "Closer," she added.

Jack wanted to take her in his arms and hold her as time swept them...somewhere new. Because time would let him hold on, he thought scornfully. That had worked when the recall device had activated and formed a vortex, sweeping them out of the past—apart. That they'd found each other was a miracle. Now they needed another one to keep each other.

"I've lost them—no, there they are."

"Bogeys?"

"Changing to intercept course," Mel admitted calmly. "They'll be on top of them in five minutes, maybe less." She adjusted her headset. "Exchanging fire."

Jack shook his head. They were not nearly far enough from Edwards for this to go unnoticed. But his monitoring of military channels showed no sign of interest.

Time was complicated, he reminded himself.

* * *

As GRANGER MOVED toward the lone jeep, his gaze searched the darkness for evidence of...what? An alien spaceship? Did he really want to know? It would change how he looked at the world, at reality. It could change how he looked at the past and the future. Was he ready for that?

And still he looked. It seemed, he admitted somewhat wryly, that curiosity was stronger than...wisdom.

The shadow of the jeep grew larger, recalling his thoughts from aliens to the more urgent need to escape. He had to get far enough away that the recall vortex wouldn't add to—or create—the alien meeting story.

He glanced down, saw some likely scrub and managed to trip without actually going down, but he was able to use the trip to twist, and hit his captor hard. The handgun discharged and Granger released a silent curse. Without waiting to see how incapacitated the guy was, he scrambled into the jeep, offering a prayer as he reached for the place where the keys should be—they were.

He cranked the jeep, shifting into gear, and hitting the gas. His mirror shattered as a gunshot hit it. Granger twisted the wheel, going into an avoidance pattern that almost jolted him out of his seat. He didn't dare turn on the headlights, so this wasn't going to end well.

There were shouts and more shots, but none as close as that last one. It had to be close to his recall time. He pressed harder on the accelerator, hoping he didn't break his neck before it happened.

Behind him, he heard the roar as some sort of pursuit began. They could use their headlights, and multiple dots of light began to pierce the darkness behind him. He saw a deep shadow ahead. It was too late to turn if it was a deep gully.

He floored it, felt the jeep go airborne, and saw the horizon pulse urgently off to his right. He didn't have time to think about it. Barely had time to react.

He closed his eyes and launched himself toward it. He contracted his body into a ball, or as much of one as he could manage, with some vague idea that it would help.

It didn't, well, not completely.

He hit the ground hard, rolled multiple times and ended up facedown in scratchy stuff. There was a bright flash behind him.

And then he heard the roar of multiple vehicles heading toward him, or so he assumed. A strand of moonlight pierced the cloud cover, enough to give him a glimpse of his watch. He blinked and looked again.

It was still fifteen minutes to midnight. He shook his arm, even though it was probably his most futile act this day. How long had it been stopped?

Too long, he realized. His recall device hadn't triggered. Almost reflexively, because he didn't want to die, he tried to trigger the cyanide. That didn't work either.

He was stranded here. With the President of the United States —and who knew what else—on the base. He'd be lucky if they only shot him as a spy.

* * *

"HURRY, MA'AM," one of the men called out. "We got incoming again."

She heard the sound of rapid fire behind her, drowning out the clack of the helicopters closing in.

She half ran forward, struggling to follow the edges of the time event and not trip on scrub while her shoulder and other bruises throbbed their complaints. The "walls" wavered and moved, but it was dark ahead, so she followed that.

A flash of light interrupted the dark, then faded, but she heard the muted roar of vehicles approaching.

"Tom!" She waited, then tried again, "Tom!"

She almost tripped over the prone figure. Her foot caught and she staggered, barely managing to stay on her feet.

He groaned and lifted his head. "Alice?"

She crouched by him, her gaze on the incoming line of lights. "Can you get up?"

"Sure...how..."

"There's no time." And all the time, apparently. Where would they end up? Which threat would they face? "I have a handgun."

Tom paused, half upright. "Okay."

"There's a...vehicle back the way I came, but they are under fire," she told him. She clutched him as he swayed and she saw his face, shadowed, but there. "In your time, if we can get back there."

"My time? You've been—"

The incoming vehicles' engines revved louder, as if they sensed Tom close, or that he might escape. She couldn't tell which. The past or the future—either looked equally dicey. But if she had to choose, she'd rather risk the future.

"Let's go." Tom took her hand, the one not holding the gun. "Which way?"

Alice turned back the way she'd come, surprised to see the tunnel or vortex still there. In its heart was a circle of light and the sound of fire being exchanged.

"Can you see it?" she asked.

"Yeah." He sounded dazed.

"How badly are you injured?" she asked the question as her own injuries reminded her they existed as well.

"I'll make it," he said, urging them forward together.

The ground was rough and the vehicles were making better time than they were.

"There's a gully," Tom panted out, one elbow supporting his ribs, she had time to note, when they paused to glance back. "That should slow them down."

There was nothing to slow down the bogeys on the other side. She wasn't a soldier, but she knew the high ground was the better position. Were they running into worse danger? Almost philosophically, she reminded herself that she was supposed to be dead. Though it was not happy to think she'd helped Tom back to die, too.

Ahead, the circle of the future seemed to be shrinking, but Alice could see the ground around the vehicle kicking up. The men there fired back but held their ground. It amazed her they'd do that. For her or for Tom? Did it matter? They could die, too.

As if Tom realized it, too, he picked up the pace, his breath coming in pained gasps. If he hurt as much as she did, he couldn't talk either. She jumped a piece of scrub in her path and came down with a jolt that put stars around vision that darkened for several seconds, but Tom kept her—and himself—upright somehow. She'd heard his gasp of pain, too.

The circle narrowed some more, but the sounds of pursuit behind them got muddier and more indistinct.

She felt Tom bunch and drew from what resources she had left in her as well.

"It's going to hurt..." he panted.

She bent her legs with him and they both leaped toward the pinpoint of light...

* * *

THE TIME RIVER was almost at their feet, Mel noticed, and the assault on their bunker was one floor away. She'd quit looking at Jack. It was too painful to see him pulsing in and out of sight—as did the team with Alice.

When they were visible on her tracking, she heard shouts and the exchange of weapons fire. Through the radio, one of the men shouted, "I'm hit!"

And then the room was engulfed in light or maybe it was the time river. Mel couldn't tell. She felt Jack's hand clutching hers and then her fingers closed on nothing...

CHAPTER 17

*T*his waking up on his back was getting old, a habit he'd like to break, Granger thought, opening his eyes to bright sunlight—and confusion.

He heard the crunch of footsteps and tensed.

"Sir?" The man who crouched next to him, Granger knew that he knew the man's name; he was part of the team, but his brain wasn't pulling it up. "Where are you hurt?"

Granger shifted, testing various body parts and replied with considerable surprise, "I'm…fine."

The man—Carl—his brain produced part of his name, held out his hand and helped Granger to stand.

Alice.

He jerked, looking around.

"The lady is fine, sir," Carl said, sounding a little surprised, too. "We're all…fine."

That implied they shouldn't be…his dots connected. They'd been under fire and he'd heard…someone had been hit.

"Both of you? All of you?"

"The Cap always said time is complicated, sir, and he was

right," Carl said, leading him around to the rear of the parked Humvee. And there, sitting on the bumper wasAlice.

His brain and his body stopped. She looked...her face was dirty and streaked with dried blood. Her hair was tangled, too. Her flight suit had multiple tears. And she looked amazing. She looked—he stepped toward her.

"Are you sure..." The question died because it was more than "are you all right?" He couldn't believe she was here—he turned to Carl. When was here? "What's the date?"

* * *

THE TWO TEAM members excused themselves and went to the front of their vehicle, leaving Alice facing Tom. *Ty.* Could she call him Ty now? Was it safe yet?

February 20, 2020. Was it truly still the future? Had they jumped forward two more days during all the chaos? The clear, cloudless sky seemed to say yes, this is a brand-new day. A new century for Alice.

"Are you really all right?" he asked, stepping closer, his eyes still showing the shock she felt, too. "When the *Ray*..." His grin was crooked. "I'm not sure what happened with the *Ray*. How..."

"I ejected," she said, wondering how to explain what happened in those last moments. "I landed out here and when I," she looked at him, knowing if anyone could believe her it would be Tom—Ty. He'd seen the time events, too. They'd just come through one. "I followed a time event to the road and met these two men."

Granger came to stand next to her, taking one of her hands as if he were afraid she was going to disappear.

"I'm going to have a heck of time writing my report," he half turned as one of the men came back around the side of the vehicle that Ty had called a humvee. "Everything okay back at home?"

The man still looked bemused, which she had a feeling was not common with them.

"Apparently, though, they are as"—the man paused as if unsure what word to use—"startled as we are by recent events." He hesitated, then added, "We have a signal from you? A device activated?"

Ty looked startled. "That's right. I might have something for them." He lifted the torn sleeve of his shirt and exposed the device, a single cuff link, she saw.

The man removed it and gestured toward the front. "I'll get this sent to HQ."

He left them alone once more and Ty took her hand again, then reached out so that he held both of them.

"I can't believe you're here. I wanted it...so much." His gaze echoed the sincerity of his words. "There's so much I want to say, to tell you."

"Do you still love me?" she asked. The words had felt true, but he'd said them thinking there was no hope. Now they were here, in his future. Was there a place for her here, in his life?

He let go of one of her hands, but only so he could touch the side of her face, smooth back the tangle of hair.

"Always. You told me to love again and I said I'd try, but I lied, Alice. I could never love anyone else."

She saw him glance past her where the low murmur of conversation from the two men was the only other sound in this desolate place.

"That seems like a lie that I can forgive," she said, a smile trying to form on her mouth. She released it halfway, still apprehensive about this place she found herself in. The words were thick and hard in her throat, but they must be said. "This place, this time, is strange to me. You're not...just because of that?"

He pulled her gently close. "Can you feel my heart, Alice?" She nodded against his chest. "When I was back there and thought you were...gone..." His chest heaved in a sigh and his hold on her

251

tightened. "I won't lie that the transition won't be challenging, but you won't be alone. And I, well, I know someone who did it, too."

She lifted her head, looking at him in surprise. He knew someone else who had jumped into the future? Questions crowded her mind, her throat, but she had time, she realized. She sagged against him once more. She had time. They had time.

* * *

THE WALL where they'd tracked the Merriweathers was a mess. Half the images, notes and articles they'd pinned there were scattered around the room.

It looked like a tornado had gone through it. Jack pushed his hair back and turned them both—because miracle of miracles, he still held Mel's hand—in a slow circle trying to assess the damage.

The intrusion was gone, as if it had never happened. That was interesting.

As near as they could tell, it was Saturday both here and where their team was. Their team that now included both Granger and Alice Merriweather.

Jack couldn't complain about her arrival in the future. From early reports, Alice had saved Granger from the past when his recall device misfired. They'd need to look into that, debrief both he and Alice and the team with them.

But for now, it was enough to know they were together. Alive and together.

Jack's computer beeped.

"That'll be the images from Granger's last device," Mel said, with a sigh. Still holding hands, they returned to the terminals. They'd already righted their chairs so they could talk to the team. But they'd managed to do it all without letting go. He didn't want to ever let go again.

They sat and each used their free hands to do what they

needed to pull up the images. There were only two and they were dark.

"They'll need some work to enhance the images," Mel murmured. "Let's shoot them off to our resident geek."

"Yeah," Jack said, but still worked on enlarging the clearer face. Something about the shape of the head twitched his memory.

"What do you think stopped the event?" Mel asked.

Jack looked at her. "This. These images. Or Alice."

"Or both?"

He nodded. Or both. Time was tricky. He kind of wished they could take a break for a while. Just long enough for him to get over the headache. And for he and Mel to spend some quality time together. Maybe even go to Florida and see his old friend Norm and Mel's Gran.

CHAPTER 18

"*A*re we doing time travel research or running a dating service?"

Mel bit back a grin at the question, though it was rich coming from Jack.

"That is the risk when we limit our team to single people," Mel pointed out. And Granger and Alice were both so happy it was a bit sickening. She and Jack had probably been as goofy at falling love, but it hadn't felt like it at the time. And to give credit where it was due, Alice was taking to the future—which she'd called "loud, chaotic, fast-moving and colorful"—pretty well.

"Until they aren't single," Jack shot back. "I sure didn't see Granger's fall from"—Mel shot him a look—"bachelorhood coming."

Would Granger be upset he wouldn't be traveling through time again? Not that staying put had helped her and Jack during the recent attacks. She shivered at the memory of how near they'd come to losing each other. She could tell Jack was thinking the same thing, based on the sudden grimness that removed the humor from his face.

A change of subject seemed in order.

"We got the report back on Granger's recall device and his dead man's watch." She handed him the folder and watched him process it. It was almost funny that Jack's brows rose at about the same rate hers had when she'd read it.

"They were fried?"

"Totally fried and without any damage to the surrounding, um, tissue in either location." Granger's tush was sore from the extraction, but not as sore as it could have been if the frying had fried flesh, too. And the watch frying had saved his life. She felt a chill that he'd tried it, even as she'd understood his horror when it hadn't worked. "Our guy is going to work on extra shielding for future versions." She hesitated.

Since debriefing both Alice and Granger, they'd been avoiding talking about the elephant in the debrief. Granger had seen President Eisenhower. And there had been a bright light and a sound that knocked him out cold. Had that event also fried his recall device and his watch? It was the only thing in the debrief that seemed likely—even though what had happened wasn't possible, according to their expert, their onsite "Q," though he wasn't quite as inventive as the James Bond version.

So Eisenhower hadn't been to the dentist that night, but that didn't mean he or Granger had been involved in some kind of alien encounter. She compressed her lips when she realized she was arguing with herself. And then continued doing it.

Because it was also true, that not believing didn't mean it hadn't been an alien encounter. Their "Q" had no explanation for how the recall device and Granger's watch had been damaged without cooking a chunk of Granger's rear. And there was the fact that the US Air Force had finally admitted there were, and had been, UFO encounters.

To this she could add the enhanced images of the possible time tamperer. The team had done their best. It wasn't their fault that they'd created more questions while answering none.

She looked at all three images, pinned where all the

Merriweather data had been. They looked lonely there on the wall. And creepy, she admitted. It could be the light and the interaction of it with the shadows of what had been, according to Granger, a chaotic scene that made them seem kind of...alien.

The long shots showed an outline that was tall and thin, but not so tall or thin the figure couldn't be human. Their people had looked at it every way currently known to man and all they'd concluded was that they couldn't conclude anything.

Which was easier to believe? Aliens or someone from the future messing about in the past? Or...both?

Only time would tell...

* * *

THANK you for taking another journey through time.

Love, courage, and impossible choices have a way of lingering —especially when the clock refuses to slow down.

🖋 The Story Continues

The battle to protect time is far from over.

What began as isolated missions is becoming something much larger... and far more dangerous.

The final chapter of the *Out of Time Stories* brings every thread together.

TELLING TIME

An Out of Time Story

Time is unraveling.

Allies are scattered across decades.

And the future itself is at risk.

As rogue time travelers make their boldest move yet, familiar faces return—and new ones step into the line of fire. The past, present, and future collide in a race where every second counts, and love may be the only force strong enough to change the outcome.

Click below to continue the adventure and reach the thrilling conclusion:

 Read *Telling Time* now

Telling Time

 Want to start immediately?

You don't have to wait.

Begin the final Out of Time mission right now.

Read the opening chapter of *Telling Time* below...

March, 2531

John—he'd had so many last names and lived so many brief lives he didn't remember his real surname anymore—looked out over the complex as a shuttle flew past the blocky buildings toward the landing pad.

His fingers twitched as he fought the longing for a cigarette. It was a bad habit he'd picked up in 1954.

"So we still don't know who they are, where they are, or what they want." Her voice was a stark contrast to her ice queen aspect. The voice was warm, charming even when Stella was annoyed—as she was right now.

He glanced over his shoulder at her. Yes, she was very annoyed.

A tall woman, she had availed herself of the options to refine her looks to the point she looked unreal, with only traces of similarities left between her and her daughter. There had been a time when he'd been half-way in love with her, but that time was lost in both their pasts.

Usually he tried not to remember that time when they'd both been excited by the possibilities—no, he corrected himself. They'd been intoxicated by the power and by the freedom to exercise that power. They'd made the future better, brighter...

John suppressed a sigh. If it was so bright, how had it ended up so dull? The world needed a few bad habits, so you knew what good habits looked like.

He'd been enough places, in enough different times to notice the increasing homogenization that had gradually over taken creativity. Or had it just been turned to innovation?

A little of both, he decided. There'd been no profit in being too original. It always annoyed someone. So they'd smoothed out the rough edges—though not the corners of the square buildings, he noted with wry amusement. It was the rounded edges that were gone.

In the carefully filtered air of this office, his lungs missed not just the cigarette smoke, but the dry air of the desert. And he missed looking up at the test aircraft shooting across the clear blue sky. He'd liked 1954. He'd like Edwards Air Force Base— Muroc it had been then—and the people there.

He'd liked Alice Merriweather. Not in a romantic way. It felt vaguely wrong with her mother somewhat in the picture.

She hadn't liked him. That was just as well, since he'd had to let her die again. Funny that the more they tried to change, the less they'd managed. Was it the other time travelers getting in their way? Or was it time itself?

He turned his back on the drab view, his hands shoved in the pockets of his drab suit pants.

She studied him for several seconds and he wondered if she sensed his disillusioned thoughts. There was no going back now. He knew that, perhaps better than she did. You had to move through time to see the scared, dark patches from their rough handling.

Stella shoved back her chair and rose, her flat shoes making a light tap as she walked to the screen that dominated one side of the office. He knew every inch of that screen, and he knew there was nothing new to see. Still, he walked over to stand next to her. It was expected.

The screen was both high tech and curiously vintage. On it they were tracking—or trying to track—the other set of time travelers.

Her hand pointed to what they believed was the first contact with them in that dry and dusty desert where smoking was allowed.

Her hands, and her fingers were long and narrow, the nails a permanent and discreet match for her skin. She tapped her chin, a sign the gears in her head were turning.

The instability around the event was impressive—and had been impressively dangerous. It had almost swallowed them up in it, too. He didn't want to go through that again if he could help it.

She shifted so that she looked at a different part of the screen.

"Is that the real first time event for us?" she asked.

There was no answer to this question. Not really. Time was complicated. What little they did know, it had been both clumsy and messy, but its impact had been small—again, as far as they could know.

That Stella kept coming to back to it puzzled him.

Had that event been what caught the attention of those other time travelers? They hadn't been able to identify anyone anomalous from the available data. And it was too dangerous to send someone back there to try and find out. The situation was too uncontrolled and the risk of unintended consequences too high.

Even with an image of the man who had disappeared with Alice, they hadn't been able to make a facial recognition match around the possible initial event—or a useful match any time since. He hadn't been able to get a DNA sample from the man, and everyone had someone who looked like them out there. All he knew was, they had both vanished as if they'd never been. And it was possible they had been erased. It wasn't like they could ask time what it had done with them.

With time travel, he wondered, was there such a thing as a first event?

"They never found her body," she said. "She wasn't supposed to disappear."

John knew his face muscles tightened. "I've found that everything can change, but the ending."

If someone were meant to die, they did. If they were meant to live, it was oddly hard to kill them. Was Alice still alive out there somewhere?

Her lips compressed. Stella didn't like the truth, but she always insisted on it.

Removing someone from their time, and then deleting them, seemed to be a more effective procedure. If time were somehow living and aware, did this confuse it? They didn't really know, not even that they'd succeeded. The bodies didn't tend to hang around.

The upside, people tended to blame disappearances on aliens. It was a handy out.

"Could we try again?"

John wanted to agree. He could go back as many times as she wanted. He could go live there, maybe. He didn't think it would change anything.

"We need to eliminate the competition first," he said.

"And how do we do that?" She asked.

"We set a trap for them," John said.

"How…" Alice stopped.

"We give them an agent," he said. "We can equip her with tracking they shouldn't be able to detect."

The perfect brows rose. "How long have you had this in mind?"

"What is time?" he said, then added, "She's perfect for it. Too smart." No need to mention that her intelligence wasn't his only issue with her.

"That's a pity," said Alice's mother and then added as almost an after thought, "I used to like smart girls."

* * *

STELLA MERRIWEATHER SAT without moving for a long time after John left her alone.

Poor John. He thought she couldn't tell he'd lost his illusions and possibly his soul. She'd certainly lost hers when she abandoned her child and her husband for—she glanced around—this.

From her place in the 1950s, lost in the shadow of a husband who wasn't even close to her mental equal, this had seemed like the dream. It hadn't been that hard to sell her on it.

She could have tried harder, of course. Other woman did. They'd pushed against the barriers, fought the system, gone toe-to-toe with the men. She could have rolled over poor George.

He'd loved her. She remembered that now with distant awe. He hadn't been good at loving, which might be why she couldn't summon the resolution to roll over him. He'd been so amazed she'd married him, so grateful, so pathetic.

Had he noticed she was smarter than he was? She still wasn't sure.

In the end, he'd been easier to leave behind than Alice.

Alice.

He—her snake in her non-Eden—had told her to bring Alice but she couldn't quite deal another blow to George. She couldn't leave him completely alone. Did that mean she'd loved him a little? Or—this was the thought she only had when she was alone—had she feared her daughter's brain? Alice had already shown signs of brilliance.

And so Stella had left her to the same stifled life she'd fled.

"I promised myself I'd go back for her," she told the silence. "And I knew she could handle it. She was stronger than me, even then."

She pressed her finger against the bio-lock and a drawer slid open. It had one thing in it: a picture of Alice taken not long before Stella left.

Stella had thousands of images taken of Alice after that, but this was the only one that felt real to her. This was her daughter as she'd known her.

As she'd left her.

She made herself think the thought. She'd left her and now time itself seemed determined to make her break her promise.

She pushed the drawer shut and leaned back, feeling the perfectly controlled air flow around her, its very perfection a mockery.

Welcome to "perfection."

She didn't have a picture of the snake. Alastor was clever. Either he'd managed to erase his image from time, or he'd always known not to get photographed.

She didn't need a photograph to remember him.

He was the most beautiful man she'd ever met. The fathomless eyes compelled, invited, persuaded. The rich, deep voice destroyed whatever resistance she'd had left. She'd even left her daughter for him.

She would have given him anything he asked for, but all he'd wanted was her mind.

That should have satisfied her. It should have delighted her. How refreshing to be seen for her mind and not her body.

Refreshingly unsatisfying in this future without warmth or humor or...love.

He hadn't loved her. Had she known it then? Had she wanted to believe he did? It felt more noble to abandon everything and everyone for love, rather than "mere" knowledge.

When had her calculation flipped? She'd told herself it was *for* knowledge, without the "mere." But the sober truth was that she'd left because he asked her too.

He'd seduced her with words. He hadn't touched, hadn't even kissed her. The Butterfly Effect, he'd said. It was too dangerous for them, for Alice. So she'd followed him, because touching each other wouldn't affect her past once she was in the future.

And then he'd showered her with knowledge, so much she'd been drunk on it. And when she sobered up?

He was gone.

In the agency records, he was listed as missing in time, presumed dead.

But he wasn't dead. Whatever she'd felt for him, kept the connection alive. And she had a feeling she knew why he'd left but she wasn't sure what he looked for.

Alice, her mind? He needed more knowledge that he couldn't get on his own. She knew that much.

She'd helped him get part of the way to where he wanted to be.

And now she had to stop him before he got all the way to... where? What?

* * *

Somewhere in time.

Smoking helped him think, so Alastor often came to this time where it was still legal. It was a pattern of sorts and therefore dangerous, but he never picked the same terrace for his smoking and thinking. Or the same continent.

The world was still a big place—one made larger when one threw in the ability to move through time. Someday he should do the math on the odds of matching him to both a time and an inconsistent place. He could go somewhere that had the capability to do that math, but he liked going old school.

And Stella would be watching all the technologically superior places. She wouldn't be able to imagine him going rustic.

She didn't know him as well as she thought she did.

Poor Stella. Poor brilliant Stella. He'd thought she might be what he needed. It was ironic that she'd been smart enough to help him realize she wasn't.

He'd almost told her. She'd have understood. She'd lost a

child, too, though left was a better description for what she'd done. Abandoned an even better one. And that was why he hadn't told her.

Her guilt was different from his.

He knew where else she'd be watching for him. He'd never said it, but he knew she suspected him.

She believed he wanted her daughter.

And he did. But not in the way she thought.

No, she'd never really known him.

He glanced at his watch. It looked authentic to the time if anyone were to look at it. Only he could see the butterfly fluttering behind the constantly moving numbers.

* * *

JUNE, 1960

It was a perfect day for flying and for watching flying. The airshow was crowded with excited spectators and a good many pilots had turned up with their aircraft.

Jack Hamilton adjusted his cap so it cast more of a shadow on his face as he moved easily toward the line of parked planes. He looked resolutely away from the B-17. He wasn't that pilot anymore. It was crazy to miss the *Time Machine.* It was long gone and he was happy no one was shooting at him. But she'd been there when they needed her.

He did miss the feeling of rising into the sky, the throb of engines beneath him, and the rush and push as the plane lifted off.

Yeah, he did miss that.

He didn't miss it enough to risk being spotted by, say, some rogue time travelers. If he were looking for him, this is where he'd look; at airshows, but not on the ground. He'd look at the pilots. So Jack didn't fly where he could be spotted and possibly photographed.

He didn't think the opposition knew who he was, even though they'd gotten pretty close to wiping he and Mel out of time. But there were easier ways to get rid of someone. Just go further in the past when they were vulnerable to accidents and such.

But you had to know who they really were to do that.

Who they really were.

Sometimes, he didn't know who he really was. The person he was, had jumped over his life, arriving in a future he was happy to live with Mel.

But unlike her, because he didn't have her photographic memory, he'd just get flashes from that other life.

His sister believed he was her grand-nephew. When he'd arrived in the future, his team'd had to believe who he was. The older him was just gone. So they'd constructed a story. Old Jack had died in a lab accident. And surprise. There was a grandson.

If his sister had been younger, she'd have noticed the holes in their story, but she was just relieved to have someone to take over for her brother.

And the things he did remember with, or about his sister, he'd had to suppress. He'd spent time listening to her remember. And he'd made sure to hug her as much as she'd let him.

He was glad about that. He'd got the news she was gone not long before he'd deployed for this mission into the past. Mel had been worried about him doing this, but it was one of time's quirks. If he waited too long, it would be too late.

But right now, she was alive out there. With the version of himself he couldn't remember?

At least Mel hadn't told him not to go see himself or Dorothy. The temptation was there, but the risk was there, too. He could be spotted, photographed even, without realizing it. So he kept moving through the crowd, keeping his gaze—if not his thoughts —fixed on the goal.

It was already dangerous doing this much time tampering. You changed time too much and it punched back.

There were ways to get around that punch. He'd learned to track disturbances in time, but it was broad stroke, more like a hammer to a mosquito. They'd been lucky. So far. But if they were going to find the opposition, they needed to up their game. And put a new face on it.

It was why he was here, why he'd traveled back in time so he could stroll around a 1960s air show and not go see his sister.

They needed someone to test their new, and hopefully more efficient, time machine. He needed someone young, strong, adept, a top-notch pilot who wasn't too risk-adverse—and someone who could believe the impossible.

That was always the tricky part.

The first time he'd told Mel—now his wife—that she could travel in time, she'd almost passed out. Ty Granger hadn't wobbled on his feet even a little. But he hadn't believed Jack either.

"Prove me wrong," Jack had challenged him. That was the thing with pilots, they liked a challenge.

Ty made the leap—literally—and after, he'd agreed with Mel that you didn't truly believe it until you did it. And even then, you wondered if you'd lost it.

Ty's wife, Alice...Jack half frowned at the thought of Alice. Her relationship with time baffled them all, but there was no question she was a valuable asset to the team. Her brain had been wasted in the fifties.

"You put wings on a washing machine," a voice broke into Jack's thoughts, "and I can fly it."

Jack stopped and studied the man leaning against a Pitts Special, using the bi-wings for shade. His cap tipped back from his head, he smiled at the small cluster of young women trying to look grownup.

If the kid was the pilot who had been flying a Pitts in air shows, then he was good. But anyone could lean against a plane, wearing the leather flying jacket, and pretend to be a pilot.

For a few seconds, his mind went back into the past, to his buddy, Rick. In the end, he'd died a hero, but he'd been more bluster than pilot.

Jack stepped closer, reaching up to touch the tip of the top wing, then walked forward, while running this hand along its edge. The name of the plane was right. Was this his man?

The pilot straightened, his gaze going past the girls to Jack. He settled his hat more firmly on his head and took a few steps in Jack's direction.

The girls hesitated, their expressions disappointed, then they moved on.

"Yours?" Jack asked. Up close, he could see his face matched the photo of the pilot he'd hoped to meet today. Third time was the charm.

"Built it myself," the man said. His manner had changed from cocky flirt to something more serious, as his gaze assessed Jack.

Jack knew what he'd see. Pilots recognized one another at a cellular level.

And the really good pilots would relax their swagger and use their eyes to measure each other.

"Nice," Jack said. He held out a hand. "Jack Hamilton."

"Connor Hayes." The young pilot gripped Jack's hand without trying to start an arm-wrestling match.

So far, Jack liked what he saw. He glanced at the bi-plane. A one seat. So that temptation was removed. There would be no joy rides today. Mel would be pleased.

Without prompting, Hayes began showing his Pitts to Jack, both the basic design and the innovations he'd added. It didn't take long before they were talking stunts—at least Hayes was. Jack's experiences were in battle.

A plane roared by overhead, drowning out their words and drawing both of their gazes skyward. When it had passed, a comfortable silence remained.

Jack patted the Pitts. She was a beauty. He felt a pang for Hayes. If he agreed to Jack's proposition, the kid would miss her.

"Can I buy you lunch?" Jack asked.

Hayes hesitated, as if he sensed there was more to Jack's question than was apparent. That was a good sign, too. The guy had good instincts.

"Sure." Hayes said, his eyes studying Jack. "I don't fly again for a couple of hours."

"My wheels are this way," Jack said, nodding back in the direction he'd come. This part both amused him and terrified him. He never knew how someone was going to react. He'd thought Ty might call an ambulance to come get him.

Jack hoped that Hayes would give him a chance to prove time travel was possible. It would save his life.

Continue the story in *Telling Time*

Telling Time

The Out of Time Stories — Complete Trilogy

This story unfolds across three interconnected adventures, each with its own love story—and a shared fight to protect time itself.

Reading Order:

Out of Time

Just in Time

Telling Time

For the most satisfying experience, read the trilogy in order.

A note from the author

Writing these stories let me explore courage, connection, and the moments that define us—no matter when they occur.

Thank you for continuing this journey with me. I hope you enjoy where time takes you next.

ACKNOWLEDGMENTS

I'd like to thank Alexis Glynn Latner, Gary Swift, and Kristin Farry for their help in making this story happen. I'd also like to thank my editing team and cover artist.

BOOKS BY PAULINE BAIRD JONES

Science Fiction Romance/Paranormal

Project Enterprise: The Cyborg Chronicles
Cyborg's Revenge: The Cyborg Chronicles Book 1
Cosmic Boom: The Cyborg Chronicles Book 2
CabeX: The Cyborg Chronicles Book 3
AzumC: The Cyborg Chronicles Book 4
MircoP: The Cyborg Chronicles Book 5
ScytheQ: The Cyborg Chronicles 6
OmnitronW: The Cyborg Chronicles 7
TalusH: The Cyborg Chronicles 8
TrackerY: The Cyborg Chronicles 9
Side story: Operation Ark: A Project Enterprise Story
Origin Story: Lost Valyr
Project Universe Series:
The Key (book 1)
Girl Gone Nova (book 2)
Tangled in Time (book 3)
Steamrolled (book 4)
Kicking Ashe (book 5)

The Reboot Books of Project Enterprise
Found Girl (book 6)
Lost Valyr (book 7)
Maestra Rising (book 8)
More Project Enterprise
Project Enterprise: The Short Stories
Time Trap: A Project Enterprise Series Short Story
Operation Ark: A Project Enterprise Story
General's Holiday: A Project Enterprise Story
Echoes Beneath: A Project Enterprise Story
Claws & Effect: The Otherworldly Pets of Project Enterprise

Other Romantic Science Fiction Stories
The Real Dragon
Nebula Nine (time travel adventure)
Open With Care (Christmas collection that includes, "Riding For Christmas" and "Up on the House Top"
Specters in the Storm: A paranormal/steampunk/science fiction romance novella

Out of Time Series:
Out of Time
Just in Time
Telling Time
Out of Time Series (Three Book Bundle)

An Uneasy Future
(A science fiction romance mystery series set in future New Orleans)
Core Punch (1.0)
Sucker Punch (2.0)
One Two Punch: An Uneasy Future Bundle

Romantic Suspense

The Big Uneasy Series:
  Relatively Risky (1)
  Family Treed (A Big Uneasy Short Story)
  Dead Spaces (2.0)
  Louisiana Lagniappe (3.0)
  Worry Beads (4.0)
  Fais Do Do Die (5.0)
  Beaucoup Fracas (6.0)
  Pirogue Wipe Out (7.0)
  Bourre Brouhaha (8.0)
  Soc Au' Lait Stiff (9.0)
  Gumbo Ya-Ya Exit (10.0)
  Boucherie Breakdown (11.0)
  The Family Way (A Big Uneasy Short Story)
  Guess Who's Coming To Christmas: The Wedding Edition
  The Big Uneasy Bundle
  An Uneasy Collection: The Big Uneasy Books 3-5

Lonesome Lawmen Series:
  The Last Enemy
  Byte Me
  Missing You
  Lonesome Mama (Bonus short story)
  (The *Lonesome Lawmen* is also available as a digital bundle)

Do Wah Diddy Die
  The Spy Who Kissed Me
  Perilously Fun Fiction Bundle (includes *The Spy Who Kissed Me* and *Do Wah Diddy Die.* Bonus: *Do Wah Diddy Delete Short Story Collection*)
  Dangerous Dance
  Dangerous Duet

Short Story Collections

ABOUT THE AUTHOR

Award-winning author Pauline Baird Jones writes *perilously fun fiction*—from romantic suspense to space opera, time travel and more. With 40+ books, a flair for humor, and a love of adventure, she creates heroines braver than they realize and heroes brave enough to love them. If you crave thrilling plots, smart laughs, and happy endings, you're in the right place!

To find out more about Pauline or her books:
http://paulinebjones.com